JOHN DOE MODERN KNIGHT

N.F. KIPP

This is a work of fiction. Names, characters, places, and incidents either are the product of the author's imagination or are used fictitiously. Any resemblance to actual persons, living or dead, events, or locales is entirely coincidental.

ISBN 978-1-7363998-0-4 (paperback)
ISBN 978-1-7363998-1-1 (ebook)

FIRST EDITION

Dedicated to Jenna Lee

CHAPTER 0

EVERY STORY HAS ITS BEGINNING

Greed is a constant trait of sentient life forms—the desire for more, unchecked by any understanding or compassion for fellow beings. Perhaps greed is not a strong enough word when the desire for more never ceases. It is the root of darkness; it spreads through hearts like a curse. Greed cannot be sated, and as it feeds, it desires more, regardless of consequences.

Bodies lay arrayed about the burning caravan that once contained refugees who had fled their homes searching for safety. Such dreams they possessed, only to be slaughtered now for their meager possessions.

Bernard had already seen far too much darkness for this scene to pull at his heart. He moved through the caravan, efficiently directing the other Knights to arrange the bodies for burial. At his order, the Knights began to meticulously check each crumpled form for any sign of life.

The green forest swayed in a gentle breeze around the road, oblivious to the violence that had been wrought.

Bernard walked over to the collapsed form of a woman pierced by three arrows protruding from her back. He bent to shift her over to check for life that had already faded. With a pull, he turned her over, only to mutter a low curse as he found out why she had been positioned as such. In her limp arms, she held a boy that had the same dark hair as her. Surprisingly, he looked unscathed compared to the rest of the caravan people, sporting only a bloody head wound.

Bernard was about to walk away, when he noticed a slight rise in the boy's chest. Muttering another curse, Bernard drew a green crystal from his belt, fumbling with it slightly as he hastily brought it close to the boy's forehead. He took a deep breath, focused, and orange light shimmered around his hand, filtering into the crystal, which lit up a soft orange before its light started draining into the boy. The headwound slowly vanished, and the boy's breaths became deeper and steadier.

Bernard moved to call another one of the Knights, but his attention was caught by the boy's pale blue eyes suddenly opening, eyes that were staring directly at him.

CHAPTER 1

A PARTING GIFT

Can you hear it?

That sound, like oceans lapping at the shore, Like a forest burning to the ground, like an intake of breath.

That is the song. Magic. At the edge of your hearing until it isn't.

It calls them. They hunger.

They are here.

—*The Last Words of Lano,*
Grand Mage of the Eighth Realm

Constructed three hundred and thirty-six years ago, the Western Workshop was a magnificent construction, a testament to the masterful craftsmanship of its creators, the dwarves. The main craft floor spanned 50 meters in length and 60 meters in width. Large windows high above let in streams of warm yellow midday light to the workshop. Great steel machines and forges were worked by the numerous craftsmen that swarmed like many ants about the floor. Garbed in thick dark grey cloth outfits that covered all but their faces, they each bore a small blue symbol, the shape of a double crescent moon sewed onto their sleeves.

Located at the far back, an elder dwarf stood at one of the worktables, examining a bluish silver metal bar. He was tall and lean, and his head and beard burst with snow-white hair that trailed down his upper back and mid-chest. He was holding up a magnifier to his eyes while examining a collection of oddly bright metal bricks on his worktable. The elder dwarf looked up, momentarily, and beckoned another worker at a station a couple of feet from him.

"John! Come here! You must take a look!"

John looked up from a glowing weld he had just soldered on a flat black board placed in front of him. He had dark brown hair plastered by sweat to his forehead, cut short to prevent strands from trailing into his ice-blue eyes, so pale and blue people would often refuse to meet his gaze.

"Coming, Bernard," John called back, setting down his torch and walking over towards the dwarf.

As John arrived by Bernard's side, he realized why Bernard was so excited. Unapparent at a distance, the bars he was examining on his desk had a faint blue light to them.

"Bernard! Where did you get Hart Steel from?!" John visibly winced as his voice cracked in the middle of the sentence, but thankfully Bernard was not the type to tease.

"I made a trade for it!" Bernard responded jovially. "One of the Tower Mages needed help with a bit of smith work and gave me a whole crate of these bars in payment!" He gestured towards a crate John hadn't noticed previously filled with bars identical to the one Bernard was examining.

"Start the forge, would you, John?"

"Sure thing." John nodded and turned to walk to the steel furnace built into the wall only eight meters away. The furnace had a large rectangular metal door set against the stone around it. Two round silvery steel bars were embedded on each side, identical and inlaid with numerous engravings and symbols that stopped at the center, leaving a portion of the bar completely smooth. John grasped the smoother part with his right hand, and closed his eyes, taking deep, deliberate breaths.

The next breath John took was magic. His hand shimmered with light blue energy that flickered about almost like bursts of flame. The feeling ran through his limbs like a warm current, familiar and pleasant. He focused and guided the feeling that flowed through him into the etchings on the handle, filling them with glimmering blue light. With a hum, the furnace came to life. The indicator runes lit up on the wall to the right of the handle, flickering with his blue magic as they engaged.

After a couple of seconds, the lights flashed intermittently before the top rune began to glow steadily, and the rest of the indicators dimmed. Bernard had laid a bar of Hart Steel within a mold John had never seen before. The mold's cavity was long and narrow, which should have precluded fitting the rectangular bar into the mold. Still, at a whispered word from Bernard, the bar shimmered green, *stretching* into a more limited form that Bernard laid gently into the mold.

He placed the lid back on with similar care before tracing his hands over the mold, whispering syllables that clashed and clattered with each other in the way that only runic words did. Soft orange light glimmered around Bernard's fingertips before the light swirled off onto the metal itself, tracing numerous runic scripts over the bar. The orange energy dimmed to reveal innumerable lines etched over the Hart Steel. The light died down, and Bernard lifted the bar and mold with his bare hand and turned to the wall behind him, walking to a square burnished steel door that rested at eye level for the dwarf. Opening the door and ignoring the loose spouts of roaring blue flames that flared out toward him, he plunged his hand with the bar inwards. He then withdrew his arm, completely unharmed. He walked over back to his workbench and sat down with a contented sigh, closing his eyes.

After a moment, John spoke, making sure to keep an eye on the indicators, "So… mind telling me what you're doing, Bernard?"

Bernard opened his eyes, looking bewildered. "I didn't tell ya?"

John shook his head no, a bemused smile playing across his lips. Bernard had been alive for over three centuries, so John expected the occasional memory slip. Bernard got up, pulling out a long sheet of rolled draft paper from one of the nearby shelves on his desk, and walked back to John, unrolling it.

He held up the sheet for John. On it was a diagram of a long sword with small, scribbled script denoting various specifics about the construction of the weapon and measurements between runes.

John looked up in surprise back at Bernard and said, "You're doing a weapon commission? For whom?"

Bernard grinned and then tapped the bottom left of the paper; and a short message was scrawled out: "Commissioned for John Doe."

John's eyes widened, a warm feeling enveloping his chest. Bernard's ordinarily pleasant smile, somewhat obscured by his massive beard, had taken on a soft quality, crinkling the corners of his eyes.

"It's your present, John; your apprenticeship is fulfilled, and it's now up to you where you take what you've learned here. I feel that I've pounded enough discipline into your head so you don't cut anything you don't mean to. I'd have been surprised if you had stayed at the workshop. Doubly so given how insistent you were as a wee lad to learn the sword. Didn't let me have an ounce of rest for a week," said Bernard, his gaze distant, looking at a scene only he could see.

A small moment of silence passed between them. Bernard's eyes were affixed to a far-off point as he fiddled with an engraving, spinning steel stylus that danced between weathered but nimble fingers; it traced silver circles through the air in almost hypnotic motions.

After a moment, John said hesitantly, "Bernard?"

It took a moment before Bernard seemed to come back to himself. He turned to look at John and spoke as if the moment had not occurred at all, "Let's get that blade out."

Bernard slid open the furnace doors before plunging his hand into the still-raging fire, bringing out the mold from within. The mold's etching had now filled with a blue light similar in color to the fire; he placed it on the nearby anvil. He then grabbed a hammer and smashed it down, his glimmering green magic flaring around his arm as he struck. The mold shattered, revealing a sparkling blue blade. Bernard gestured at one of his shelves, and a box dislodged and floated towards him, an orange light surrounding it. He snatched the package from the air and opened it to reveal a sword hilt that, despite the polish, John could tell, had been in use before.

Pulling the hilt from the box, Bernard muttered something under his breath as he slowly slid the hilt onto the flat end of the blade, the metal seeming to sink through the hilt embedding deep inside it.

Bernard sighed deeply stepped back from the sword and turned to gesture for John to step forward. "Well, go on."

John nodded, feeling stunned as he stepped forward and slowly grasped the hilt of the sword and lifted it, marveling at the sensation. The blade shone under the light overhead, spreading a blue glow around. The sword itself felt light, though not overly so, and moved with ease as John swiveled it.

Bernard's voice broke John from his thoughts. "Now, how about one last spar before you head on your way? After you're gone, I'll only have Merlot to help keep me in shape."

"Yard in five?" John replied, mirroring an all too familiar statement of Bernard's.

"Good lad. That's the spirit." Bernard nodded approvingly, a flash of something passing over his face so fast John couldn't identify the emotion. He patted John on the back before walking away. "See you in the yard; bring your new sword as well."

John nodded and watched him walk away before turning to grab the scabbard that laid askew on the table. He sheathed his sword and buckled the scabbard to his belt before turning and walking towards the back of the workshop, where two giant doors were set into the wall. One of the doors had been swung open presumably by Bernard to let in the soft morning breeze. Stepping through, John squinted his eyes against the sudden exposure to the bright light, which seared against them. Blinking rapidly, John felt his vision clear to take in the courtyard. The space was cobbled with stone except for the four training rings spaced at each corner, whose floors were covered in dirt.

Bernard had retrieved an elegant looking blade that had a green hue to its steel. He was in the closest of the four combat arenas, a generous term for the dirt squares boxed in with wooden posts and frayed rope. Bernard swung his blade in the closest arena in slow and gentle cuts, first high, then low, and then again maintaining slow, gentle motions. He had stripped off his gloves and overshirt, revealing a muscled physique with arms twice the size of John's and massive stretches of scar tissue that traveled over his entire torso and on to his left arm.

Following his example, John stripped off his overshirt and gloves and took a moment to enjoy the cool breeze drifting over the yard. John placed his right hand on the sword's pommel, adjusting the sheathe slightly with his left hand and feeling for a better equilibrium. John drew fast but slowed once the blade exited the sheathe, bringing the iridescent blue steel through the air in a gentle, unhurried arc.

The hilt fit perfectly into John's palm, and it almost felt as if he was swinging air itself, which caused his reach to overextend. John stumbled. He readjusted his feet for a firmer base and turned slowly in circular swipes, becoming surer of the motion as he grew used to the weight of the blade. The circles of the blue steel grew surer and more even till John felt that he had gotten somewhat used to the blade's size and weight.

"Ready, John?" Bernard's voice had a mocking lilt to it as he called from behind. John turned to see him standing at the edge of the ring posts.

John nodded, and his chest thrummed as his magic reacted to his sudden burst of adrenalin, flushing through his system, making his limbs feel light as air. Bernard leaped past the wooden posts with effortless agility and strength that John had all too often been on the receiving end of. Standing across, Bernard twirled his blade in a lazy but fluid pattern, leaving his guard entirely open.

Or so it seemed.

John brought his blade up into a diagonal guard and waited. A moment passed before impatience hurried him, and he lunged his blade, flashing forward only to be parried to the side. Bernard's blade flew back in return, and John ripped his hand downward, sending a blast of magic—blue and slightly translucent—that sent Bernard flying into the air, chipping his green magic shield now visible from the damage.

Bernard spun, regaining control of his body's orientation, and ripped his hand toward John, sending vibrant green energy at him. John attempted to dodge, but his blast was too quick, slamming into him, sending him tumbling across the ground to slam into a wooden post, making a dent in his magic reserves.

Bernard was already charging forward and bringing his blade to bear. John rose to his feet and desperately deflected a blow that left his arms numb and unable to defend against three slices to the gut, which further whittled his shield and reserves down. It was futile to get into a magic contest with Bernard. John wasn't quite sure how old he was, but he was the only craftsman in the workshop who had the reserves to fuel his forge well into the dark of night and back into the light of day with no visible signs of exhaustion. He swung his blade at John, who angled another desperate block across his blade's path, sending Bernard's blade skittering away and jarring John's from his hands and into the dirt of the field. Bernard's sword did not stop swinging toward him, but this did not elude John's sight as he dropped under Bernard's blade and rolled, grabbing the slightly dusty sword hilt and swinging at Bernard's legs. Bernard leaped backward into an acrobatic roll that belied his age, coming back to his feet in a motion that looked unnaturally easy. He swayed on his feet, his left hand still gripped firmly but not crushingly on his sword hilt.

Bernard looked at John the way one would a particularly bothersome nail that refused to be hammered down. He then sprinted forward and brought his sword down in a crushing swing. It broke past John's guard, taking another chunk from his magic reserves, which were dwindling at a rapid rate. John lanced his blade forward, letting Bernard flick his blade aside only to take advantage of the slight opening by slamming his shoulder into Bernard's chest, sending a bright flash of green light through the air as John glanced against his barrier.

He retreated, receiving a glancing slash for his efforts that further drained his reserves entirely as his magic shield faded away in a shower of blue sparks.

Bernard did not follow; instead of halting, he said, "All right, John?"

"Never better," John bit back, frustrated. How was it that he still couldn't even stand for more than a couple of minutes against Bernard even after over a decade of training? No matter how much he practiced, it seemed, Bernard was still his better.

Bernard nodded, a small understanding smile beginning to stretch across his face. "Look, John, I know that—""

"I'm fine, Bernard," John cut him off, his voice light as he stood up. "I'm just going to catch my breath for a bit. I'll see you at lunch."

Bernard hesitated for a moment, his face looking old in a way not related to age before he nodded and turned, exiting the ring through the gate. John slowly pushed himself to his feet. He grabbed his sword from the ground and sighed at the accumulated dust on the blade. Reaching into a pocket, he pulled a loose rag and ran it up and down the blade before he sheathed it and began to slowly walk back to the workshop.

It's not like John wasn't used to losing to Bernard. It was just that being used to something doesn't always make it better. He had been training with Bernard for the better part of ten years, and still, he felt no closer to even approaching his mentor's skill level. John entered the work area to find that a couple more of the crafters had come down from their quarters above. He continued on his path back to his room. He had everything he needed packed for tomorrow. There was nothing more to do. He laid down with a sigh on his bed. John would have dinner at the communal hall tonight, and that would be it. In the morning, he would be leaving. Perhaps he would be more excited if he had someone to share with the accomplishment or journey.

Regardless, the other apprentices and John had long since diverged to the point they no longer talked. John was the only apprentice at the forge who was leaving, abandoning the crafter life and the safety it entailed. It made sense; it wasn't outright maliciousness; the fact of the matter was, John just wasn't going to be around that long.

CHAPTER 2

A SUBTLE DOOM

As a rule, Quests are either mortally perilous or generally uninteresting, with perhaps some other events transpiring that may divert attention.

The level of danger will depend on the Quest. Still, a general rule can usually be applied: unless particular conditions are the Quest's withdrawal by the requester, the Quest must be completed. Withdrawal rarely happens; thus, as a general rule, Quests are either successful or complete failures.

On the reverse side, someone who fills out a Quest is obligated to pay the agreed-upon reward and the Lost Difference (unknown factors that occur during the Quest that increase the danger).

(Excerpt from Zayne Dallard's *Encyclopedia Adventuria Volumes 1–3: Never Say Die Edition*)

The early morning sun the next day had just touched the tip of the mountains when John went to knock on the assigned address's door. The streets were quiet as John walked, making his way through the tangled streets of Leonardo's District.

The district was distinct from the rest of the City of Lights by the number of workshops that called it home. Some sellers were set in moderate two-story buildings, while others were towering in steel glass monoliths filled with light. These buildings' defining feature were the tall glass spires that emerged from various points, reflecting glittering rays of sunlight across the streets.

The other defining feature of the district was why John was here.

He saw the darkened building tucked into a corner of the district, noticeable by the absence of mage light fixtures comparable to the surrounding buildings. John stepped up to the stained wooden door and gently tugged the rope made of thousands of silver threads to the right of the door, which itself had no visible handle.

Gentle chimes sounded through the air, and the door opened inward, seemingly of its own volition. John's heart thudded hard against his ribcage, and he paused to take a deep breath, followed by another, trying to fill the pit in his stomach.

When he felt relatively steadier, John finished his walk to the door and then past the entryway he had wanted to cross his entire life.

The Gargoyle Tavern was a local tavern in the City of Lights, and despite its relatively smaller three-story size, it had a specific style that John couldn't help but love. The structure was of hard grey stone with large gargoyles posed alongside the entrance's polished silver doors. John felt his stomach seemingly flip flop as he stepped up to the doors and grasped the smooth steel handle. The cool steel against his palm steadied him slightly, and he pulled open the door, letting it fall shut behind. John stepped into a room paneled with dark brown wood, lit only by the dim lighting set above and in the walls. The tables around the room were surprisingly thick and circular. Arrayed around them in wooden chairs were patrons cloaked in an incredible variety of clothes made more apparent by how each group often differed dramatically from one another.

A group of patrons obscured by tattered navy cloaks huddled in the back of the tavern: the Council Guard, not surprisingly.

They were the Garrison force for the Cities on the Cold Mountains and served the Stone Council enforcing the Common Laws and manning the City Wall. These guards had probably just come off duty on the wall.

Several other patrons were scattered around the tavern with a couple at the tavern head; by the barkeep sat a man with long dark hair framing a brooding face, set with eyes closer to burnished gold than any other color John had seen. His dark brown skin was marred only by a few small scars on his face that nearly faded with age.

He was slumped onto the bar counter for support, clutching a large bottle of shimmering red liquid. A forest green cloak was draped around his shoulders, and a braided leather belt clasped a longsword with a long hilt with a cord. A bracelet beaded with gold and silver on his left wrist caught John's eye. The bead patterns almost looked intentional and may have meant something, but John had no idea what. He realized the man was slumped over into a dark grey porcelain mug half full of a thick looking red liquid as he got closer. A health potion, John realized.

Lon, one of the workshop apprentices, had decided to chug three after a couple of the older apprentices told him that they would make him strong. It had done the exact opposite, sending him to the hospital for three months and setting back his apprenticeship for longer; not as long as the older apprentices who had been kicked from the workshop.

A long moment of silence passed before John hesitantly spoke, based more on a feeling than anything, "Zayne Dallard?" John stood awkwardly as the man gazed at him for a while before he made a vague gesture at the stool next to him and said, "John Doe, I presume?"

He waited for John to nod an affirmative before he continued, "Sit. I'm the Party Leader to interview you." He held out a hand. "Zayne Dallard, Adventurer and Guild Master of the Raven Fallows." John shook his hand and said, "John Doe," nonplussed.

Zayne looked amused. "That's it, no title? Usually, people have something…" he moved his hand about as if to pull his meaning from thin air.

John chuckled awkwardly, feeling his cheeks flush. "Well, I haven't thought of one yet…"

Zayne's smile quirked, and he nodded, scratching with his pen at the notepad in an unsettling manner.

Before John had time to start worrying about what exactly he wrote down, Zayne looked back up at John with weathered brown eyes. "Need some basic background first. Is the City of Lights your current residence?"

"Yes. I was an Apprentice of Bernard the Forge; he works at the Northern Workshop."

Zayne nodded as he made a couple of notes before he looked back up at John. "Think Bernard did a commission or two for me awhile back. Quality work that. So, in your application, you mentioned you're interested in the Scouts? Not as an objection to continuing that route, but you listed five years Forge Apprentice under Bernard the Crafter. You will be more than welcome to a senior position in the Master Trades Camp if you're having any second thoughts about your application for the Forward Expeditionary Legion."

Despite the offer, Zayne looked as if he was speaking from a script rather than his own words. As if this wasn't his offer but someone else's.

"I'm sorry, but I would prefer to continue my application to the Forward Expeditionary Legion."

Zayne shrugged and stood up. "Your loss, come on; let's get to the test."

His loss? John's gut twisted. What did Zayne mean by that?

Finished with his explanation, he abruptly stood up to walk to the back of the Tavern. John hurriedly followed, scraping his chair backward, and rushed to follow him. John caught up to him as he got to the very back of the tavern, where a door was set against the weathered stone, made of solid steel with telltale glints that indicated some possible Mage Steel but likely not Hart, Macon, or the equivalent.

Zayne turned the handle and opened the door onto a courtyard of beaten dirt, crates stacked in a corner by a decently large wooden shed.

John followed Zayne as he walked to the center of the field before turning to face him, slinging his green cloak smoothly onto his left arm before he tossed it to the ground a distance away. Zayne wore a polished grey tunic that fell over the top portion of his dark emerald greave plates, which looked to be made of segmented metal that didn't seem to inhibit his movement much, if at all, judging by the ease of his walk.

A single broadsword hung in a scabbard by his side, which he spun out skillfully into his right hand, holding the blade in a simple guard position across his torso.

"The test is simple. We spar. If you don't go down too easy, I'll offer you a company contract." His tone was light, but his expression was set in a stern frown, his dark eyes glaring at John confrontationally.

John's heart sank, but he drew his sword, though he did not flourish it, letting the blade fall to his left side at a relaxed angle. Sweat beaded at John's forehead as he focused on keeping his breath calm and even, examining his opponent.

The moment broke, and Zayne, with astonishing speed, closed the distance between the two as he sliced towards John, nearly cutting into his side before John angled his sword in a desperate downward deflection. John resisted the urge to disengage for breathing room, and instead of taking advantage of their locked swords, he twisted his palm outward and let loose a hastily concentrated magical blast.

Blue energy ripped forward, slamming into Zayne's torso, lighting his mage shield up a bright orange and sending him tumbling through the air. His body twisted into a spin, and he pointed his feet back towards the ground, landing smoothly on his feet.

Zayne was skilled. John could tell he was far better than him even with just the brief exchange, but John wasn't going to give up now. John leaped at Zayne, swinging his sword in a low to high stroke blocked by a brandishing of Zayne's steel brushing John's to the side. Pain seared through John's skull, and he crumpled to the ground, feeling like the world had turned upside down. The top of his forehead was numb, as if severe head trauma had caused his magic reserves to dip a significant chunk. Rolling across the ground, John rose a couple of feet from Zayne, who was holding his sword in a guard stance.

John charged forward, swinging his blade down hard, which was surprisingly only barely deflected by Zayne's own. This left his sword askew; there was finally an opening. John swung his sword, blade first, into the side of his neck, feeling his sword grind against Zayne's magical shield sending angry orange magical bursts outward in return.

John spun away from a rising strike that nevertheless scored a path over his magical shield across his chest, marking a bright blue line across his torso. John swung his hand down, channeling magic to a concentration at his fingertips, then releasing, sending a wave of blue streaking outward, which ripped through the field between them, blazing towards Zayne in a shower of rocks and dirt.

Zayne brought his left hand up sharply and stone shot from the ground, protecting him entirely from the blast, which dug into the stone, ripping chunks from it before fading, leaving the pillar withered but intact. John suddenly felt his left foot drop as a hole seemed to spontaneously open in the ground underneath him, burying his entire left leg up to the thigh, leaving his right leg arched out awkwardly.

He was pinned but not entirely helpless. He took a deep breath and focused on directing his magic down through his hand, releasing another blast that ripped apart the ground his leg was stuck in, freeing him just in time to manage a weak block against Zayne's sword, which sent John's skittering away. Zayne's sword struck his stomach, and his magical shield dispersed in a shower of sparkling blue.

John was done.

Zayne, on the other hand, looked entirely ready to keep going, and even with his limited external magic sensing capabilities, John could tell Zayne's reserves were still relatively high. A pit dropped inside his stomach. He should've taken it as a sign he wasn't ready when he still did that terribly against Bernard after all these years.

"I think that's enough," Zayne said and sheathed his sword, his face an unreadable mask. A long moment passed between them as John started to break into a cold sweat, his stomach continuously twisting in discontent.

Zayne finally spoke, startling John from his thoughts, "Solid work, John. I've got a spot for you in the Expeditionary Legion. Not sure why your heart is so set on it, though. The Master Trades Camp is far safer."

John shrugged, desperately trying to hide how relieved he was. "If I wanted to spend the rest of my days crafting magical items, I would have stayed at the Western Workshop."

"Fair enough," said Zayne. Another long moment of silence passed as Zayne continued to examine John.

"You're in."

Instant relief flooded John, nearly taking his legs out from underneath him. Zayne continued, "You can settle which of the Guilds you join whenever. We're in a bit of a situation right now, though." Zayne grimaced, his still youthful features scrunching together.

"Is this because of the Barons?"

Zayne nodded, his face creasing in a frown, and went on, "I won't lie. It is. The Adventurer Guilds in the City of Lights are understaffed, desperately so, due to the Barons in the Lower Lands pulling in anyone willing to trade conflict for a coin to fight their war. Most of anyone who's not interested in that has long left for other cities further from the Barons. Fortunately, the City of Lights gets its supplies from the Mountain Hold within the Cold Mountains. *Unfortunately*, we haven't heard from them in a week, we've already sent one tram down. No one's returned. Without Igni, the City of Lights and the rest of the mountain cities will run out of mineral supplies in three months or less and food in half that; if the situation isn't dealt with soon, another nation will take over."

John's gut twisted painfully at the thought of Bernard trapped in a City of Lights ruled by the Amelion Imperium or the Hart Kingdoms.

Zayne sighed, running a hand through his thick dark hair. "As we're shorthanded with the war going on, I'll be surprised if I can get ten adventurers, and normally, I wouldn't do this without twice that many. You," he looked pointedly at John, "wouldn't have a choice if you choose to sign up for the Guilds now. The Council already put out a Priority Contract, and most of the Free Guilds have already packed up and scattered months ago before they get pressed into the War by any of the passing Barons."

John kicked himself for not realizing the Free Guilds had already left. The workshop orders had declined dramatically, but it hadn't occurred to John till now that the Free Guild members would abandon the city they called home. Some of them had been here for a hundred years. The city couldn't be under that much threat, could it?

John responded, realizing he had been silent for a little too long, "That just means I don't have a choice. Bernard isn't going to leave just because a war is going on in the Lower Valleys. Stone's breath, I don't think he would leave if the War came up here."

Despite the confident-sounding words, John's voice was anything but shaky and jangled. He couldn't back down, though; he had spent the better portion of his life dreaming of becoming an adventurer and seeing the Realms. This was what he wanted, right?

Zayne thankfully didn't seem to notice and turned, running a hand through his dark hair. "Let's go get those forms."

CHAPTER 3

A SINGLE KNIGHT

Five peoples coexist in the Thirteen Realms: the humans, the elves, the dwarves, the clockwork, and the fae. While they vary in appearance widely among themselves, they are, in essence, more similar than different. All peoples have inherent magic, with no race having advanced capability by intrinsic virtue. Even the lifespans of the peoples are inherently similar based on the intrinsic strength of magic.

Still, despite that, the peoples share more in common with each other than the other life forms in the Realms. It is not uncommon for disputes to arise based on superficial differences…

(Excerpt from H. Dallas,
Modern Conflict of the Realms)

The forms turned out to be a three-hour affair that left his hand aching and his eyes irritated as he stepped back out into the natural sunlight. The streets were quiet as he made his way through them to the closest Inner Tram station.

Zayne had directed John to stay at the Knight's Rest Inn, located directly beside the Ann Side Railway Station, from where they would be leaving in the morning. He would be there later, but one of the party members should be at the platform; John was to show the staff a steel card Zayne had given him that would let them know John was with the Expedition.

Walking up a couple of flights of grated metal steps, John emerged at the top of one of the tram station platforms, mostly empty. He only had to wait a short while for the tram to arrive. The tram drifted into the station, coming to a stop and disgorging its passengers, the City of Lights citizens: humans, elves, dwarves, fae, and clockwork. The Realms' known sentient peoples were all relatively humanoid and varying in size, with the slender fae being the tallest, stepping with grace through the crowd. Their skin varied with all the rainbow hues contrasted against the dwarves, elves, and humans' pale and dark complexions. The dwarves stood a little over a meter usually but had naturally powerfully built arms and chests. The human heights, while sometimes matching the elves, were generally shorter. The clockwork moved in all the peoples' shapes but were made of gleaming silver, bronze, and rare gold sparkles. Their features were mechanized, shifting, and flashing as they blinked orbs of silver metal.

The clothes and people, typical of the City of Lights, varied widely. A group of humans strode by to John's left, covered in bright reds and oranges that carried long halberds over their shoulders. They wore bright white half-capes draped to the backs of their knees and sewn with symbols John had only seen on heavy grade armor. He walked past them into the tram, finding open seats with relief. John relaxed into the soft cushions, and with no more than a gentle tug, the tram began to move.

It drifted through the city, following a smooth, curved path over the street, hovering on a cushion of magic. Ancient stone and modern steel buildings passed by before being replaced with lower stone and wood buildings, so suddenly, one would think they had left the Realm entirely.

The tram flew low before stopping at a similar stone platform to the one John had entered.

"The Council Center," a soft voice chimed from overhead.

The tram slowed to a halt, and a few of the passengers got out, but more came in, finally filling the tram to the uncomfortable capacity John had dreaded. The tram restarted, and they soared above the streets, illuminated by soft yellow lamps.

"The Market District."

The doors shut and the tram continued its path ducking in and out above the streets. They stopped and the voice said, "Ann Side Railway Station."

John stood up and moved towards the doors, slipping through the crowd of people outside. The late afternoon sun shone dimly on Ann Side Railway Station, refracting off the puddles that remained from the rainstorm from earlier as John walked down the steps in the sight of the countless inns and taverns on each side of the street.

The buildings were arranged almost on top of one another, with blinking signs or massive posters declaring their rent availability. How was John ever going to find the Knight's Rest Inn?

"Look a little lost?" a warm but slightly rough voice spoke from behind John. He turned to see a dwarf with a dark, well-trimmed beard and flashing bright yellow eyes. He was clad in a dark red fabric under metal bracers and chainmail with a sword attached to each hip.

John grinned somewhat awkwardly. "Yeah, a little."

"Maybe I can fix that. You John Doe?" John blinked, caught off guard, then nodded.

"I am."

The dwarf held his right hand up to shake. "Name's Lon Silverstone. I'm here to get you to the inn." John grasped his hand and shook. Releasing, he turned to gesture for John to follow him, "Come on, we're at the Knight's Rest Inn."

The Knight's Rest Inn was thankfully not too far from the station platform as John followed Lon through the fading but still present crowd at the platform and down the steps. They crossed the street and entered a small market district, coming to a stop at a large building of dark brown woods and emblazoned in bright gold lettering over the doorway: "A Knight's Rest."

Lon walked to the door, inset into the stone, and grabbed the handle, pulling open the door to allow them in. The tavern room was spacious with wooden tables and chairs and lit warmly by the lights hung overhead. Various people sat around, eating and chatting with each other. The bar had a door that led back to a kitchen that emitted the warm scent of food, making John remember that he hadn't eaten since morning.

Lon and John walked almost to the tavern head but then diverted to one of the circular tables immediately to the right, occupied by four people, eating and pouring over tattered yellow maps.

A gorgeous elven girl who looked close to his age—which for elves, John supposed, meant nothing—was at the table; she had striking silver eyes and delicate, elegant features. Deep purple hair was draped around her shoulders and contrasted sharply against her beautiful deep amethyst eyes.

She was animatedly talking to another older female elf with timeless features only recognizable as an elder by her silver hair. Her dark skin and steel-grey eyes reminded John of… someone, though precisely whom, had escaped him.

A clockwork sat on the edge of their seat next to John, staring intently at the table with what John would have described as looking lost in thought. They were crafted from a silver metal as a humanoid but distinctly mechanical body. The clockwork wore a large black cloak over their form and had two green glowing magic cores that made up their eyes gazing at the table.

The group's final member was an older bespectacled dwarf with grey streaks that ran through his dark beard at Lon's left. His nimble weathered hands worked over an object so small that they obscured everything but the silver glint of metal.

Lon coughed, and the group ceased their activities and looked up in eerie unison at Lon, who then spoke, "Zayne got another spot filled for tomorrow."

"Uh, I'm John," said John. They scrutinized him for a moment before turning back to their previous activities.

Lon muttered something under his breath and then turned to John, vaguely gesturing at one of the chairs. "Take a seat," he said. "We've got some food if you're hungry."

John nodded. "I am, thanks," he said and sat down, sliding his chair in to sit down as Lon did the same, albeit without the awkwardness inherent in John's movements of sitting at a table with strangers.

The food on the table was vast, so John elected to grab some pieces from the trays closest to himself. The meal turned out to be a couple of baked potatoes doused in a portion of one of the thick stews on Lon's insistent recommendation, a torn half loaf of fresh bread, and a whole smoked turkey leg.

As John took his first bite of turkey and potato, Lon said, "With the addition of John, Dallard feels as if we have delayed as long as we can for more people. We move out tomorrow at 5:30 am. All of you heard the details of this Expedition when you signed up. It's likely dangerous, but there's little choice—"

"I still don't see why we don't just ask for some help from the Legionaries; make 'em work for a living for a change," interjected the older dwarf.

"You know why, Trajan; this isn't the Legionaries job. They're only under contract for civil protection."

Trajan nodded, frowning, and said, "I know what their rotten job is, but they won't have much of one if the city runs out of supplies."

"It can't be helped," said the older female elf. "They will have their own trials to face in our absence." Her voice was soft but firm, and it seemed to resolve the topic as Trajan sighed, nodding in acquiescence to her point.

"Marcila is right," said Lon. "The city will have enough to deal with while we're gone with the Barons in the lowlands. Now let's go over the current plan."

Lon grabbed a stack of paper and laid out the first five in the center of the table, placing them so that the sketches met and formed what John realized was a map of mine tunnels.

He spoke, a solemn expression set on his thickly bearded face, "We will be traversing the mountain tunnels in a tram that the city has procured for us. The journey to the Mountain Hold by Tram takes a some hours. We are to keep an eye out for the two previous expeditions. Besides that, there is little we know about the situation ahead. The loss of two expeditions would preclude any more investigation even if we had the manpower to spare, which, as you all know, we don't. We also can't abandon the Mountain Hold; whatever's happened, there's a city and its people down there who may need our help."

The table was quiet in response. A part of John wanted to twist with anxiety. The closest he had gotten to a lethal situation was a malfunctioning forge that drained near his entire reserves just to protect himself from the explosion.

John was unconscious for about a week, and the physicians had said he was lucky to be alive.

This was different. John was walking into this knowing full well that over half of first-time adventurers never made it back. Worse, it wasn't as if anyone seemed confident of any degree of success. Still, this was what John signed up for, right?

While Bernard had rarely spoken of his father and never of his mother, he had told John parts of his own life. He had himself once been an Adventurer. John remembered this from his younger days when Bernard told him stories of his adventures. John had seen how Bernard's eyes had sparkled when he had spoken of his companions and how his scowl had deepened when he spoke of his enemies.

John wanted to have those experiences. No doubt or fear that welled up inside him could push him away from this. Still, the thought didn't change the pit that was starting to develop in his stomach.

Lon looked around the group and said, "Questions?"

"Is this the best use of the city's resources, especially with the Barons at the gates?" the clockwork said in a distinctly metallic sounding voice.

Lon frowned. "That's not for us to decide, Seven."

Seven shrugged. "Still worth asking."

No one else spoke; Lon sighed and stood up. "All right, down here at 5:30 geared and ready."

Lon turned to John, reaching into one of his pockets and pulling out a small silver key. "Here," he said, holding out the key towards him, "room for the night; the number should be on the key. I'd recommend getting some sleep—" he looked at John then shook his head, "never mind, let's go for a walk."

"I'm sorry?" John said, confused before realizing Lon was indeed serious as he grabbed a cloth bag from a pouch at his belt and grabbed two loafs of hot bread, a hunk of cheese, and two turkey legs, one of which he handed to John. He reflexively grabbed the paper wrapping. Lon stood and beckoned towards him until John rose and followed him out of the Inn.

The cold night air hit John like a wave, making him suddenly aware of the sweat that had broken out on his skin as well as his deep, heavy breaths. Lon's broad, heavy hand gently patted John on the back.

"Easy, John, it's alright. It's not what Zayne or I wanted for anyone's first mission."

John nodded. They continued down the street, and John felt the shakiness wearing down somewhat, at least enough for his stomach to remind him that he was hungry. Taking a bite of the turkey leg, John focused on the feeling of the night air blowing over his skin like a thin ethereal coating of ice.

John and Lon walked through the quiet streets lit by the occasional lamp, which sent rays of light reflecting onto the pools of rainwater that had collected. The walking kept John focused on moving, and for some time, they moved through the rain-soaked streets, slowly eating and intermittently talking about subjects unrelated to tomorrow. John had the feeling that Lon had done this before with more adventurers than John knew. That wasn't saying much anyway since John knew Bernard and a couple of the other Guild crafters; that was it. John had completed the mandatory schooling from the workshop under the guidance of Bernard, who had been as strict with regular schooling as he was with the sword. The other apprentices had been older than John. This made it difficult for him to find friends with whom he could relate; not to mention his inability when it came to making friends in general.

John would have felt lonely, but he thought that one would need to have made deep friends first before saying they were lonely. Until John accomplished such, he would hesitate to say he was lonely. Perhaps "friend-averse" was a better term. Either way, that feeling was always present; the one that was actually bothering him was the tension that had settled in his gut since the inn's conversation.

"Looks like you're thinking pretty hard, kid," said Lon. "Can't claim to be an expert on dealing with feelings, but I know the sweats;" he used a term that John had never heard, at least not in this context.

"Sweats?" John asked.

They had traversed to the quite literal edge of the city before they stopped. A low stone wall of a meter and a half high was all that separated them from a sickening drop to the valley floor below, usually shaded in darkness that now glittered with thousands of fiery lights. John knew those indicated the thousands of soldiers camped only a small distance from the city walls.

Lon nodded. "That sensation of intense foreboding, the pit in your stomach, the ice on your skin; it's because you're afraid."

Before John could interject with a halfhearted defense, he raised his hand. "Don't tell me you're not scared; either you're lying or stupid, and I hope it's the former. Zayne told me you were capable. I believe him. Just because you got some moves doesn't mean you don't have the right to be scared. I am, and I've got more than a century on you."

He sighed a deep, gusty breath, looking out across the valley before us, and continued, "Mostly everybody gets them before their first mission. It's your emotions going haywire as you're confronted with the possibility of death. The stuff going through your head is specific to you, but it's what your mind seized on to explain the fear it just felt."

"I'm not worried about the mission," said John. Lon looked at him with a raised eyebrow. John wilted slightly under his gaze and fixed the sentence. "Okay, I am worried about the mission, but that's secondary; I guess to what I'm worried about right now."

The night air's chill had descended into his hands to the point John had to call a little magic to them to chase away the awfully cold numbness.

"So, what're you worried about right now?" Lon's question caught John somewhat off guard, even though it shouldn't have.

After a moment's pause where John tried to order his thoughts, he began, "I've always wanted to be an adventurer. It probably started with the stories my guardian, Bernard, told me. Now that I'm here, I feel—" John broke off, not knowing how to describe the tension coursing through him.

Then, Lon said, "Zayne seems to think you know your way around a blade, and I have no reason to doubt him. The worst thing you can do right now would be to shake yourself up, whatever you need to do to get the energy out or else you won't sleep."

John nodded, and Lon patted his shoulder before walking away. John continued walking in the opposite direction, eventually finding himself standing on one of the walls of the city. The lowlands stretched below; the lights from the small villages that had once dotted the landscape extinguished; John hoped by the villagers to avoid attention and not by the masses of light that remained: the Barons armies whose numbers swelled with every passing day even though they were dying by the thousands on the battlefield. They splayed across the valley in their hastily erected encampments and fortresses blazing with a light that indicated there were more soldiers gathered down in the valley than possibly people in the whole city.

Supplies would never get through. The city would run out of food, and that would be it. They would have to negotiate with one of the armies for supplies, which would mean that the city would be occupied, leading to the end of its independence. The City of Lights, the only home John had ever known, would be forced under the rule of a King.

Before the Stone Council, there had been a King of the Mountain, preceded by hundreds of Kings, who had developed unfortunate magical tendencies towards the darkest branches of magic.

John shivered as, despite his magic generating warmth, a trail of ice ran down his spine. There was a restless feeling to the night. Something moved, not noticeable by sound but by something instinctual. John spun, looking around the dimly lit streets, searching down the street's channels trying to find…nothing, just dark buildings lit by the dim lanterns in the street. Not a single soul walked these streets. Yet as John walked back to the Inn, he couldn't shake the feeling that he had not been alone at the overlook.

INTERLUDE 1: WHAT MOVES IN THE DARK?

It is unfortunate that hatred is the most resilient emotion for some individuals. It is the curse of free will that inflicts such feelings indeed. If they had no choice, they wouldn't feel this unhappiness, this anger, this hurt.

The man indeed, if he could still be called that, hadn't enjoyed himself like this in centuries; the arrogance of those "immortals." What is immortality when death's grasp can still be granted by everything except the flesh's infirmities? To live forever young but forever be at the mercy of those around himself was a fate, that was… unacceptable. Yes, that was the word. He would change this. As he had grasped mastery of the arcane, he would gain knowledge of the Realm around him. Just as the Six Kings of Hate and Darkness had done. Yet, why was he lying on the floor?

Who was the older man? What was he doing here? What was he doing with—

CHAPTER 4

INTO THE MOUNTAINS

It was approaching 5:00 am when Lon pounded on his door, rousing John from a sleep filled with darkness and something worse. John got ready, blearily pulling on a dark blue shirt that was a shade different from black and a pair of similarly dark pants but grey. John's black boots came up to his calves and were well worn around the ankle, making each step nothing more than a muffled impact.

Strapping his sword and belt to his waist, John passed through the door of his temporary room at the inn and walked down the hallway, stepping to the left to enter a lift. Which upon his entrance, smoothly dropped downward just as it had flown upward. The back wall was glass so John could see the many floors that seemed to rise ever upward. The lift slowed and came to a halt on the ground floor, letting John out into the dining area from the previous night. The room was mostly empty, except for his would-be Guildmates.

John started walking toward them, maneuvering between the scattered tables. His company, as he believed the term was, was straightening and tightening a dazzling assortment of weapons and armor that may have even slightly impressed Bernard. The armor pieces were likely of magical variety, given the faint glimmer around the metal. Armor, at least in the old sense of the term, was reasonably useless if one had a shield ring and magic unless the armor was designed to work in conjunction with the ring.

Zayne was wearing dark brown leathers with his sword hung at his side and a large, beautifully carved longbow over his left shoulder. Three gold rings glimmered on the fingers of his left hand. One John identified as a shield ring and another as an earth element ring, but several others were a mystery.

Such things were expensive and not useful unless your life was on the line. John might have considered trying to craft or even buy one with his savings from the forge if he didn't also know the dramatic magic stamina reduction they entailed. While this wasn't an issue for older magic users who had developed reserves, at 19, John's reserves just wouldn't be deep enough.

John put a halt to his flighty thoughts to focus on Zayne, who was in the middle of the circle that the rest of the company had formed around him. Zayne nodded at John and then spoke, "We move as soon as you have prepped your gear."

"I am prepped," said John. He looked at John strangely for a moment as if trying to determine if he was serious.

A moment passed before something flickered across his eyes, and he simply nodded, then turning to talk to the elf girl, elven woman, and the clockwork.

"We will be going in a tram cart provided by the city along with what food and basic equipment they can spare. As we travel through the tunnel, we will be on the lookout for anything that could indicate where the previous expeditions led. The city's trip should take only a couple of hours, but we should be expecting trouble. Two trams of adventurers don't go missing for no reason."

Zayne paused to pull some crumpled papers from his pockets. "Trajan and Lon will act as the first shift main guard for the tram, Aysel." Aysel nodded. "And Marcila will take the second shift. Seven." Seven looked up, glowing eyes focusing on Zayne.

"And I," Zayne said, looking at the group with a face that betrayed nothing, "will act as the main expeditionary unit for any external tram operations that may occur in transit. In case of my death, Marcila has this command."

Marcila inclined her head slightly and said, "Of course."

"Alright, let's move."

Wait, why didn't he have a group? John would have asked this question, but the group was already on the move. They followed Zayne out of the Knight's Rest into the darkness that was only illuminated by the streetlamps about the street. Passing quietly across the stone paved street, they crossed over to the tram station. At the top of the stairs, a single car sat perhaps 15 meters in length. An older woman dressed in the station uniform handed a key to Zayne, whose blue silver glint pinged something in John's memory, a conductor's key, John remembered now. John had made a couple of those keys; they served to allow people to channel magic into whatever device they wished to power. The tram key, in particular, was an expensive commission because of the quality of the metal needed and the level of time to detail the magic channels.

Zayne waved the key before the wide door at the very front of the tram, which slid open to reveal the insides of what looked to be a hastily remodeled passenger tram. Beds were stacked in bunk arrangement near the back, with eight beds in total. Crates likely filled with supplies occupied the tram's midsection, leaving only the central portion free for the train console, and the two seats in front for the conductors.

The rest of the company headed towards the back of the tram. John's path was halted by Zayne's hand on his shoulder, "You mentioned you worked in a workshop?"

John nodded. "Yeah?"

"The tram runs with a single conductor's magic output, and if you worked at the workshop, you must've done magic channeling. That's the only absolute basic requirement for powering a tram. I know a bit about channeling, but my efficiency isn't of note. Same for the other adventurers. Could you do it?"

Huh, he had been relegated to a magic battery already. If that hadn't been Zayne's original intention in the first place. John attempted to push back the negative thought and responded again, "Yeah."

He changed his path and walked towards the console gingerly, taking the left seat. This sea of blinking lights and levers couldn't be too hard to figure out, right? Pushing out everything but the console from his thoughts, John examined it, observing each button lever and the panel. Slowly it came together. There was only one red lever controlling the throttle. The metal handgrip was obviously for power. The dials were still a mystery, but that was in part because they were inactive. John took a deep breath, grabbed the handle, and began running a current through the system, which came to life, with flickering lights and a hum.

On a panel to his left, the first of seven lights came to life, blinking blue before solidifying and triggering the next to start blinking. John could feel his magic racing towards the back of the tram, engaging systems as it went. John felt the magic drain decrease as the initial startup finished with the final blue light blinking on.

The tram vibrated below, and John was almost tempted to engage the throttle, but steadied himself enough to turn to Zayne and the rest of the party, keeping his hand on the steel power grip. The rest of the party strapped themselves into the side seats, except for Zayne, who walked forward, sitting in the chair next to him.

Using his free hand, John awkwardly gripped the belt, pulling it to buckle over himself. Zayne buckled himself in first, showing more foresight than John had, and reached his left hand forward to grip the secondary handle in front of him. Immediately, John felt his magic drain rate decrease another chunk as Zayne started providing secondary power.

"Engage," Zayne's sudden command almost caught John off guard, but years of conducting magic and taking orders from Bernard allowed him to keep the flow steady as John pulled the tram handle slowly down.

The tram seemed to vibrate for a moment before they shot forward, seemingly vanishing inside the dark tunnel ahead within an instant. The transparent viewports on the side of the tram suddenly filled with darkness that changed to rocky slate grey as Zayne engaged the tram's lights, demonstrating a far better understanding of the console than John.

One of the dials John could interpret glowed with a small but easily legible blue number, *150 lph.* They were going incredibly fast John realized. So fast if they hit a wall they would disappear in a pancake of metal and unfortunate life.

John shook himself slightly; he needed to get a hold of himself.

"Output stabilized," John said, getting a strange look from Zayne before he thoughtfully cocked his head.

"That the term in the forges?"

As nervous as John was at this point, there was nothing to do but watch the dials and channel magic through the tram. "Yeah, we usually run the forges all day, so I'm used to running in a team of two."

Zayne nodded. "I thought your magic capacity was abnormal for someone of your age, but that makes sense."

"Most of the crafters I knew had larger reserves than me," John responded, not ignoring his party leader's attempt to make conversation.

Zayne nodded. "I hear the first months as a crafter is another world of exhaustion."

"It is. I couldn't even move some days after work. Still, you have to do it, or else you won't have the proper reserves to craft anything."

His reserves were at least an asset now. Would Zayne have even recruited him if he didn't need that particular talent?

The silence stretched as time passed, only broken by the occasional mutterings between the company too low for John to make out even if he had been trying to listen. Zayne focused on reading a small book bent and folded along several pages in his left hand. He shifted his hand for a moment, making the title visible, emblazoned in fancy gold, "The Cold Mountains."

John cautiously refocused his gaze on what he could see of the dim tunnel blurring past his eyes through the windows, just the tunnel's cragged rock and the seemingly endless track stretching into the infinite darkness.

INTERLUDE 2: THE FALL OF THE CITY OF LIGHTS

He ran through the darkness, relying on memory and reflex to safely maneuver between the camp's empty structures. It was unfortunate that while the sky was overcast, the city's light was still a barrier. Any approach would be spotted early, and the solider didn't doubt they would be torn to shreds in a rain of steel fire if they dared to approach. Still, he did his job and finished his run, halted by the middle-aged man, breathing in quickly to try and steady himself. The man turned, and the solider was thankful for a moment that the darkness shrouded the man's face too. He had seen enough horrors for one night. Still, he was a professional and had a report to make.

"Sir, the MP is in place."

What an MP was, the soldier hoped he never found out.

"Good," the man said; his voice was cracked like the surface of cooled lava. "Give the signal."

One of the knights next to the man garbed in a full segmented plate that shifted freely around his limbs clicked a button by the collar of his neck and said, "Detonate." A single croaked word, and the world itself seemed to flash as the city's lights instantly flared a bright searing white that illuminated the valley, still not reflecting off the paint covered armor that lay in wait before the lights went out.

CHAPTER 5

BETWEEN A ROCK AND A HARD PLACE

Something was bothering John, and it wasn't that he was racing through a pitch-dark tunnel under a rocky mountain. An antsy feeling like electricity was cycling in his chest.

Perhaps it was the way too attractive elven girl who sat in the seat closest to the console's left. Her face was…distracting, and John wasn't quite sure why.

So, John focused ahead at the terrifying abyss that the low lights from their transport could not pierce. If the track dropped ahead, they wouldn't notice to perhaps 10 meters, and by then, it would be far too late.

This might have happened to the other expeditions; a dark thought crossed his mind before John shook it away. If needed, he should be able to telekinetically slow the flight to the ground enough to ensure survival.

He hoped.

With that pleasant thought finished, John once again focused on the darkness ahead of him, and the unpleasant mental sensation returned. He closed his eyes, and the sensation went away. John opened his eyes, and it returned even more potent; that wasn't normal.

"Zayne—"

"I feel it too." The handsome man's face twisted into a grimace as he glared up ahead. "Slow to stop."

John focused, reducing the current flowing into the tram, and the vehicle slowed to a crawl, that John cut as Zayne drew a short line across his throat at him. The tram stopped, but the inner lights remained on. Zayne's hands scrambled over the board till they found a red switch, which he flipped, cutting all the internal lights entirely.

Now the dark abyss was inside too.

"Wh—" a feminine voice hushed from the back. Was that Aysel?

John's attention was scattered by a distinct something scraping over the metal roof. The rest of them stirred in their seats.

"John, 100%. Now."

John rammed the throttle forward and groaned as magic was slurped from his reserves into the train, causing the external lights to flicker on.

There were curved teeth, approximately way more of them than John was comfortable with, staring at him from outside the viewport. The skeleton head of a dragon glared through the window with a single, ruby-filled moving eye. This was all John saw as the wheels engaged, causing the tram to shoot forward, and the skeletal head vanished from the viewport. The tram cannoned forward through the abyss, and first, one red sparkle then another appeared as the lights of the tram scattered off a horde of humanoid skeletons with a single ruby eye set in each of their skulls.

This was all John saw as the tram smashed through the skeletons, sending pale white bone fragments flying onto the viewport. The bones chattering off the surface alerted the rest of the tram's occupants to the sight outside.

"Zayne, what's going on?" Marcila's voice was calm and steady, and Zayne replied in the same manner, "Mountain Bones; they can't break through the tram, though. Why are they—"

Suddenly, the bones vanished, only to show an empty abyss, with no track. They were falling.

John reached for his magic, not knowing what he was trying to do but spreading it outward to try and grip the metal to slow, and stop the fall. The tram tugged, slowing momentarily before the weight bore down on John like the mountain itself.

He broke.

CHAPTER 5.5

ON THE BENEFITS OF NOT BEING DEAD

The cold penetrated every fiber of his being. John couldn't move or breathe, not that breathing was an option. John found himself surrounded by thick, dark water, at least he thought so. Something grabbed him and pulled, dragging him deeper, or was it upwards? His lungs burned too much, and John swallowed something liquid. Hands like iron gripped him and pulled; suddenly the water was gone, yet John could not breathe. Hammered beats occurred on his chest; it expanded, and John coughed murky liquid out over his already soaked clothing. Next to him, Aysel was kneeling, visible under the glow of soft blue light from an undetectable source. She was soaked to the bone as John was, her hands still pressed over his aching chest.

"Th—" John collapsed into a coughing fit, choking up even more dark liquid. Another moment passed. Magic sparked then flowed inside him, and finally, the pressure on his lungs eased. John tried again to speak. "Thank you." The instant the words left his mouth, they felt inadequate.

Her face brightened for a moment before her expression dimmed again. "You're welcome."

They were alone on what looked like a rocky outcropping set a distance above a massive pool of cave water, which expanded into the darkness so vast that John couldn't see the other side. Aysel must have carried him up, John realized. They were both soaked, and John could see the chill already beginning to seep its way into Aysel's frame as she shivered.

John concentrated; he could feel that his magic reserves were still depleted, but he knew how to weave at least a simple heat spell. Grasping at his magic, he spun the energy and bent it around them until heat flared around them, causing their clothes to steam. The steam came to a hissing halt, and John reduced the heat to ambient warmth. Aysel's chills receded, and she spoke, "Thank you as well." She pointed upwards, and John followed her gaze to the space above.

Multicolored glowing crystals were sticking out of the cavern's stone, providing just enough light to pierce the gloom up to the tram tracks. That is where the tram track should have been and where now only bent and torn steel remained.

John looked around trying to peer further into the dark but the light the crystals provided was dim at best.

He turned back to Aysel, "The others?"

Aysel shook her head. "I do not know. I found you by chance when your body bumped into me as I swam out. No one else has surfaced. I…" she trailed off.

John's heart sank, he looked around again. Maybe the other adventurers had surfaced further than the light of the dim crystals could reach. He shook his head shaking the thoughts away, he was being far too hopeful. "So we're on our own."

"Yes."

The water lapped against their stone outcropping, the only sound that disturbed the silence for a moment.

John felt around at his belt for a sword that he already knew was missing. He glanced at the murky waters grimly. What even was the chance…? There was a faint tingling as his hand moved seemingly of its own accord, raising out and over the dark water. A splash, and then a corded hilt slapped into his hand out of a spray of water that doused him. The sheath had come off at some point, but the silver-blue blade was intact.

Releasing a strangled exclamation, Aysel jumped back slightly and said, "How'd you do that?"

"I... I'm not sure?" What had Bernard done to the sword? That wasn't him. Was it?

Aysel shook her head, dismissing the question despite his short answer. "It's not important. You have a weapon, which is more than we could say before."

John nodded, looking around the cavern, which answered the question of where the strange green was coming from. Faintly glowing crystals were embedded into the cavern walls above, decorating the slick cavern walls otherwise smoothed by centuries of water.

Torn and bent steel jutted from the roof wrenched apart, creating a massive gap where the rails suddenly both misaligned and *away* from each other. There was no way the tram had broken the track that way, which meant—

"I don't think this was an accident," John said softly, trying to keep his voice steady against the adrenalin flooding through his veins.

"Agreed, but that just makes it more imperative we get out of here." Aysel's face was stoic. They sat down on a rocky outcropping at the edge of a dark pool of cave water. The cavern walls were made of sheer rock weathered possibly from eons of water running down the walls.

How were they even supposed to get out of here?

"I—" Aysel clapped her hand over John's mouth, holding her free one up to her lips, before pointing at her ears. What was she trying to convey? Voices, rough and still distant but definitive, sounded from overhead, "Did those fools send another tram down?"

"Who cares? There's no way they survived the fall," another, higher voice responded.

"Fall or not, we still have to check; you know that the General doesn't accept anything but eyewitness reports," a third and distinctly low voice cut the conversation to a close. Rock shifted as footsteps shuffled about, and a beam of light suddenly shone down on the still displaced water into which they had crashed.

The light traveled over the water, drifting slowly toward their rock, and fear clutched at John's stomach. A soft but firm hand grasped his wrist, and a sensation like warm water trickled over his skin; the light passed over him, shining straight through where his body should have been on the stone below.

"If any survived, they're not here," said the second voice, and the two others murmured various assents before the thudding footfalls walked away. Aysel released her grip on his wrist.

They looked at each other silently. Anxiously, John tried to push the anxiety down. What were they supposed to do?

Aysel whispered, "Do you see that slightly protruding rock?"

She pointed upwards to the left at what looked like a slick cavern wall at first glance, but as John looked closer, he saw that the rock did protrude outward if only by a hand's span. He nodded, unwilling to use his voice out of caution.

"Can you throw me up there?" Aysel asked.

He didn't know. John had enhanced his strength before with magic in spars with Bernard, but this…

"I'll try."

Aysel nodded and lifted her left foot slightly, and placed it on his platformed hands.

"Now."

John jerked his torso and arms upward with a heave, sending Aysel up as she leaped upwards, her arm outstretched, catching onto the stone with her left hand. She then jerked her body once more upward to another small outcropping two meters up, catching on with her right arm. She repeated this, scaling what had looked like a sheer rock with ease until she got to the top, where she pulled herself over, vanishing.

A long couple of moments passed before a rope was tossed over, landing on the rocky outcropping in front of him.

"Climb."

Her voice, though quiet, carried efficiently to his ears in the near-dead silence of the cave only broken by the lapping and dripping of water. John grabbed the rope and started pulling himself upward. The rope was taut, and John heaved his body upward, his magic easily aiding each pull. He arrived at the top and saw Aysel peering warily down the dark tunnel.

She turned to him, revealing bright silver pupils.

John remembered that elves could see in absolute darkness, a supposedly useless fact that Bernard had told him. She reached out a hand and grabbed John's, turning and pulling him deeper into the dark abyss where soon John could not make out anything.

The dark pressed down on him, his sight gone his only guide her firm grip on his hand, pulling him further in. Each step impacted unevenly against the stone, and John found himself having to continually try and prevent himself from stumbling over the rough stone. They moved through darkness until suddenly, Aysel halted. Then she pulled once again, continuing forward.

And suddenly, the darkness was broken, a speck of yellow light up ahead piercing the curtain. Aysel went on, and John realized the light was coming from a glowing light in the wall that came from a glass bulb.

As they got nearer, the sounds of clunking and chinking, almost like those from the workshop, reached his ears except these were far louder and more discordant.

The reason became apparent as they crept ahead, crouching and peering out onto the Mountain Hold lit with innumerable lights. Shapes moved below, which John realized were people: dwarves, elves, and humans clad in chains to each other, shepherded by figures in smooth armor that glimmered crimson as they passed through the lights.

The metal bones of a massive construct rose from the center of the city from where they could hear the sounds of construction; the light flared brilliantly on the ring as the metal was welded.

Aysel tugged at his arm, gesturing toward a path that ran down into the city from the outcropping. They moved slowly, still crouching, only rising as the stone surrounding the city passed over their heads as they descended. Entering the street level, they cautiously looked around. The surrounding buildings were dark, the only light coming from the streetlamps.

Thud, thud, thud, the march of boots caused Aysel and John to glance at each other momentarily in panic before they threw themselves to the left, pressing up against a small stone alcove. Figures garbed in full dull grey steel marched past a group of people in torn clothing. The people were bent over and huddled in the middle, carrying an assortment of what looked like mining tools.

The group passed, leaving the street empty, and Aysel moved forward; John followed. They moved through the streets, the clink and whine of what sounded like tools growing louder as they moved deeper into the city. They passed broken merchant shops with smashed windows; then a jewelry shop, "Balin's Values!" where gold valuables lay scattered across the ground like grains of sand.

Foodstuffs had been emptied of its contents; windows were shattered across the ground in the dim light from the streetlamps. Carefully they maneuvered around the glass, finding more stores completely untouched and not raided.

A magical forge's front, "Seven Wares," was knocked down, the forges inside torn apart and scattered across the ground.

Aysel dragged John through the empty gap where the window of a "Georges Staves and Wands" had once resided. They crouched behind what had probably once been the seller's desk, the tramp and grind of stone and metal roaring in his ears before it faded gradually. John peeked out from the side of the desk. The room was torn apart, wood and precious metals scattered about. A single box lay empty on its side a short distance away.

Emblazoned on its side was "Hart Steel."

"Food and Hart Steel," John murmured to himself

John wondered what was going on. Hart Steel was valuable, but so were the gold and jewels scattered across the ground. They differed only in that Hart Steel was necessary for magical circuits and channels. He heard more tramping and pulled himself in tightly behind the desk, as did Aysel, whom John was now staring directly at.

The tramping stopped suddenly, and John heard the clinking of metal grinding from what sounded like the store's immediate front.

The sound of moving armor faded into indistinct vibrations, to nothing.

His hands were shaking, John realized, and he forcefully clenched them. John looked at Aysel, her face indistinct in the darkness. She stood up slowly, peering over the counter before gesturing at John to move. He stood up and followed as she led them back out of the shop, peering out the broken window opening before exiting entirely back onto the street.

Aysel led further into the city, drifting by the edges of buildings and cautiously peering around the corners on the alert for whoever these people were. The clanking that had been quieter on the outskirts was growing louder until the reason for the sound became apparent as Aysel gestured for him to look around the corner.

A gigantic machine constructed of glimmering metal shot into the air, the metal was bound by railing in an almost cone-like formation. In the center of the construction, a swirling red orb of magical energy hovered, casting a baleful glow.

John's vision swam, and he pulled himself back around the corner, trying to calm the sense of vertigo that had turned the world shaky. The feeling passed, receding to something smaller but still nagging, of something being distinctly *wrong*.

Aysel also seemed to be steadying herself. Once she did so, he followed her, this time away from whatever was going on in the construction, into the city's relatively darker outskirts.

John followed with no complaint: equal parts having no other idea and refusing to make a sound out of fear of being heard. They traveled through the empty streets, which John now realized in the closer light of the red, was scored with magic damage running the length of the street. An entire storefront had disappeared into a gaping hole in the ground they steered clear from.

SCREECH!

John's thoughts scattered away as a thunderous crash rumbled through the block. Aysel and John spun as around to see a massive cloud of dust erupting from the construction spot.

Three figures sprinted from the cloud of dust, unlike the previously seen soldiers in armor. The figures sprinted towards them and then right past as the sound of metal footsteps pounding the ground behind them, grew to a roar as another squad of armored figures burst from the dust after them.

Aysel and John turned and ran. The air around Aysel seemed to shimmer green for a moment as her speed increased dramatically. Magic flowed through John's limbs, lending them speed and strength, speeding his run after her until they had both caught up with the running figures who had swerved around a corner. One of them turned, revealing a somewhat youthful male face. He drew a long blade in a flash, seemingly longer than he was tall, pointing it directly into John's face.

John halted, raising his hands, "We're not with them—" he said before more footsteps burst into the alley, revealing three heavily armored figures clutching halberds pointed at all of them.

One swung at John with no hesitation, and he desperately responded by sending his sword into a block, gritting his teeth at the heavy impact that jarred his arms.

On instinct, John stepped in, sliding his blade along the shaft, spinning the halberd away from the armored man's body, and swung in a heavy cut, slicing straight through the armor with the high-pitched screech of tearing metal. The armored man fell, and something cold settled in John's stomach.

What had he just—?

A halberd flashed towards his neck; John tried to block, too slow, and braced his mage shield. A long but narrow blade entered between the halberd and his neck as one of the figures thrust a dagger in between the parrying sword. A feathered shaft sprouted from the armored figure's chest, sending them to the ground, his blade tumbling out of his hands.

Aysel rolled around, grabbing the dropped sword, and swung in low, slicing at the legs of the final armored figure clearing through the metal with a tearing screech. The armored figure tumbled down as Aysel finished a spinning reversal of her blade into the armored back.

Suddenly, there were only five uneasy allies. They looked at each other before the sounds of tramping metal alerted them to the present being still dangerous. The figure with the dagger looked back and forth between Aysel and John, hood shifting with her movement. She finally spoke in a low voice, "Come."

John looked at Aysel, who shrugged and responded in kind. "What else can we do?" John didn't have a response; He turned to the one with the dagger and said, "Okay."

CHAPTER 6

REBELS WITH A CAUSE

John and Aysel followed the cloaked figures through streets and alleys twisting and turning with seemingly no rhyme or reason, each building looking nearly the same until they arrived close to the outskirts. A house tucked in behind three others only accessible through a narrow alley turned out to be their destination.

The only source of illumination was the eerie red glow permanently cast over the city from an unknown source. The figure with the bow stooped down slightly by a section of the stone walk at a dark home's walls. The figure pressed their hand down, and soft brown light swirled over the stone, illuminating several glyphs before the ground shuddered and tore apart.

Stone steps led down into the darkness and the figure took the lead stepping down them. John and Aysel glanced at each other before they followed. The tunnel was dark, but as the sound of stone sliding back into place ceased, soft yellow light lit up along the side of the tunnel, revealing more grey stone.

The group continued walking forward until they emerged into a larger, bigger area with three beds lined up in the far-left corner and a kitchen and pantry in the opposite corner. The center of the room had a table surrounded by eight dark blue cushioned chairs. The three accompanying figures shed their cloaks to reveal two humans, possibly around John's age: one a boy with dark brown hair tied back in a ponytail and piercing dark brown eyes. His bow was still slung across his back; the other a girl had bright green eyes and long red hair that fell loosely around her shoulders. The third and final member was a dwarven woman, older than the other two, whose hair was a deep onyx black, and her eyes a fiery red.

They were all garbed similarly in simple, flowing dark cloaks, under which they wore dark shirts, and pants tucked into their boots. The dwarven woman stepped forward and said, "Who are you two?"

Aysel responded, "We're an expedition from the City of Lights, our tram—"

"—Fell into a pit?" the dwarven woman interrupted. Aysel nodded.

"The track was one of the first things those stone chewers cut," the dwarven woman continued, "I'm surprised they didn't find you."

She sounded suspicious. John said, "We're telling the truth. I'm actually from the City of Lights."

Her glare turned towards John before a flash of recognition appeared. "Wait, aren't you that kid Bernard of the Western Workshops took in?"

John nodded, somewhat dumbfounded, until her features finally cleared through his memory. "Karat?" he said.

Her face softened as she smiled. "I can't say this is how I imagined our next meeting, but all the same, it's nice to see you again. John, was it?"

John nodded. Karat owned a jewelry store that Bernard had sold products to and bought materials for, for as long as John knew. John had met her multiple times between the various meetings she'd had with Bernard, who had called her an old acquaintance, something he had never expanded upon.

Either way, John was glad to see a person that didn't want to kill him.

"What happened, Karat?"

Karat sighed, sitting on a nearby chair and said, "You'll probably want to sit down. The story's a little complex."

John sat in a nearby stuffed chair. Aysel mirrored his actions on another thick cushioned seat. The human boy and girl also took seats, but theirs were located right by Karat, flanking her on each side.

"It started some weeks ago; a tram went missing on the way to the city; no warning, just dropped out of communication. The Minister of Stone was found dead in his chambers, seemingly having dropped dead for no apparent reason, at least none that anyone could determine. Then people just started disappearing, and that's when those armored figures you just saw started appearing. They called themselves the Hemlock Guard, and the Council said they had been hired for our protection. It didn't take long before they started rounding us up to build that machine. Old Man Abrams was the first to refuse, and they killed him. The survivors in hiding were discovered. I ran into Martin and Silvia here, dodging the patrols to scavenge for food."

Karat spoke the entire time calmly, showing little to no emotion. She looked exhausted; she had dark bags under her eyes, and she was drooping on the chair. The tall boy whom John assumed to be Martin had busied himself with finding a bag of tea but seemed to have trouble keeping enough magic current flowing to power the pot. John stood up and walked over to him and said, "Here, let me."

Aggrieved, tired eyes stared out from under his curtain of brown hair before what John said clicked through the almost physical current of tiredness that rested over him. Martin stepped aside, and John placed his hand on the kettle handle, letting his magic run through the system, causing the kettle to heat up and steam to begin hissing out rapidly.

John lifted the kettle, passing it over each of the five cups. Martin grabbed three, and John grabbed the remaining two, which he brought back with him to his seat, handing one to Aysel.

Martin handed the other two cups to Karat and Silvia, who both cupped their hands around the drink in oddly similar motions. John looked down at his cup and felt a faint flash of resistance to drinking the tea. How did he know they could trust them? John shook the thought away and took a sip. Unfounded paranoia was just going to drive him over the edge sooner. John could trust Karat. Bernard trusted her.

It wasn't like John had any spells that could detect poison anyway. With that morbid thought, John took another sip. Aysel cocked her head and nodded along to Karat's words attentively.

John noticed his cup was shaking, sloshing its contents about and some over the side, spilling dark red liquid onto his pants. John blinked, and the liquid reverted to translucent green tea again. He set the cup down at the side of his chair and clenched his fist tightly, trying to eliminate the trembling. He couldn't let the pit in his stomach open up anymore. What would Bernard do?

He didn't know.

John was sure he wasn't ready for where this adventure had led. He had thought he was, but it was becoming increasingly apparent that his fantasies of adventure had lacked the terrifying reality of it. Fear clawed through his thoughts, sending them into a whirlpool of darkness that was sucking him down.

Something warm landed on his shoulder, and John looked up to see that it was Aysel's hand; she was looking at him with an expression that John couldn't quite place. The sight of her broke his train of thoughts. Aysel's mentor Marcila was most likely dead, and she wasn't losing her senses. He needed to get a hold of himself. He took deep breaths until he felt the world's equilibrium right itself.

Karat was taking a big sip of her tea before placing the mug down.

"So, what now?" he said, a cross between an honest question and a plea for a solution.

Karat frowned. "We need to take back the Mountain Hold, but that's a hard task especially considering you have all the resisting forces I know of in this room. You didn't come down here with anyone else, did you?"

The others… John had been trying very carefully not to think of what had happened to them. Aysel looked down before saying, "We were part of a larger expedition, but a section of the track was out…the others didn't make it."

Martin straightened up in his chair, brow furrowing before he said, "Silvia and I spotted a group of guards when we were arranging the distraction. They had some people we didn't recognize chained to each other."

John's stomach twisted; a blue spark traveled over his cupped hands, and suddenly his tea was boiling again. John took a deep, shuddering breath; he may have only been an adventurer for a little less than a day, but he knew the rules. If any of the party was captured, the remaining members had to do everything they could to rescue them.

And what else were they supposed to do? The City of Lights had been taken; his home. John couldn't abandon his home, and Bernard. A small part of him wanted to run, flee in terror and go anywhere but here. John pushed the thought aside and said, "We have to rescue them."

Karat sighed.

"They've been taking any citizens who won't work to the City Center, which they've converted to a prison. Rescue won't be easy. The place is crawling with guards. A straight-on approach won't work."

"What about the sewers?" Silvia interjected. "They lead under the entire city?"

"Wouldn't they be under guard too?" Aysel asked.

Silvia shook her head. "At first, the Hemlock Guards attempted to search the sewers for anyone who may have hidden out, but they're so expansive it's impossible to look everywhere. Especially because they need most of the guards dedicated to forcing people to work on that machine the both of you saw."

"What is that machine?" Aysel frowned.

"We're not sure," Karat said. "But it's what they've been focusing on building since the takeover. Either way, the first step is freeing the rest of your group; we need all the hands we can get."

"It's dangerous," interjected Martin, face creased in a deep frown. "I thought we decided it was too risky before."

John grimaced and made to respond, only for Silvia to speak first, "We decided it was too risky because we only had three people. We have two more now and a fully qualified adventuring group waiting for rescue."

Martin didn't look satisfied, but he nodded and focused back on his drink. A moment of silence passed before Karat once again spoke, "We can help you, but you have to help us in taking back our city."

Aysel nodded. "The Adventurers' Contract would require us to do so anyways."

Karat smiled faintly at that. "Well, that's dealt with, then. Martin, we'll need the maps."

Martin nodded and moved to a far corner of the room with a desk, chair, lamp, and a massive pile of papers. He grabbed one of the stacks and walked back, overlaying the sheets one after another. The sheets formed a giant map marked with writing, indicating guard patrols and camps spaced throughout the city. Karat prodded along a couple of green markings interspersed through the map.

"These are the entrances to the underground of the city, and this," she pressed a complex located near the outskirts, "is the prison. It's guarded by the Hemlock Guards day and night, but most of their forces have been concentrated at the machine, especially because of our attacks on the structure. Besides that, we don't have much else to go on," she tapped on a section of the map a fair distance from the prison where a red circle was scrawled, "as the machine has been the main focus of our attacks."

"So, what would you propose?" asked Aysel, looking thoughtful.

"They won't be expecting us at the prison," interjected Silvia. "One of us could set off a decoy attack on the machine while the rest exit through one of the sewers."

"That would leave that person exposed," Martin said.

Silvia shook her head. "Not if they were fast. You, Karat, or I know the City well enough to escape even on our own.

We need as many of us as possible at the prison if we want to succeed."

"It's still risky," Martin replied, grimacing.

"It's all risky," Karat said, drawing both Silvia and Martin to look at her. "But if we don't take the risk, we'll get caught eventually anyway."

CHAPTER 7

SECOND ROUND, FIGHT

In tribute to their ancestors, the majority of cities constructed by the dwarves reside within hollowed-out mountains. These cities are not just inhabited by dwarves, though, and are vibrant communities filled by all of the peoples. Their relative isolation from the world, in general, is seen as an advantage by their residents as the natural defenses of the city make them difficult targets to conquer. This isolation can have slightly negative consequences as they are entirely reliant on their lines of communication that run to their neighboring cities.

(Excerpt from H. Dallas, *The Peoples of the Realms*)

As John walked the streets after Martin and Silvia under the dim city lights, he could not shake the uneasy feeling that had accompanied him from the hideout. Karat and

Aysel had split off to cause a distraction and were supposed to meet them after the breakout. It had not escaped John how little the three had been willing to tell Aysel and him about the details of their plan. The mistrustful looks Martin had been giving him would have tipped him off anyhow.

They turned a corner onto a smaller street lined with mostly intact houses, aside from the odd shattered window. They halted in the center of the street, lit by a couple of dim lamps. Martin bent down, waving a hand that trailed crimson light over a section of the street, which slid back to reveal a set of stairs. Silvia stepped forward first, red hair swaying slightly, and began descending. Martin looked at John and gestured with his chin toward the hole. "You're next."

John nodded, not seeing the point in arguing, walked ahead, and began stepping down, passing under to see another similar street as above except for the ceiling being markedly closer than the cavernous rock formation above the first level. He stepped down into the faintly green-lit tunnel courtesy of Silvia, who was holding her hand up and letting off a small but bright green light.

John reached the bottom and stepped to the side. The tunnel was paved with cobblestone inset with houses and other buildings similar to the city's portion above; broken and smashed windows and doors abounded. The light in the tunnel was scattered, emerging from the still-standing streetlights casting the surroundings in dim yellow light. The light from overhead vanished with a clunk as Martin stepped down, and the stair entrance sealed shut behind him. He reached the bottom of the steps and turned back and forth, looking down the tunnel for a moment before looking at Silvia. "Straight and to the left?"

Silvia nodded. "Should be."

Martin took the lead, walking down the city street and holding his hand aloft to leave a red light on their surroundings. In turn, John followed along with Silvia as they walked with only the faint echoey steps to break the silence.

They continued for some time like this, passing by numerous buildings without light and life, blurred together in their abandoned state. Unfortunately, this time left John to his thoughts, which drifted back to Bernard and his home. Was the City of Lights still free? Had the Barons invaded already? What was even going on in the Mountain Hold? Unanswered worries clawed at his mind.

Clink.

John paused, looking around the street. What was that?

The street shaded under the streetlights remained empty. John continued stepping forward, carefully placing each foot on the ground to minimize the noise.

Only his and the other faint footsteps of Silvia and Martin broke the silence.

Clink.

That wasn't his imagination; he spun, looking about himself only to once again find nothing.

Silvia's voice interrupted his thoughts, "John, what's going on?"

Silvia, features cast in sharp relief from the overhead streetlights, was looking at him in alarm, a hand gripped to one of her long daggers that hung underneath her cloak.

John responded, feeling somewhat sheepish for alarming her. "Nothing, I just thought I heard something."

Silvia nodded. "The Underground can play tricks like that; just keep moving."

John did so, swiveling his head up and down the street every so often, but the road remained empty. Despite this, his trepidation remained.

Clink.

John did not spin, but he searched the gloom around him until a flash of bone-white caught his eye on a beaten building. His eyes traced the bone upward to a massive skeletal leg, up to an all too familiar draconic skull with a single harsh red eye.

John froze cold, fear sinking through his limbs, deadening them.

Martin called out, "Hey, what's the idea? We need to—" his voice dropped off suddenly.

The skull stretched its bony maw and *roared*, a sound that deafened as much as it tore at the ears. An arrow shot through the air, chipping, slamming into the eye, and dispersing in a shattering of wood. Magic raced through John's system, lending him speed as he ran forward.

"Run!" he cried.

Martin and Silvia did not need him to say that and shot forward as they ran as a group.

The skeletal dragon fell to the ground with a leap, lacerating stone, just missing Martin and sending a cloud of dust into the air. They continued running, and with another bounding jump, the skeletal dragon rose over them, impacting the street ahead, glaring balefully at the group.

John halted, not knowing what else to do; he drew his sword from the loop he had placed it through on his belt. The silver-blue blade glimmered in the green light, still cast by Silvia's hand. Martin drew his bow from over his back, and Silvia drew two long daggers from beneath her cloak.

In a flash of viridian light, an arrow shot from Martin's bow, lancing through the darkness and crashing into a shower of green sparks against the red eye.

Despite it being a skeletal dragon, John had a distinct feeling that it was insulted. Like a whip, its bony tail lanced toward John from the darkness. He flared his magic, and the tail clashed against his sapphire shield, sending magic sparking from the impact and taking a hefty chunk from John's reserves.

Silvia sprinted past him, red light shooting over her limbs as she leapt into the air, soaring to land on the skull. The dragon roared and shook it's head trying to shake Silvia off, but she caught on to the empty eye socket, preventing her from being thrown.

John sprinted forward himself, magic lending his legs speed, aiming for one of the frontal skeletal legs, and swinging. His blade clashed against the bone, sending painful vibrations into his hands, nearly jostling his sword from them. The bone cracked and dented but remained as a whole unbroken, and the claw ripped to the side, slamming into him, denting another bit of his reserves and sending him through the air, only to painfully collide with the front of a building.

Blearily, John saw Martin jumping and rolling backward to dodge the massive tail, which slammed deep craters into the street with every miss. Silvia still clung on to the empty eye socket, but her body was tossed about like a leaf as the dragon moved about.

John struggled up to his feet and charged, ducking under a bony claw, that tried to swipe him in half, and slammed his sword once again into the spindly leg. His blue magic splayed about his arms as an ear-splitting crack ripped through the air, the bone collapsing, sending the beast towards the ground.

John backpedaled, trying to avoid the collapsing skeletal body, and managed to make just enough distance as the tail came slamming down on where he once stood. The draconic creature collapsed without the support of its right foreleg and was now struggling to rise with its remaining three.

It emitted another colossal roar, a grinding vibration against John's eardrums that made him wince and clap his free hand to one of his ears, which did little to dull the sound. Silvia, right next to the cavernous maw, painstakingly climbed her way upward as John saw a bit of blood dribble from her ears. Her left hand clasped onto a bony spike on the forehead, and with her right, she drew her dagger, slamming the blade directly into the evil red eye.

The roar stopped, and in the sudden silence, John's ears continued to ring before his magic filtered through them, allowing for sound to once again filter into his mind. The now dull red eye, no longer glowing red, turned into obsidian stone as the skeleton collapsed, sending Silvia into a fall from the remaining meters. She landed with bent knees to absorb the impact, which turned into a full collapse onto the ground.

Martin and John rushed forward; they arrived at Silvia's side, who looked exhausted, eyes partially open, ears bleeding red. A shimmer of green light ran over her features, and Silvia looked slightly better, the color returning to her cheeks. "Well, I guess it wasn't just the Underground playing tricks."

Her dry statement caught John off guard, and despite that, he couldn't help but snort, followed by the same from Martin, who looked at him for a moment, and the tension that had been underneath the surface since John had met him dimmed.

"Are you alright, Silvia?" Martin questioned, face twisted in worry in the red light he was still emitting from his left hand.

Silvia nodded. "I think so."

They gave each other long looks, and John had the vague sense of intruding. He thus turned slightly, looking about the street, eyes catching onto the skeletal dragon, which was utterly lifeless, disconnected now from the events of the world. Its right foreleg, shattered by John's strike, had caused the skeleton to collapse, so its unbroken foreleg was on top.

Was it the same dragon that John had encountered on the tram tracks? It looked similar, but John couldn't help but wonder if there were perhaps *more* of them.

"We need to keep moving," Silvia's voice broke John from his thoughts, and he saw that she had risen to her feet and lit her hand once again with brilliant green light interplaying with Martin's crimson light. Martin extinguished his light as Silvia took the lead once again, Martin following behind her, leaving John to now take up the rear.

They moved down the street at a hastened pace, minutes turning into nearly an hour before their march halted in a section of the underground city with a couple of large buildings that were just as abandoned as the rest. Martin pointed at a section of the rocky ceiling and said, "Right about there is probably the best entrance point; past there should be the City Center."

A question occurred to John. "How are we going to get through?"

Martin smiled fiercely. "Like this."

He drew an arrow from the quiver at his side and whispered under his breath, the red light encircling the arrow, leaving faint, glowing marks. He pulled the arrow back, pointed up at the ceiling, then released it. The arrow flew up, impacting the roof and piercing through enough to hold in the rock.

Boom!

Red flashed in a dazzling display, ripping through rock in a massive explosion; the rock collapsed, causing the stone to fall, crashing into the buildings below, and leaving an enormous gaping hole revealing a well-lit grey ceiling. Martin drew back another, muttering something under his breath and rereleased.

The arrow flew, embedding itself into the ceiling before a glowing red, slightly translucent rope dropped down to the floor below.

Silvia grasped on and started pulling herself upward, followed by Martin; John grabbed on after the rope, and started pulling himself up. The rope seemed to hold his body and then release as he dragged himself upward, arriving at the gaping hole just after Silvia and Martin.

He pulled himself up into a basement-like room with thick stone walls and lighting provided from overhead by several dim yellow bulbs. Martin and Silvia had moved to a stairwell and positioned themselves just out of sight of anyone coming down. Martin had drawn an arrow to his bow, and Silvia was gripping her dagger.

Martin jerked his neck at John, gesturing behind himself, and John followed the nonverbal command, moving over to stand behind Martin. John rested his hand on his sword and waited, straining his ears to hear the approaching footsteps.

Nothing. Not a single sound. No hammering of approaching footsteps. No raised voices.

John, Silvia, and Martin looked at each other uneasily. Martin tentatively stepped forward and began walking up the stairs, easing a foot on to each step, followed by Silvia and then John, who nervously held his sword hilt. They moved up the stairs, reaching another floor filled with what looked like offices for the numerous officials who had once worked there. The halls were lit by overhead lights interspersed in the ceiling.

Some portions of the wall were blown out, chunks of stone littered over the floor; as they moved down the hallway, they had to pick around the rubble. They reached a split, and Martin led them to the right before opening seemingly at random a door to his left and ushering the rest of them inside. They entered a staircase and moved up the steps, passing the first and second floor and stopping at the third. Martin pushed slightly at the door and scanned outside before stepping through, followed by Silvia and then John, who stepped out into a corridor filled with closed doors.

"Is this really where they keep the prisoners?" Martin whispered; John felt increasing discomfort. Where were the Guards? They hadn't entered quietly, and if people were kept imprisoned here, shouldn't there be *something* to prevent them from escaping?

Silvia moved to one of the doors and tried to open it. "Sealed," she murmured. She pulled out her dagger and ran the blade through the gap of the door, emitting a small green light. She then pulled again, slowly opening the door to reveal a room filled with crimson armor stacks. They were in rows, some halfway through construction, others assembled as a full set.

Martin said quietly, "No good; it's just a storage room."

Silvia nodded in agreement and shut the door. They crept further down the hallway, testing a door every so often, only to find more suits of armor and rooms full of weapons. They arrived at the end of the hallway and encountered another door; Silvia ran her blade down the crease and then pulled, edging the door open to reveal five figures chained to the walls.

"It's them," murmured John, feeling a small drop of relief.

They looked far worse for wear, but John immediately recognized them: Zayne, Marcila, Lon, Trajan, and Seven. They looked unconscious and were bound by steel rings to flat boards that were tilted loosely upward. John made to step forward, only to be barred by Martin's hand. "Wait, this could be a trap."

John frowned but let Martin step forward slightly. Martin reached into a pouch at his belt and withdrew a silvery metal ball, which he proceeded to roll across the floor. The ball made its way forward, moving swiftly and stopped dead a couple of meters from the party members. The metal glowed red for a long moment and then continued rolling, coming to a stop in front of the party.

"There were wards, but they should be down," Martin explained.

John nodded hesitantly and once again attempted to move forward. Martin didn't stop him this time. He stopped before Zayne, who looked unconscious; examining the steel bands that bound him, he found that they were quite literally seamless, only smooth steel.

Martin and Silvia moved up. Silvia stepped farther forward and drew her dagger, bringing down the blade on the steel band, but unlike the doors, the blade stopped, unable to cut through. She frowned and turned back to them. "The metal's resisting any manipulation; it must be enchanted."

"Can you break the enchantment?" asked John, cold worry coiling in his stomach.

Silvia shrugged. "I used to work as an enchanter, but these are levels above anything I've ever done. I can try, but I could end up triggering something."

A moment of heavy silence passed between the group; John wanted to speak but was unsure of what to say. He couldn't abandon the other adventurers, but there didn't seem to be a way to get them out. Once again, he found himself contemplating what Bernard might have done in this situation, but this time a thought occurred. The bars holding his compatriots looked like solid metal but didn't look to be magically forged. Magic forged steel was solid. His sword was made out of it...

John drew his blade and walked forward, pressing the sword against the steel band. The blade edged onto the metal but did not cut through entirely. Focusing, he channeled his magic through the sword, causing the blade to glow a soft blue and slowly cut through the metal band. With a final jerk, the blade cut through the first band, and John moved to the second, and third; Martin and Silvia stepped forward to help Zayne's body off the platform. The final band finally came loose with a clatter, and they pulled Zayne free and laid him on the floor. A moment passed, and then Zayne's eyes flickered open, glancing around frantically before they landed on John.

"Looks like you found us," he croaked out.

John smiled weakly. "Yeah, Aysel, and I found some help."

Zayne nodded, eyes flickering to Martin and Silvia and then to the still trapped party members.

"Can you get the rest free?" he asked, and John nodded.

John went to Marcila's side and ran his sword similarly down her restraints, and with Martin and Silvia's help, lowered her to the floor. They repeated the process with Lon, Trajan, and Seven.

They all came to consciousness slowly at their release from their bindings, Zayne being the most alert as he was the first to be released.

"I've been through a lot, but I thought for sure this would be the end," Zayne said, gaze focused directly on John. "Thank you."

John shifted uncomfortably, not knowing how to respond to Zayne's solemn words. The problem was solved as Marcila spoke, her face creased in worry, "Where's Aysel?"

John did know how to respond to that. "She's with a woman named Karat; they're causing a distraction right now to keep troops away from the center."

Marcila nodded and rose to her feet, the rest of the group also doing so.

They moved across the room where John now realized their weapons had been tossed in a pile. They armed themselves and then looked back at John, Silvia, and Martin.

Martin said, "Follow me. We'll be going out the same way we came in."

He turned, going to the door and pulling gently. He eased it open, peering out, before beckoning towards the rest of the group to follow him. They arrived at the hallway and headed towards their makeshift entrance point.

Their steps echoed loudly in the silence, yet they remained unimpeded by any guards, a detail that was starting to worry John. Where were the guards? Was there so little point in guarding captured prisoners for whoever was in charge? Surely the distraction wouldn't have drawn *every* guard away.

They continued their somewhat silent march down the halls, turning down a staircase and then another, reaching the basement area. The red translucent rope still hung there, and the party members were ushered down after Silvia, who went first.

As Zayne was climbing down the rope, John's ears caught the faint sound of thuds, soft now but growing progressively louder. He looked at Martin. "Martin, do you—"

Martin cut him off. "Yes," he drew an arrow from his quiver, and John made to ready his sword only for Martin to shake his head. "Go, I'll be after."

John wanted to argue, but he knew that would be a waste of time. He slipped his sword into his belt and ran over to the rope, beginning to shimmy down after Zayne. Martin had backed up to the edge of the hole and drew back a shimmering arrow.

John dropped to the ground. Martin released his arrow into the depths of the basement and leaped onto the rope, sliding down.

Boom!

An explosion of red light visible through the hole erupted in the room with a cacophonous roar. Martin slid to a stop at the bottom of the rope, and pressing his hand against it, the rope dissolved into sparkles of red light.

"That won't delay them for long, and we need to run."

The group needed no further urging as it ran after Silvia, who was holding a hand up that lit the surroundings in a warm green light. John and Martin ran at the rear of the group, and John couldn't resist the urge to look back.

Behind them, visible even from a distance they had covered, a *swarm* of red armored figures emerged from the hole they had created, simply dropping to the ground and then turning in an almost mechanical manner to run after them, except for the ones who drew longbows from their backs, arrows launched.

They were going to get cut down as they ran. John's mind raced for an option, anything. For some reason, his mind latched on to when he had *tried* to stop the crash of the tram. When he had reached out in an attempt to halt the fall of the vehicle, he hadn't needed to try and hold a lot of mass; he just had to block it.

Not really knowing what he was doing, he bent his magic, folded it, and then let it spring backward. A massive wall of blue light shimmered into existence, causing the incoming hail of arrows to glance off in showers of blue sparks.

Following the rest of the group, John turned as they ran through the dark streets with only Silvia's light as a guide.

They turned street corners every which way as Silvia led them deeper into the maze of buildings. Around another bend, John realized they were once again in somewhat familiar territory as Silvia's light glimmered off the service ladder they had used to enter the underground. Silvia started to climb, followed by the rest of the group; Martin stayed at the bottom, bow drawn on the lookout. John stayed by Martin's side. The sound of trampling feet was still audible through the sound's direction, and thus, the enemy force was impossible to determine.

Martin's red light was the only source of illumination now taking up the duty after Silvia had reached the surface. As Zayne climbed up, John realized that only he and Martin remained at the bottom. Martin jerked his head at the ladder, but whatever he was about to say was void as an arrow smashed into his magic shield, causing him to stumble back.

John turned to see the guards once again, bows already let loose with more arrows flying their way. John desperately called on his magic, attempting to create a barrier as he did before the blue energy coalescing just as the first arrow sparked off on impact.

A thousand other arrows collided in the next second, and John gritted his teeth as each impact drove his reserves closer to empty. The hail didn't let up raining down until suddenly the blue wall vanished as John's reserves depleted. A vibrant red wall sprung up the next instant as Martin stepped forward. "Go!" he shouted. John hesitated. If he left, there was no way for Martin to get out. He would be cut down by the hail of arrows that even now hammered against his shield. He glanced up once to see the rest of the party surrounding the hole outlined in Silvia's green light.

John drew his sword and swung, channeling every last piece of magic he had left through his limbs, directing his blade into the ground. His sword sliced through rock, and he poured everything he had into the blade. In the next instant, the ground exploded in a cloud of dust and rubble.

They fell.

CHAPTER 8

AN EXPLANATION OF SORTS

He was returning to consciousness the second time in a short period; John's head felt like an overworked furnace at the workshop. Jumbled thoughts moved through his exhausted mind. He was surprised to find himself alive and his limbs felt intact. Pitch dark clouded his sight until a small red glimmer caught his eyes. The glow grew into a full-blown crimson light pressing back against the darkness, revealing that he was in a tunnel, laying on top of a pile of crumbled rock and street. A little distance from him, he saw Martin lying back against the tunnel, left hand holding up the crimson light.

He looked at Martin, mottled brown to pale blue, and despite himself, John couldn't help smiling. They were alive. The smile faded as he attempted to shift his body, which immediately protested the movement as he realized his magic reserves were empty, the passive regeneration of mana getting sucked to his injured body.

Those injuries felt like they covered every inch of him. He was lucky to be alive, he realized. He had spent all of his mana to break the floor beneath them. He very well could have died if he hadn't stuck his sword through the rock beneath them.

His sword! He tried to feel around for the blade. Nothing. Back in the cave with Aysel, he had managed to summon it. What if he could still…

He raised his hand, calling.

There was a shift and grind of rock; he felt a familiar hilt slap into his palm, far lighter than it should have been. He channeled magic to his other palm, and his tired magic reserves formed a low light, enough to see that he was holding his sword's hilt attached to the warped broken metal.

John's heart sank.

"My sword," he whispered.

Martin's raspy voice broke him from his thoughts. "I'm sorry," he said as he looked at John with an unreadable expression.

"It's all right," John said, not knowing how else to respond.

A moment of silence passed.

Slowly, John felt his magic reserves filling once again as his injuries were dealt with for the most part. He once again tried to move, and this time there was no pain, though he still felt exhausted. He slowly crawled from the pile over to Martin, joining him leaning against the wall, still clutching the broken hilt.

"That was some fall," he said after a while.

Martin nodded. "Yeah."

"Any idea where we are?"

Martin attempted to shrug but winced as he shifted his shoulders. "Probably an old mine shaft. I used to explore them when I was a kid."

Another moment of silence passed before Martin spoke again. "Think they'll come down after us?"

John looked up into the gaping abyss above and thought for a moment. "They probably think we're dead. No reason to, right?" The last part felt more like a hope than an answer, but Martin nodded, seemingly satisfied.

Minutes became hours, and finally, John felt his magic reserves nearing full once again. Martin had dropped his hand and the light, and thus the only blackness had been visible for quite some time. Raising a hand, John channeled his magic, casting their surroundings in blue light.

They had landed in a sort of tunnel, and while the collapsed rock sealed one side, the other end stretched outward until John's light could no longer illuminate the darkness within.

"How deep do these tunnels usually run?" he asked.

Martin cocked his head thoughtfully. "Hundreds of kilometers. They cross and intersect everywhere."

"Do you think we can get back to the city through them?"

Martin shrugged helplessly. "Supposedly, all the tunnels should have been mined from the City, but we could just end up going deeper."

"Do we even have another option?" John replied dismally.

Martin sighed and shook his head. "No, we don't. I suppose there's nothing else for it then."

Martin began shifting, pulling himself to his feet. John mirrored his actions, and Martin stepped forward, taking the lead down the tunnel, handheld red light shining forward. They walked down the tunnel, and the monotony began to set in. The tunnel would sometimes deviate back, in turn-offs behind them, but they continued forward, hoping that they were headed in the right direction.

The air smelled slightly stale and dusty, itching at John's nose. Their march continued when John noticed that the path was ramping upward slightly, and they emerged into a somewhat wider stone passage. Martin looked down the hallway before pausing and walking over to a section of the wall. A series of lines were marked deep into the stone. Martin ran his palm over the symbols before turning back to John. "We're in the main passage if we head that way," he pointed down one end of the corridor, "we should exit back into the city."

John nodded and made to turn the direction Martin had pointed before something stopped him, and instead, he turned to look in the opposite direction. The tunnel extended into the darkness that his light could only pierce so far into, leaving a stretch of the abyss that his eyes could not penetrate. Something that was a feeling but not so much as a thought worried at the edge of his consciousness.

"John?" Martin's voice broke John from his thoughts, and he turned to look at Martin, his face furrowed into a concerned frown.

John found himself without an explanation, but he tried. "I—I'm not sure. I just feel that we should go that way."

Martin frowned. "That way just leads deeper into the mine tunnels. We need to head back; the others don't even know what's happened to us."

John frowned and nodded, understanding and agreeing with Martin's logic, but despite that, as he made to step away, he found that he had only stepped further down the tunnel. Frowning, he tried to turn but found his body completely unwilling to comply.

"Martin, I can't move away."

"What do you mean?" Martin walked to John's side.

"I mean just that." John tried to turn, but his feet just carried him forward another couple steps, "I can't walk away."

"What are—" Martin walked up next to him, and his face twisted from surprise to mirror the worry John knew must be apparent on his face.

They each tried to move backward, but every attempt caused their bodies to walk forward as if their bodies' controls had been overridden.

"I don't think we have much of a choice," John said, his gut twisting.

Martin nodded. "Eyes up, then."

They moved down the tunnel, the odd feeling of being driven forward persisting with each of their steps. Martin's red light illuminated the tunnel, which continued further downward, sometimes branching off, but the force driving them refused to allow any diversion in their path forward.

They continued forward, the darkness held at bay only by Martin's crimson magical light. Each step John rebelled at but found himself unable to do anything. Minutes turned to hours. They had walked forward so long that the feeling of trepidation had long since disappeared in John replaced by the frustration of their continued progress. How many kilometers under the mountain were they now?

Martin's light held back by the stone walls around them suddenly stretched farther as they stepped into a chamber; the only visible surface was the floor as the walls and ceiling vanished; presumably, such a distance away was clouded in utter darkness. Only the floor was visibly shaded under Martin's light around them, disappearing into the darkness farther out.

"Where are we?" murmured John, amazed at how massive the cavern must have been.

Martin had no response, shining his red light into the ink blackness. John lit his hand, and while the relative quantity of light had increased, the place's actual size was still undeterminable. John realized that his steps still refused to be turned back, so he walked deeper into the cavern with Martin.

Each step echoed, increasing the tension twisting at John's gut.

Each step brought them further into the room until they could no longer see the hole they had entered. Still, John and Martin were driven forward, until abruptly, they halted.

A moment of silence passed. "Should we go back?" Martin asked.

"I—" John cut off as something seemed to shift in the darkness. "Did you see that?"

Martin shifted, jutting his face forward, trying to peer through the gloom. "No, what is it?"

John shifted his hand forward, trying to illuminate the darkness further. Nothing.

He walked a couple more steps forward, and his light suddenly reflected, revealing a metallic shine. Another step ahead revealed that the shine was, in fact, a sword improbably embedded into the floor of the cave. The blade glimmered a pale blue under John's light, sparking and dispersing and somehow refracting over the blade in blue sparks. The hilt was comparably darkened, and on instinct, John reached for it.

Martin grabbed his wrist. "Are you crazy!?"

John looked at Martin, surprised by the vehement reaction. "What? I was going to—"

"Get yourself killed," Martin interjected. "Whatever force brought us down here, it could have meant for us to find this sword. Are you just going to trust that?"

John hesitated, thinking over what Martin said. He was logically right, but something at the back of his head nagged at him. Not quite a thought, but a feeling; this sword was important. More than that, as he stared at the blade, he couldn't help but feel that this sword was…different, a sensation, at the edge of his senses, a hollowness that he had felt all too often.

"I don't know, but I can't just leave it here."

He looked at Martin, who stared back at him with a slightly incredulous expression.

"Why?"

"It feels lonely."

Martin's expression further deepened in disbelief, but John was no longer paying attention; reaching forward, he grasped the hilt. Cool metal pressed into his palm, and he pulled, not expecting the sword to leave the ground without any magic enhancement to his strength.

The blade came free, and John stumbled slightly, not ready for the lack of resistance. The blade glimmered strangely under Martin's red light. Despite himself, John waited a moment, half expecting Martin's prediction to come true and for the next dangerous thing to occur.

Nothing happened. The feeling ebbed away, and John was left with the sword in his hand.

The blade's hilt fit smoothly into his palm, and when he shifted the sword, it moved lightly with a strange lack of heft, as if the sword was much lighter than it should have been.

He turned to Martin, who had taken multiple steps back as if anticipating an explosion. At John's gaze, Martin shrugged and cautiously stepped forward once more. He spoke somewhat abashedly, "I guess there was nothing to worry about after all."

John made to reply, but a faint click caught his ears before he got a sound out. He spun around looking for the sound, fearing yet another skeletal creature, but saw only a large rock that had most certainly not been there before. He emitted a half yelp and hastily stepped back a couple of paces. Martin drew his bow, preparing to knock an arrow, only to pause at the rock.

"Where did that come from?" Martin murmured, moving back towards John, albeit far more carefully.

John had no reply, but any response he would have had was cut off by a sharp *crack*, and the stone in front of them split open. Rock crumbled, and dust blurred the already dark air but not so much that it obscured the distinct form of a towering humanoid. They had dark grey skin similar to the stone they had just seemingly emerged from; they had no hair, and their eyes seemed to be formed by gleaming topaz, as a strange light to them caused them to glow slightly even in the relatively dark cave only lit by Martin and John's lights.

"Greetings, John Doe. I have been waiting for you."

John backed away further, surprise battling fear.

"Wha—"

"Do not be alarmed. I mean you no harm, nor you, Martin Kol."

The creature's head shifted to direct its gaze toward Martin, who stood there, jaw slightly agape and bow relaxed next to John.

A moment passed before John gathered himself enough to respond. "Who are you?"

"I am called Treemor, and I have been waiting for both of you."

John responded, feeling off-balance entirely, "Waiting?"

"Indeed, I have waited for over millennia to see you stand before me. I confess that I am relieved that the wait is over. There is not a terrible amount to do down here."

"I—" John tried to determine a response and ended with, "I'm sorry?"

Really, was that the best he had? John kicked himself in his head.

The being of rock shifted with a crunch and grind of stone. "It is immaterial. You are here now, and that is what matters. Seeing as you have the sword, I will proceed to show you to your next destination."

The creature turned and began to walk away, each rocky leg lifting and crossing a vast distance to bring themselves forward.

John looked at Martin, whose mouth was slightly agape. "Do we follow?" murmured John.

"I don't think we have much of choice," Martin responded in a similarly quiet voice.

They followed in Treemor's wake as they walked further into the cavern.

Eventually, after an indeterminable distance, Treemor stopped, and Martin's light glimmered off a massive pile of metal that revealed itself to be armor upon closer examination. Gauntlets, breastplates, greaves, and other pieces were all tossed in a messy pile. The metal glimmered surprisingly bright in Martin's light, seemingly not touched by the length of time they must have been there.

"I'm sorry for the mess; my hands aren't particularly suited for sorting," Treemor held up their massive stone hand articulated with three fingers each.

"Where did all this come from?" Martin asked.

"Various people have come down here over time, for items of value, but in return, I ask for something."

A knot began to form in John's gut. "What are you asking for the sword?"

Somehow Treemor's face twisted to form an expression similar to surprise. "The sword? Oh no, that was here long before me. I can claim no ownership of that blade. These items, on the other hand—" he gestured grandly at the pile of metal behind him, "—are most certainly mine. I am a collector, you see. Some of these items are well over a thousand years old. The histories are simply incredible. Why this gauntlet here—"Treemor retrieved an old, inscribed gauntlet from the pile— "Was crafted by Bernard the Lionhearted, a Captain of the Knights of the Dawn."

"The Knights of the Dawn?" Martin questioned, his puzzlement shared by John.

"You haven't heard of the Knights of the Dawn?" Treemor said, bewildered. "They're only the guardians of the Thirteen Realms. The ones who guard against the darkness."

"Thirteen Realms?" John said, confused. "Wait, the Thirteen Realms? There's only seven."

Treemor shifted with a rumble of stone. "Seven? That's not right at all. You must be mistaken."

"He's right. There's only seven," Martin responded.

Treemor did not speak for a long moment. Finally, he said in a voice far softer than previously, "It truly has been a long time."

A long moment of silence passed before John hesitantly said, "You said you were waiting for us. Why?"

It took a moment, but John's words seemed to rouse Treemor from his reverie. "I have been waiting on the orders of the Grand Mage Lano for a pair of humans who he said would be named John Doe and Martin Kol who I presume to be you two as you rather aptly match his description."

"Who is this grand mage?" John questioned; he had never met anyone of the sort.

Treemor responded, "Oh, he is quite the character, by far one of the most fascinating humans I have ever met. It is why I agreed to give his message to the pair of you."

"What message?" Martin asked suspiciously.

Treemor responded evenly. "That in your current endeavor you have already lost."

John's mind spun. "Lost, what do you mean lost?"

Treemor raised its shoulders slightly in an approximation of a shrug. "I do not know; he asked for me only to relay this message to the next pair of humans I encountered along with their—your—names."

A long moment of silence passed as John and Martin tried to wrap their minds around the simple yet stunning words Treemor had said.

Treemor spoke up, "I am sorry. It seems the Grand Mage Lano's words have distressed the pair of you."

"It's alright," John responded somewhat faintly, trying to figure out which way his mind was spinning. "Just a lot to process, you know."

"I understand." Treemor nodded.

Martin spoke; his voice had an edge to it. "Why?"

"I do not know," responded Treemor. "The Grand Mage did not share his reasoning, only that I must be here to relay this message to the pair of you."

John frowned, but he shook himself from the spiral of thoughts flowing through his mind, regardless of whether they still needed to get back into the city.

"Do you know how to get to the Mountain Hold from here?" he asked Treemor.

Treemor nodded. "I do," he pointed behind himself toward a shadowy section the room not yet pierced by Martin and John's light. "That way, you will find a set of stairs that will lead you to the city proper.

John looked at Martin. "We should go then."

Martin didn't respond for a moment, then he nodded. "All right," he spoke softly. John noticed Martin's grip on his bow had tightened.

John looked at Treemor. "Thank you; we need to go."

Treemor nodded slowly. "Of course, good luck John Doe and Martin Kol."

Martin took the lead, walking toward where Treemor had pointed his red light, finally finding the edge of the stone wall and a deep cavernous hole lined with chiseled steps that stretched upward into oblivion. They walked in silence. John noticed that he had no idea how long he had not seen the sunlight. It felt like a long time; he hadn't slept since before he had entered the mountain, and now his eyes were starting to weigh down like lead. Still, he marched behind Martin, not complaining.

Martin had said nothing since they parted from Treemor, and they continued onward in silence for some time, the floor slight angling upward, the only indication that they were hopefully headed in the right direction.

Time stretched; their steps continued their path. Martin's red light finally caught an opening ahead, which they stepped out of to find themselves suddenly at the Mountain Hold, or to be more precise, above it.

The buildings stretched out below were cast in a baleful red light from the machine that stood in the city center. The construction was still going on, specs of people worked about the device. The red orb seemingly had increased in size, though strangely, the mental sensation he had felt before looking at it was significantly lessened.

They were back. John looked about, trying to locate a way down from the outcrop they stood on top of. He finally located a set of steps almost invisible to the left due to how well they blended in, carved deep into the wall.

Martin had extinguished his light, the red glow cast by the machine just enough to see their surroundings. John took the lead stepping down the stairs, carefully followed by Martin. They were so high up the city under the Cold Mountains, the buildings looked like little more than children's toys. They continued their careful descent down the steps. John found himself easing each foot onto the step below to make as little noise as possible despite the probability of noise carrying the vast distance to the ongoing construction.

If they were discovered up here, there would be no escape. Faint echoes of the clink of machines were the only sound audible through the otherwise thick silence.

John and Martin had traversed around halfway down the steps now. They were eye level with some of the taller buildings. From this height, the buildings seemed more like toys, their rectangular shapes rising to attach to the ceiling of rock above. With every step, John's scabbard bumped against his leg, reminding him of the strange sword he had found and taken. Even now, John was unsure why he had taken the sword. Though it was not as strong now, the strange feeling of loneliness had remained at the back of his mind.

John took another step down onto the hard rock.

They were approaching the bottom of the stairs now; John had no doubt someone would spot them immediately if anyone were looking. John reached the ground, followed by Martin; they were surrounded by the city's buildings, some with broken windows and doors.

"Where do we go?" John asked Martin.

Martin hesitated momentarily, looking about himself, evidently trying to orient.

"This way, I think," Martin murmured, striking out through the streets following a map only he could see. They crossed through large streets back to the smaller alley's backside buildings; each step they took, John's trepidation increased as he half expected red armored soldiers to appear suddenly.

The streets remained empty and became somewhat more familiar as Martin led him through sections John could have sworn he had seen before. The broken windows and abandoned buildings they passed almost looked almost sad. With no people to manage and maintain them, they were but reminders of the life that had once passed so easily through these streets. After an indeterminate amount of time, they arrived at the back-alley John recognized as the hideout entrance. Martin stepped forward, bent down, lifted the entrance door, gestured John forward, and followed behind. John stepped down into the hideout.

It was quiet, edging on his nerves and making him rest his hand on his recently acquired sword. There was light ahead, and he stepped forward to find a rooms worth of weapons pointed directly at him.

Zayne held John at sword point, mirrored by Marcila. Lon had collected a green sphere of light in his palms and looked ready to set it loose. Seven's left arm had shifted into a wicked-looking short blade. Trajan had drawn an old looking ax. Karat had her sword ready at her side. Silvia had her dagger out, ready to slice forward. Aysel was at the forefront, sword gripped tightly in her hands.

John halted, as did Martin, and John raised his hands palms open to indicate peace. "Uh… we're back?"

Dead silence. No one moved.

Lon dropped his hands and the green sphere disappeared. "John, how in the blazes are you alive!?"

John was taken aback. "I—I'm not sure?" What even was the response to that question?

"If it is John," Zayne's voice interceded, his sword still pointed at John.

"If it is me?" John questioned, confused and somewhat angry at the strange treatment. "How am I supposed to prove that? I've only known most of you for a couple of days. The only person I met any length of time ago is Karat."

Zayne's sword lowered, a look of relief crossing his face. "That's one way of proving it."

The rest of the room lowered their respective weapons, and Marcila stepped forward, looking John and Martin over. "We were sure the pair of you had been lost to the depths."

"We're okay," murmured Martin, and John noticed that when he said this that he locked eyes with Silvia.

John nodded mutely in agreement, not sure what else to say. His eyes met Aysel's, whose expression was strange, her face was blank, silver eyes unfocused. John forced himself to look at Marcila, who began to speak again, "With the return of you two, we can begin to plan our escape from the Mountain Hold in earnest."

"Wait, *escape*?!" bellowed Martin. "What do you mean 'escape'? Aren't you guys supposed to help us free our home?"

Karat shook her head and sighed, "It's worse than we thought, Martin; we've found out just what they've been doing to the citizens."

"Doing?" Martin's voice softened incrementally as he looked at Karat in confusion.

"There was a reason we didn't find anyone else in prison," said Karat, looking anxious. "Through some dark magic, they were one by one turned into the soldiers. Without them, we have no force large enough to fight back."

John was shocked, but Martin replied first. "How is that even possible?!" His voice was stretched and thin.

"We're not sure," said Marcila. "But we were there long enough to see the effects firsthand. It's why we were concerned if it was you two or just your bodies controlled by their magic."

The room was silent, and John found himself stuck between disbelief and horrified acceptance. Was this part of what Treemor's message had been discussing? John opened his mouth to interject before closing it again. What was he supposed to say? A rock golem had told him that they were doomed to failure? Who would believe that?

"Karat?" Martin had turned to Karat, whose face was neutral.

After a moment, she responded, looking directly at Martin, "They're right, Martin, it was already a fool's hope to try and stand against their forces, but they're able to use magic to control people, which means we're up against a force we can't possibly hope to match. All of the city's inhabitants have been taken."

Something pricked at the back of John's mind. If their enemy could control people, why hadn't they taken control of the other adventurers? He didn't quite know how to address that as he looked at the adventurers in the room.

Martin looked mutinous but merely nodded once at Karat before taking an empty seat, staring down at the table. A moment of silence passed before Zayne spoke, "That being said, escaping the city won't be an easy feat as we no longer have the tram. We will need to acquire one, along with determining a way to bridge the gap in the track."

"That's no easy feat," Lon said. "The track alone is hard to fix without the materials and the skill to forge the metal."

Trajan interjected, "We'll walk out if we have to but staying here is worse than a death sentence."

Seven clipped, "We must acquire another tram, and we must create a temporary fix for the track or examine the alternate routes to see if they have been cut off."

"There are only three other tram exits that go to other mountain cities," said Karat. "They're also severed. A repair would require metal crafting knowledge that I'm not sure we possess." Karat's gaze landed on John in that instant, and her eyes narrowed as a thought seemed to occur to her. "Unless… John, do you think you could do it?"

The room's attention suddenly focused on John, and he tried not to fidget under their gaze. In the broadest terms, what Karat was asking was feasible if he had the supplies, the forge, and the knowledge of the length of the expanse he was attempting to fix. Under the weighty gaze of the party, he knew that he only had one possible answer.

"I can try."

CHAPTER 9

ACTION AND REACTION

There had been only one place to go to get the metal needed to repair the track, a place that John had no desire to go, yet he found himself following Zayne there anyway.

The group was split, with Karat as the first leader taking Lon, Marcila, and Trajan to the tram depo while Zayne led John and the rest of the group on a material finding expedition. Unfortunately, most of the material available had already been taken to the ring's construction in the city center. They had waited for the relative nighttime even though there were no sunrays in Igni as Karat had noted that work still ceased despite knowing that the workers were imprisoned in their metal suits of armor.

They crept through the streets to the edge of the construction. The site was free of the red steel armored workers having achieved an uneasy silence at night. Steel machines stood about erected like ancient monoliths illuminated by the work site lights dimmed to a low glow.

They had crept through a gap in the buildings into the worksite. They moved through the site, and John found himself in the middle of the group by Aysel and Seven.

Aysel was yet to say a word to John since his return, which would not have bothered him except for the glances she kept giving him when she thought he wasn't looking.

The worksite was abandoned of any activity. John found this strange as without daylight, the work could have continued, but there were definite breaks in the construction where the workers were locked back in their cells in the buildings near the city center, a significant distance from the metal ring. The ring itself remained as it always did, with the red energy casting a baleful glow below.

As they stepped through the relatively darkened worksite, which pulsated with the unnatural red light from the center of the construction, it felt like they were walking through a graveyard and each small sound hammered like a drum on John's senses.

As they reached a pile of metal rails set by some construction equipment that towered into the air before disappearing into the darkness, they stopped, and Zayne turned and beckoned at John. John slipped around the group to come to Zayne's side as he gestured at the metal railing.

"Will this work?" Zayne whispered.

John bent down, examining the steel running his hand along the length. The rail was similar in size to the standard track, and the length was perhaps 10 meters. Four rails should do it, John thought as the gap was far less than 20 meters in span.

"They should," he murmured back to Zayne. "Grab four," he guessed as he had no real idea how large the gap they were spanning was. Two rails may have been able to do it, but he hoped that four would ensure that they had enough material to repair the track. Zayne nodded and beckoned the other members of the group forward. Martin and Silvia picked up a rail using their magic to enhance the strength of their limbs. Zayne and Seven each managed to lift a rail, leaving John and Aysel partnered up on the fourth and final rail.

John took a deep breath, focusing his magic through his limbs as he bent down and lifted the rail with Aysel mirroring his action on the other end. He grunted slightly at the weight that he suddenly bore, but his magically enhanced strength did not fail.

Zayne retook the lead, moving out of the worksite, followed by Martin and Silvia. John and Aysel took the third spot, and Seven brought up the rear showing no strain whatsoever from the large rail he was holding.

They hastily exited the site and traversed the streets to the tram station located at their exit point. It was awkward moving with the heavy rails on their shoulders, but they managed to maneuver through the streets, which somewhat lost their red glow as they moved farther away from the massive construction.

The streets were barren, and John found himself wondering at the abandoned buildings they passed. A store called, "Rock and Slate Confectionaries" looked to have formerly sold ice cream along with other desserts. While abandoned, the city contained the reminders that people had lived here, people who were now trapped inside those red carapace-armored suits. A morbid part of John wondered if they were still aware of those suits, able to see all their actions yet powerless to stop them.

They turned off from a street and started moving through back alleys behind a building, with broken letters no longer illuminated but still readable as "Bazaar Superstore!" Moving the railings through the buildings was a task, and John became nervous as they carefully maneuvered their packages through the back alleys.

Finally, in the dim under street lighting that remained, John spotted the tram station located at the end of the rail. The building that housed the trams looked deserted as ever, but he saw a tram car slowly crawling out.

The stairs up to the platform were hard to manage with the rails, but they eventually reached the top where Karat was waiting alone with the rest of the members evidently in the tram. Her hand strayed to her sword upon their appearance, but on recognition, she merely stepped to the side, allowing them access to the flat cart drug behind the tram. They settled the rails down in parallel and grabbed the loose straps, tying them over the metal as securely as they could.

The tram's inside was significantly less set for travel than their previous one, having only the regular seats for passenger travel.

John looked at the front to see Trajan trying to keep the tram powered, but the flickering lights indicated that he was having trouble keeping a steady output going. With a grateful nod, Trajan stood up, allowing John to take his place. John grasped the handle and began to emit his magic through the system, causing the tram to come to life with a gentle hum. John looked behind to check if everyone else had piled in; he was satisfied to see everyone buckled in or, in Zayne's case, walking forward to join him in the second seat.

Zayne sat down and nodded at John. "Let's go."

John engaged the tram, and they rolled forward into the darkness. Slowly, after a distance, Zayne turned on the light showing the tunnel and rail stretching ahead. They proceeded for quite a distance, crossing the ground much faster than Aysel and John's walk up the passage.

Finally, the light caught the glimmering edge of the bent track. "Stop," Zayne ordered. John needed no telling as he braked fully and disengaged the engine immediately but leaving the lights on for those—save for Marcila and Aysel—who had no vision in the absolute darkness. The tram stopped, and they piled out, and John was relieved to see he had not underestimated the gap. The question now was how to fix it. Bernard had once taught John how to weld metal without a furnace, but they first needed to realign the track rails.

He turned to Zayne, feeling odd telling his leader what needed to be done, but he shook off the sensation. "We need to bend the track back into alignment."

Zayne nodded and stepped forward. Orange light glimmered around his legs, and suddenly he shot into the air with a massive leap, clearing the gap and landing on the other side quickly. John tried not to gape at the impressive display of magic enhancement and instead turned to the railing bent upward on his side. He gripped one rail and let his magic flow through his arms, and the metal slowly began to bend. He edged it downwards, and following his example, he saw Seven start bending the other side, the screech of protesting metal adding to his own. Zayne mirrored their actions on the other side, aided by Marcila, who cleared the gap with a leap that gave off a small purple glow.

She and Zayne both bent their rails, and with a groan of metal, they began to shift. As relative flat alignment was reached, they stopped, and John wiped his brow of sweat that had accumulated from the heat of the constant magic output.

He turned to see that the rails had already been unloaded by the rest of the group. They had been separately laid end to end. Multiple gazes focused on him as he walked forward to the middle and bent down. Bernard had taught him how to heat his magic when he was younger, before he had even used a forge, and he recalled the lesson as he bent over the railings.

The two ends were of similar size, so that wasn't an issue, but he would have to heat and then cool them without creating a weak joint, which would cause the track to snap and for them to fall for a second time into the abyss below.

Focus, he chided himself, and concentrated on the ends, letting the others fade away. Forging a bar without a furnace was difficult and produced an inferior result, but there wasn't another option.

He brought his hands to each rail and began to let his magic flow to the ends, focusing on heating each part while keeping the rail straight. He lifted, straining at the rail' weight, which suddenly decreased as Seven grabbed one end and Silvia raised the other. He brought the rails together, running his magic through the joint, lighting the steel bright orange and melding it within itself to change the two into one. Slowly he withdrew his magic, and the rail's radiant orange glow dimmed until once again the metal returned to its natural shade, now as one steel rail.

John released a ragged breath he didn't realize he had been holding. He grabbed the next set of rails and repeated the process turning steel fiery red and melding the beams together with Karat and Aysel holding the ends this time. He turned and grimaced at the next issue, mending the actual track.

They ran the rails onto the other side into the hands of Zayne and Marcila until the minimal amount necessary remained on their side. The rails they had stolen were wider than the ones already laid down, but having worked with tram's before, John knew the vehicles had methods of dealing with shifts in the sizes of tracks, so he could only hope theirs would as well. He grabbed the first rail end and brought it to the track's battered end, and began heating up the metal. He brought the ends together, gripping the broken track so that both ends met. He channeled his magic, and the metal slowly became orange-hued. Then, ever so slowly, he fused the metal ends together, using his magic to push and prod at the metal to fold and meld the rail into one whole.

John grabbed the next piece of the somewhat warped end of the track and began heating it, turning both sides a cherry orange before slowly bringing them together into one piece. He stood up, looking over to the other side at his next task.

John backed up a couple of steps and tried to calm his nerves at jumping the gap. He ran forward, arriving at the edge, and *leaped*, forcing magic through his legs to send him flying into the air.

He soared forward, almost flying with the power of the leap. His feet hit solid ground, and John sighed in relief as he stood with Zayne and Marcila, both of whom did not acknowledge his noticeable relief of clearing the gap. John bent to his next task and began heating the rail to repeat the process. He finished, and a weight settled in his gut as he realized that they were going to test if his repair had worked.

"Finished?" Zayne's words knocked him from his thoughts, and John nodded in response.

Zayne leaped back across the gap and ushered the rest of the group back into the tram. The vehicle came to life with a hum, the lights on the forefront flickering on, causing John and Marcila to both turn their heads from the incredibly bright light. The tram rolled forward, hitting the new rail with nary a visible shift, traveling slowly across the gap, for a time that seemed to stretch into eternity before suddenly the tram had passed over. John released a breath he hadn't realized he was holding as the tram came up, stopping between Marcila and him.

The doors swung open, revealing the rest of their group, and John stepped in after Zayne, following him up to the pilot seats, one of which contained Karat. By the flickering of the lights he could tell Karat was struggling to keep the output stable. Seeing them, she smiled in what looked like relief and stood up, letting the tram power down entirely.

"It was more difficult than I expected," she said, "keeping the output steady; glad I don't have to any longer."

John nodded, a half-smile on his face. "You did better than most as a first try."

When John had initially tried to power a forge, he hadn't been able to get the necessary power right for days, which had ended up reminding him of Bernard, and worry once again filtered through his mind. Karat stood up, allowing John to take the pilot seat; he cautiously settled down, finding the panel that thankfully shared most of its design with the first tram. He gripped the handle and began running power through the system. The tram hummed, and John looked at Zayne, who had taken the seat next to him, gripping the secondary power handle and decreasing John's required output.

"Let's go," Zayne said, and John grabbed the throttle, pushing forward.

The tram's engine hummed. They shot forward into the darkness.

INTERLUDE 3: THE DESIGNS OF THE DARK

The construction of the portal was going well. The city's subjugation had been an easy matter with the magic he had wrought into his soldiers' armor. Once encased, each former resident had merely been another soldier to do his bidding. There had been some unforeseen disruption, but the instigators had fled after destroying one of his pets, but such a minimal act was little more than a minor crinkle in the grand plan.

They could have been pursued, of course, but what was the point? They had been nuisances and had now removed themselves of their own accord. Fortunate indeed.

A small part of Kar Dun's mind had questioned, worried that perhaps the group would try and seek this flesh form out and rid it of its ability to carry it at their will.

The group had not done so, likely fearing their remarkable soldiers, much better than the unruly masses they had been. The group had instead feared that they would be killed and had run for help; a mistake.

He were close, oh so close now, to the completion of the portal.

The dominion of the Kings would return.

CHAPTER 10

CONQUERED

Time had been short below the mountain; now left with nothing but time to occupy his mind, John was worried. As far as first missions for adventurers went, John was pretty sure this one qualified as having gone poorly. The entire Mountain Hold was under the control of a hostile force that was constructing something in the city center that John could only assume meant something bad.

They were going back to his home, the City of Lights, which itself had armies at its doorstep, eyeing the city as a possible location to house themselves.

He couldn't help but wonder if perhaps this was all a terrible dream that he was set to wake up from any minute from now in his bed back at the workshop where life was not so dire. He rather doubted it.

The tram continued its path forward, quickly approaching its destination.

They were so close now that red daylight could be seen at the edge of the tunnel, and they quickly traveled towards it, emerging into the momentarily blinding light. John slowed the tram to a halt.

At first glance, everything seemed to be normal. The late evening daylight filtered through the tram's windows, revealing the city John called home still standing. As they began to exit the cart, the smell of smoke in the air brought John's guard up.

They emerged onto the empty platform; the streets similarly were free of people. The city was quiet in a way that John had never experienced, a quiet that clawed at his ears as Zayne led the group forward down from the platform and through the barren streets. The creak of signs swaying in the wind echoed through the seemingly empty streets.

"Where are the people?" Zayne voiced the collective thoughts of the group.

Almost as if in answer, the sound of rapid footsteps came around from a bend, revealing a group of steel-plated soldiers, a broad red double-headed axe emblazoned upon their shields. They stopped, and weapons were drawn, pointed directly at them.

"You are out during the curfew. Stand down and prepare to be arrested," a voice bellowed out from the mass.

Zayne answered, his expression carefully neutral, "What curfew? We just returned to the city—"

The voice interrupted Zayne, shouting, "Stand down!"

The soldiers shifted with a clatter of steel, readying themselves.

Zayne seemed torn and opened his mouth to respond but had to dodge back as a halberd suddenly lanced forward, slicing at his stomach. The rest of the soldiers followed the halberdier's lead, launching themselves ahead to cut into them, and John found himself fighting two at once, one with a sword, the other with a halberd.

He ducked a sword slice at his head and drew his sword to parry a follow-up halberd slicing at his stomach. The sword came swinging back around, and he had no time to parry it; he braced his mage shield, and in a shower of blue sparks, the blade fell off.

Attempting to take advantage of the staggered soldier, John lanced his sword into the soldier with the blade slicing straight through a hazy green barrier raised far too late, cutting through the steel armor like paper, sending the soldier to the ground.

John spun, desperately blocking the halberd that came swinging at him, and stepped forward into the halberdier's guard. He channeled his magic through his arm and shot his elbow up, smashing into the faceplate of the guard, sending him stumbling back, red-colored magic swirling from the spot he had just struck.

Something whistled, and instinct had John ducking down to the ground as a large blade cleared the air where he had once stood. John swung his sword out to cut at the third person who had interjected themselves into the fight. The soldier dodged back, avoiding John's blade, and John had to spin to parry the original soldier with the sword.

He was surrounded, and the halberdier was recovering. John swept his sword up to parry a strike, only to wince as he felt his magic reserves take a hit as the second soldier bit into his side with his blade. He thrust his hand out as reflex, sending a wave of blue energy outward to collide with the dual sword wielder, which sent them flying backward to impact with a crunch into the brick behind them.

The first sword wielder and halberdier attacked in unison, and while John managed to deflect the first strike, the halberd glanced off the shield over his abdomen, causing John to reel back. He dodged aside as the sword tried to slice into him, narrowly avoiding the blades at his stomach. John's stomach clenched as he faced his attackers; he shot forward, trying to slip through the guard of the halberdier, only to be warded back by another cut he managed to deflect to the side.

John found himself backpedaling as red light glimmered on the halberdier's blade, and hastily, he threw himself to the side as a blast of energy shot through where his head had just been. The explosion obliterated a section of building behind them, but John had no time to look backward as he was re-engaged.

Ducking under another slash, John channeled his magic through his arm, shooting his palm forward, letting loose a massive magical blue blast. The magic ripped on. The halberdier brought his palm up and a red shield thickened in the air before him. The sword wielder was not so fast and was sent flying backward, armor denting under the impact. They slammed into a building and crumpled to the ground.

The halberdier lashed out, lancing their blade towards John's chest, and John had to let himself fall back under it.

He threw himself forward as the halberd passed over where his upper torso had just been, slicing forward. His sword cut through the halberdier's armor like paper with an ear-shattering squeal of metal.

The halberdier collapsed, and John found himself suddenly with no enemies, and quickly, he surveyed the rest of the group. The other armored guards had been brought down, and as he watched, Zayne cut down the final guard with a wicked fast sword slice. A moment of silence passed before Zayne spoke, "Those weren't the Council Guard."

Marcila responded, looking down at their attackers, "No, but that symbol is not unfamiliar to me; it is the mark of the Red Baron."

"The Red Baron?" John's heart sank as he began to connect the dots. "None of the Barons should be in the city."

"It looks like they are," Zayne's voice was solemn as he looked around. "Come on, we need to find a place to wait out this curfew. I don't know where though. I imagine the inn won't let us in even if it's still open; same goes for the Guild."

A moment of silence later, an idea popped up in John's head.

"The Western Workshop," he said.

His loud voice startled the group, who turned to look at him, and he flushed slightly under the combined attention.

"The workshop is accessible from a back door, and I know the code even if it's locked."

"The workshop's on the other side of the city, though, isn't it?" responded Marcila.

John grimaced and nodded; how could they even get there without running into another patrol or worse?

Trajan interjected, "We're not exactly flush with options right now. I say we go with the lad's idea."

Marcila nodded, her face formed into a small frown. "I'm just saying that crossing such a distance will be difficult. We don't even know how many guards there might be."

Zayne spoke, his face furrowed in concentration, "We don't have much of a choice; we have to get off the open streets."

There were no further protests, and Zayne took the lead through the empty streets. They moved quickly, not towards the city tram but through the empty streets. Every time they passed a corner, John half expected soldiers to come crashing down on them, but the roads remained unoccupied.

The silence was tense, stretching over the streets like a taught string. The group moved as quietly as possible but still maintained a pace that was almost a run. Streets that John knew by heart passed by as he followed Marcila.

The tram track that ran overhead was empty of any trams, and the doorways remained fastened shut. It was eerie as they strode over the paved streets, looking about for any more of the soldiers that had attacked them. The tramping of boots alerted them to stay back every so often as groups of soldiers passed by; but the group could quickly hide in one of the alleyways that lined their path.

Time passed, and some of the buildings became more familiar to John; he realized they were close now to the workshop. Marcila led them through a back alley, and John recognized the back of the workshop protruding taller than the surrounding buildings. A tall door was inset into the wall that surrounded the building's rear, and Marcila turned, gesturing for John to come forward.

John stepped up to the door, which had a single handle attached to the wooden frame. He grasped the cool steel and focused, allowing his magic to feel what felt like thousands of possible channels but only letting the current run through seven of them. With a soft click, the door unbolted, and John gently pulled it open, allowing for the rest of the group behind him to file in.

The familiar sparring courtyard was filled with many crates that had not been there when John had left. They maneuvered their way through the crates to the back of the workshop where the shop door barred their way.

Marcila turned to John. "You should probably be the one to lead; they should know you, right?"

John nodded uneasily; he had known most of the people behind this door for a large portion of his life. They wouldn't turn on him, right?

He pulled the door open to reveal the workspace of his former home. A hundred eyes fell on him; workers sat around the workshop, eating dinner, piles of notes strewn about their desks.

"John?" a familiar voice called out, and John spotted Bernard sitting at a table with three other craftsmen. He looked surprised, and his brow was creased as he gazed at John's eyes, flicking behind him to examine the others. "Who are—Karat?" Bernard interrupted himself, and his brow furrowed further.

Silvia stepped past John, walking up to Bernard's table. "Hello Bernard; it's been a while."

Bernard nodded vaguely, eyes drifting through the rest of the group, his mouth tightened almost imperceptibly before he turned back to Karat and John. "No need to tell me why you're here. I presume you've likely encountered some of our occupiers."

Karat nodded. "That's correct; what happened here, Bernard?"

Bernard sighed, frowning. "The Barons happened."

"The Barons?" echoed Karat. Zayne walked over to the rest of the group following him; John noticed that they were uneasily eyeing their surroundings, including the workers.

The attention on them had only increased, and John felt the heat rising to his face.

"The Barons," Bernard repeated heavily. "They invaded the night you left; took the whole city. Council Guard barely gave an iota of resistance. There were far too many of them. We're under curfew now as they squash what resistance there is in the city while they set up whatever puppet of a government we'll have."

John's stomach twisted into a knot. Despite the encounter from before, hearing the loss of his home's freedom from Bernard was something different entirely.

Zayne spoke up, his tone strained in a way John hadn't heard before. "We can't just let them do this."

"We didn't *just let them,*" Bernard responded sharply. "We can't just mount a resistance; we can't match them."

"But Bernard," Karat interjected. "You were—"

Bernard interrupted harshly, "It doesn't matter what I was; I'm just one man. A very old man."

John was confused; what were they talking about? Distinctly, they were talking about something to do with Bernard's past, but what?

A moment of silence passed. John wanted to say something, but he had no words.

After a moment, Bernard spoke softly, "You may have shelter here; there are rooms to spare above the workshop." Bernard looked at John with an expression John had never seen on his face before, strained tiredness of someone stretched too thin. "I'm glad you're all right, John. Can you show them to the rooms near your old apprentice quarters?"

John nodded mutely, words fighting to emerge from his throat, but he knew that any attempt to speak would be an unintelligible jumble of words.

He led the group up the stairs. The stares of the rest of the workshop had subsided for the most part. He moved down the familiar hallways and gestured to the doors without nameplates; his room still had his. The members of his group split off, and he went to his room, stepping through the door and making sure to close it firmly behind him.

John slumped to the floor of his room, back against his door, his mind blank.

How had things gone wrong so quickly?

CHAPTER 11

A SHORT TALK

War is a constant in the Realms. The balance of power is ever-shifting. For example, the Red Barons, a disparate group, seized power after the military toppling the formerly democratic government of the country of Hanlo. Unfortunately for the Barons, their alliance only lasted as long as it took over the country before the factions split and the civil war divided Hanlo. Even now, the Red Barons fight desperately among themselves and with others, searching to gain an edge in their strength.

(Excerpt from H. Dallas,
Modern Conflict of the Realms)

John woke in his bed in a confused daze. For a moment, he had been expecting to be still underground until the weak morning sunlight streaming through his window reminded him of his new-old location. He moved in a familiar daze to get ready for the day and just stopped himself from pulling on a pair of work gloves.

Moving down into the workshop, he was harshly reminded that things were not as usual; the absence of the clang of metal and hum of furnaces failed to meet his ears. Workers sat around the workshop, talking in low, hushed voices, some fiddling with their tools or scribbling on paper, but no actual forging was happening.

John spotted Karat, Zayne, and Marcila near the back in deep conversation with Bernard, who was fiddling with his bench tools. John walked toward them, maneuvering through the tables and finally getting close enough to hear the tail end of a sentence from Bernard, "—out of the question. Those days are long past."

Zayne opened his mouth to respond before noticing John. "Glad to see you're up. Did you sleep alright?"

John half shrugged and nodded; he had no desire to discuss how he had tossed and turned into the early morning. Zayne didn't press and turned back to Bernard. "If that's the way you see it, I won't press any further, but we can't just do nothing."

Bernard glanced at John before he responded, "What do you plan on doing? The City of Lights is under occupation by an army far greater in size than the city's entire Council Guard *before* they attempted to stop the Red Baron's army. There are hardly any adventurers left in the city as you should well know."

Zayne looked nearly as old as Bernard as he sighed, nodding in acquiescence to his point.

"What would you say we do, though? We're bound to complete our contract and report back what we found to the Stone Council."

"The Stone Council has been dissolved; there's no one to report back to," Bernard replied weightily. "That's a no-fault dissolution of the contract."

"The people in the Mountain Hold—" Karat tried to interject.

"Will have to find a way on their own," Bernard said. "We're under occupation. There's nothing we can do."

Zayne's frustration was evident on his face, but after a moment, he nodded, sighing deeply. "If there's nothing to be done, then I'm not sure what the next course of action is."

Marcila spoke, "If there is nothing to be done, perhaps, we should focus on leaving the City entirely."

Karat's face was unreadable, and her tone flat. "I will not abandon my home."

"There is nothing you can do," Marcila's voice was calm. "We would need an army; doesn't the City of Lights have some other allies?"

There was a solemn moment of silence.

"The Seventh Federation," Silvia suddenly said. "They're allies with both the Mountain Hold and the City of Lights."

"Their borders are three hundred leagues away; how would we even get there, much less ask for help?" interjected Zayne, grimacing.

"The City has vehicles," Bernard now looked thoughtful as he stroked his beard, "They could be accessed if you could get into the depot where the cars are stored. You would have the ability to travel there. It's likely under guard, though, and there's no way you could fight through the guards they likely have surrounding it."

"So, we'll just have to be quiet," Marcila said calmly. "We can't stay here and leave both the Mountain Hold and City of Lights to their respective fates."

Zayne nodded, "I agree with Marcila."

"As do I," a soft-toned voice spoke, and John turned to see that Aysel had walked up behind them. Her mouth was set in a determined line, and her silver eyes gleamed.

Despite the current circumstances, John couldn't help but feel the same distracting feelings that had beset him at the beginning of their trip into the mountain. She was astonishingly pretty, but that wasn't quite it. She had demonstrated just how capable and determined she was in the mountain, and for some strange reason, that made his stomach wobbly.

John pushed his disarrayed thoughts to the side and refocused on the conversation that had continued.

"If you're all determined to set out, then I will provide what assistance I can." Bernard's tone was stoic.

Zayne nodded, looking relieved. "Thank you."

It seemed that the conversation was over as Bernard got up, but not before giving a meaningful look to John, which he understood well enough was an order to follow him. Bernard walked out to the back area of the workshop. It was empty, and John found himself glancing at the sparring area where it felt like he had only just lost to Bernard again.

"I hadn't thought you'd come back in such circumstances," Bernard spoke softly.

John shrugged, not even sure where to begin with the frankly awful cascade of events. "It's not what I expected."

Bernard snorted, a half-grin flashing across his face. "Adventuring never is." A moment passed. Bernard spoke again, "I see you have a different sword; can I assume the other one failed?"

John grimaced, feeling a flush of shame at his loss of Bernard's gift. "I—I'm sorry."

Bernard dismissed the apology. "It was a sword, and I assume it served its purpose in making sure you made it back even under these circumstances. I'm surprised you found a replacement so quickly."

The sword's circumstances resurged to John's mind as he recalled Treemor's words, which now he supposed were starting to make an uncomfortable amount of sense.

It came out before he could stop himself. "In the mountain, I met a being made of stone. He said his name was Treemor and that in our current endeavor, we had already lost. That's where I found the sword."

Bernard's brow rose as he nodded. "Where did you meet him? I had heard that you had encountered only those you brought with you."

John grimaced. "I was separated when we were freeing the rest of Adventurers along with another person, Martin. We met Treemor underground after we got separated from the others while helping them escape from captivity."

Bernard nodded, looking thoughtful. "I've heard of spirits possessing nature before; what you encountered was likely one of those."

"And his warning? He made it sound like he'd been down there waiting for us for a long time."

Bernard's brow furrowed, and he didn't speak for a moment.

"I won't say dismiss it, but worrying about it will do no good either. Just stay wary and remember the skills I've taught you; you'll be fine." Bernard half smiled in a way that made John unsure if he meant it.

John nodded anyway. "All right."

"You say you found the sword down there, though?" Bernard continued.

"Yeah," John nodded again. "It was embedded in the floor of the cavern, yet…"

John trailed off as a strange thought occurred to him.

"Yes?" Bernard urged him.

"Treemor said that the sword wasn't his. He had a huge pile of weapons and armor, but he distinctly said the sword had been there long before him."

Bernard nodded, stroking his beard, his eyes focused on the blade. "Could you let me examine it?" he asked after a moment.

John drew the sword from his side, and the blade shimmered in a distinct blue hue under the sunlight. It was strange, John thought as he handed the blade over, but the blade felt better balanced than the sword Bernard had made for him.

Bernard held the sword by the hilt and ran a finger down the edge. John thought he saw something flash in his eyes.

"This is a fine blade. I daresay it's more than the equal of your previous one," Bernard said after a long moment, handing the sword back to John. "You'd be served well to keep on using it."

John smiled a little relieved at Bernard's approval. Whatever he had felt when he was near the sword for the first time had abated. However, a strange part of himself felt strangely attached to the blade.

CHAPTER 11.5

A SECOND ESCAPE

For their attempt to escape the city, Zayne had organized them into three squads. The first was led by himself with Seven, Lon, and Trajan. The second was to be led by Karat, grouped with Martin and Silvia. Marcila led the final group with Aysel and John.

The first two groups were tasked with obtaining the two-car that would be needed; the final group would open the bay's door that the car was stored in. The bay itself was on the far side of the City of Lights, as Bernard had informed them. They would leave that night, worried that any delay would lead to their location being discovered, especially considering the encounter they had already had with the guards.

The streets were deathly silent as John followed Marcila, who had cupped a small purple light in her palm that glimmered off the cobblestones slick from the rain only an hour previously.

Marcila's steps were so light that John couldn't even hear a whisper of their collision with the stone street.

Aysel mirrored the feat with slightly less skill, causing the occasional click, but John's steps in comparison were unable to remove the soft thud of impact, which blared into his ears.

The buildings around them were dark, making them little more than indistinguishable shapes until Marcila's light cast them into sharp relief. Every step scratched at the back of John's mind, worrying him that any moment the Baron's soldiers would emerge and attack. They continued forward unhindered, sliding through a back alley and then emerged onto an overhang, under which John could make out a massive blocky building shape in the moonlight raining from the two moons.

"That should be the hangar," Marcila whispered from the front. Then she jumped.

She vanished into the darkness; her light extinguished. There was a small whisper against the ground and the shadow from John's left disappeared over the top, indicating that Aysel had followed her mentor, leaving John by himself.

Grimacing, he jumped, and the air battered him as he fell. He poured his magic through his legs, bracing them…

Blue flashed as he felt his legs collide with solid stone.

The jolt through his legs had not caused him to fall, and he saw that Marcila had reignited her purple light. The roof they had landed on was made of flat grey stone.

Marcila and Aysel were standing with their backs to the drop zone, and upon his arrival, Marcila beckoned him forward.

"Follow me," Marcila whispered, walking to the edge of the roof before placing her hand down on the top and violet light flared up in thin lines, tracing a square. There was a soft rustling grind as the sheet of rock floated up, separated from the roof. Slowly, Marcila moved it to the side, setting it gently down with barely a whisper of sound.

From the hole emerged soft yellow light. Marcila bent down for a moment, sticking her head cautiously through the gap, and, after a moment, pulled herself forward to land on the ground below. Aysel glanced down and leaped, and John followed, looking long enough to see the vacated floor below before he too jumped.

They were on a walkway above the ground of the main floor, where large vehicles formed of grey and crimson metal were arranged around the hangar. They were sharply angled, long with narrow fronts that split out to a broader frame. There was no sign of any guards till a pained grunt echoed through the hangar space, and John spun to see a guard up on a platform on the far side being lanced through the chest by Zayne standing behind him.

Seven, Lon, and Trajan filed in behind him, scanning around the room before they took the stairs down to the floor, walking over to Marcila, who had approached one of the cars pressing her hand against a hatch on the back, purple light flaring before the door opened down and she slipped inside.

Zayne walked down the stairs, swiveling his head around the room. He turned to speak to Marcila. "That's both our groups; where's Karat and hers?"

Marcila shook her head. "I don't know," she turned, surveying the area. "We need to get the door," she said to Aysel and John. She pointed at a booth on the far left side of the area.

They walked over, and John was immediately struck by how simplistic the setup was. There were three large levers glancing up, likely aligned with the three massive doors. The car they were stealing was located on the hangar floor in front of the central door.

He reached out to the central switch and looked at Marcila. "This one, you think?"

Marcila eyed the switch, and after a moment's contemplation, nodded. "Yes, but don't pull it yet; we'll wait for the rest to get here."

John nodded, and after a moment's hesitation, settled himself in the chair. As each second stretched while they waited, John became more anxious. Where were Karat, Silvia, and Martin? What could have delayed them?

The creak of a door opening behind him caused John to spin around, looking up at the walkways as a figure stepped through the door.

It was Silvia; he sighed with relief as Martin and Karat followed her through, shutting the door behind them. They took the stairs to the second car, which Karat opened with a flash of green-lit magic. Martin and Silvia filtered in behind her.

The car that Zayne had entered began to hum, and a couple of minutes later, Karat's ship began to hum as well.

"Now," Marcila's words nearly startled him, but John pulled the lever regardless, and with an entirely too loud grind, the doors began to open, rolling upward into the building.

John's hand instinctively found the hilt of his sword, the unfamiliar grip settling into the palm of his right hand. The door had opened, allowing moonlight from outside to filter in, illuminating the path that led outside the walls. A road trailed down the mountain, running parallel to the other routes that connected to the city.

John followed Marcila and Aysel into the transport closest to them, and as he stepped inside, he shut the door behind himself. Karat was at the front with seats lining the sides of the car where Martin and Silvia were; John quickly settled himself into one of them.

The ship began to move, visible from the window as they drove forward over smooth stone, heading out of the door following the road trailing down the mountainside. The moonlight was the only illumination as they moved on driving down the road.

As the road narrowed, Zayne's car took the lead. The engine's rumble underneath them was relatively quiet, but given the dead silence previously, the noise seemed incredibly loud. Looking out the back window, John expected the alarm would be raised at any moment and a flood of other cars would emerge to chase them down.

Nothing emerged. The City of Lights was dark, only a few of the buildings shining any light at all. John wondered if Bernard was looking out even now into the darkness. The path twisted and turned down the mountain, and they got closer and closer to the edge of the forest. Only as they entered the first copse of trees ahead of the forest, John felt a slight modicum of his tension dissipate. The car traveled at a speed that felt slow compared to the tram they had taken into the mountain. They passed into a thicker forest canopy, which eliminated most of the moonlight, and John saw through the front screen that Zayne had flicked on his lights.

Karat copied, following behind Zayne on the road through the now dense forest.

The inside of the car was quiet. Martin and Silvia had seated themselves across from John and Aysel. The silence continued until Silvia broke it. "I'd never been to the City of Lights before. I didn't think we'd have run into something like that."

Aysel nodded and then said, "I hadn't thought that someone would conquer the City in our absence…"

Martin grimaced. "It's some bad luck, that's for certain, like a mirror image of the Mountain Hold."

John almost bit out a frustrated response, but he stopped, reminding himself that Martin's own home had been conquered. They were all in this situation together now. Now was probably not the time to ask, though.

"Will the Seventh Federation help us?" John couldn't help but voice.

Silvia responded first. "I mean they're allies with the Mountain Hold and the City of Lights, right? Why wouldn't they?"

"Alliances don't always mean something." Martin looked morose. "I've read enough history books to know that saying you're allies doesn't always mean they'll spend the resources, especially considering we're already conquered."

Aysel shook her head. "Nations are obligated to answer their treaties. If they don't honor them, who will make treaties with them?"

Silvia nodded, smiling slightly, seeming to like Aysel's answer more.

John felt torn, and he remembered well all Bernard had taught him about the nations histories. Treaties would be honored just as soon as they'd be shunned, depending on perceived benefit and risk. Sometimes an honorable leader would follow through, but they could delay for years. He was looking at Silvia's face, though he couldn't bring himself to say anything that would shoot down her hope.

Instead, he concentrated on his hands.

CHAPTER 12

JOURNEY OF LEAGUES

They had driven through the night until the morning light had begun to touch the tips of the trees. The trees were thickly arrayed around the road, and Zayne's car had taken the lead. John had traded places with Karat to allow her a break to get some rest. Despite his apprehension, the controls were only a little more complicated than the tram's. Magic still had to channel through the vehicle, and while he had to steer, it was relatively simple to keep on following Zayne.

The road wasn't paved like an actual street and instead was akin to a wide dirt path, but the wheels that carried the car had little trouble traversing the terrain. The leaves of the trees stretched overhead. John found himself wishing to leave and see the outside without the barrier in front of his face.

They hadn't stopped even to eat, instead distributing dried rations they had packed in their bags. Given that their destination was three hundred leagues away their traversal should take less than two days.

The hum of the car and the roll of the wheels must have lulled him to sleep; when he next awoke, the sky through the window was once again dark. The car had stopped, and he could see in the overhead lights that Aysel and Silvia had broken from a low discussion while Martin was seemingly also stirring himself from sleep.

Karat stood up from her seat and stretched out her back. Martin stood up and opened the back door; John followed him out to see that Zayne had already walked out with a lantern illuminating the space between the two-car.

"We'll stop for tonight, and reach the territory of the Seventh Federation tomorrow," he said to the assembling crowd. "This far out, we can probably have some light as we set up camp for tonight and a fire."

The group dispersed. Seven and Lon went into the woods, probably to find firewood. The rest began pulling out food from the car, and Zayne put his hand to the ground and made a drawing up gesture to create stone seats set circularly around what would likely become the firepit.

John helped pull a package of food out of his car, sitting himself down with the rest until Seven and Lon returned with a pile of deadwood in their arms. They set the wood in the center, and Lon bent down, clicking his fingers once; a small flame flickered to life on top of the logs.

Soon they were all sitting down around the fire, enjoying the warmth as the chill of the night began to creep in. Karat and Zayne looked exhausted as they ate their food, not surprising, given how they had been running the cars for a large portion of the day.

The conversation around the fire was quiet for a while before Seven spoke with a slightly mechanical inflection. “I can’t help but wonder if the Baron’s forces may guess where we’ve gone.”

Lon responded, playing with the edge of his beard. “Even if they have, what would they even make of it? They could try and chase us, but that would require a diversion of some of their forces to track us down. They may just let us go.”

“I would assume very little about our enemy,” Trajan murmured.

“Which one?” Marcila asked. “While the Baron’s forces are perhaps the most immediate threat, what we encountered under the mountains is more disturbing. Whatever was controlling those ‘Hemlock Guards’ as you called them has a plan that we still do not understand especially considering their strange construction.”

Trajan frowned. “Both. They are each dangerous, and they must both be somehow dealt with. The Adventurers’ Contract would have us do nothing less.”

A moment of silence fell as they all focused on their meager meals. Although John had heated his food with magic, it tasted rather bland. The conversation resumed but did not take up the same topic as before. Now it was dispersed between the group members talking in quiet voices about various issues. To his left, Martin was talking to Lon about some of Lon’s past adventurers. To his right, Aysel talked to Marcila about a magic technique that allowed one to cloak themselves from sight.

A part of him wanted to attempt to join either of the conversations, but as he sat there staring at the fire, all he could think about were the recent fights in which he had engaged. He had pushed it to the back of his mind, but now he couldn't help but think about the lives he had most assuredly taken. It bothered him how sudden it had been, how he had never even seen their faces.

"John."

He heard a voice, distinctly feminine but with a strange metallic tone to it. No one looked like they had spoken to him. It was almost as if—

"John."

Almost unconsciously, his hand found the hilt of his sword. He waited, straining his ears to catch a whisper of the voice, of where it was coming from. A long moment passed as he listened to the crackle of the fire, the low murmur of voices, and the sigh of the trees in a gentle breeze. Nothing reached his ears. Had it been his imagination, a trick of the wind?

Almost without thought, he gazed up into the sky into the inky blackness sprinkled with tiny white specs. John didn't know how long he gazed at the sky, but eventually, he realized that except for Seven, the rest of his companions had packed themselves away into the sleeping bags that had been brought. He took his from inside the car Zayne had driven and laid it out along a grass section by the car.

As he fell asleep, he thought he almost heard the voice again, "Joh—"

Early morning sunlight hit his eyelids, disturbing him from sleep. Any dreams he may have had did not survive into his memory as he rose, sitting up and stretching out his back, which felt somewhat cramped from having slept on the ground.

Zayne, Marcila, Karat, and Trajan had already arranged themselves around the rekindled fire against the chill of the morning. John slipped out of his sleeping bag, rolling it up and stacking it on the pile that had already been arranged, and grabbing a meal pack before sitting on the ground close enough to feel the heat from the fire.

Marcila and Karat were quietly talking as Zayne and Trajan focused on eating their meals. John decided to focus on his unappetizing meal pack, poking an unidentified piece of noodle-like substance before internally shrugging and beginning to eat. As other party members began to rise and eat, the low conversations started again. Aysel sat next to him, having been awoken herself, and John found himself uncomfortably aware of how close she had chosen to sit. He focused on his food, spooning tasteless matter into his mouth dedicatedly.

The meal finished up without the night's talk, and John followed Karat into the car. He settled himself in his previous seat, as did Aysel, Martin, and Silvia. Karat took the controls at the front again, and the car hummed to life. They turned back out onto the road following Zayne's car. The boredom from the first ride quickly set in again, and John found himself wishing he could be driving instead, if only to have something to focus on.

"What about you, John?"

John blinked and turned, realizing that Aysel had just asked him a question; and by the way Martin and Silvia were looking at him, they had also been participating in the discussion.

An awkward smile found its way to his lips, "I'm sorry I wasn't paying attention. Could you repeat that?" He kicked himself for zoning out. She had hardly said a word to him since the prison escape in the Cold Mountains.

Aysel thankfully repeated her question. "We were discussing where we were from."

"Oh," John said intelligently, nodding out of reflex. "Well…" he paused a moment to gather his thoughts. "I'm from the City of Lights. I lived at the Western Workshop. Bernard, the man you met trained me since I was young both in forging and with sword and magic."

"Really?" asked Martin. "That explains why you recommended we go there. You probably could guess that Silvia and I lived in the Mountain Hold. I was a scouter for fire lizards when we were finding a new place to set up mining equipment."

Silvia chimed in her answer. "I worked for the City Council managing the City System."

John nodded in understanding. Every city and nation had a system that stored documents that could be downloaded by the populace for enjoyment or work purposes and allowed lines of communication that unfortunately were limited to the city as the wires that carried the data were seldom run too far.

"I've just been an adventurer. Marcila trained me," Aysel finished.

John nodded, rolling over their words. "So you have a fair amount of experience with this kind of stuff?" he asked Aysel.

Aysel shook her head, a half-smile turning her lips upward. "No, not with *this*," she said, "But in general, I've been on a couple of adventures, acting as guards for a couple of caravans. I've even fought a dragon."

"You too?" Martin grinned.

Aysel's eyes widened in surprise. "You've fought a dragon?

"Sort of." Martin turned his hand from side to side. "When we were breaking into the prison, a skeletal dragon attacked us."

"Really?" Aysel said. "How'd you deal with it?"

"Silvia stabbed it in the eye after John took out its leg," Martin replied.

"Did you encounter anything with Karat?" asked Silvia.

"No," Aysel shook her head. "We planted the explosive and set it off, and then we hid. When only you came back with the rescued adventurers, we feared the worst."

Silvia turned to Martin and John. "What did happen to you guys?"

"We—," John paused, trying to think of how to best approach what had happened. "We fell into an underground tunnel system. We met a being named Treemor who showed us the way out."

"A being?" Silvia questioned.

Martin answered, "Some kind of rock person, super large; said he'd been down there a while along with some other strange stuff. He was helpful, though."

"It almost sounds like you're describing a Mountain Spirit," Aysel said. "Marcila told me about them once. She said that they would form when enough ambient magic concentrated, taking the materials from their environment to develop their body.

"Huh." John had never heard of a Mountain Spirit. "I guess it could have been. I've never heard of one of those, though."

"It's pretty rare to meet one. They usually live as far from the peoples as they can."

John nodded at the new piece of information but had little to contribute otherwise. They fell into silence for a while. The forest rolled by the front window. The conversations were relatively sparse throughout the day, and John eventually switched out with Karat sometime late in the afternoon.

As the sky darkened, the forest canopy began to lighten, and the road took on a smoother quality. Finally, the group was free of the forest, and a massive city filled with multicolored light struck John. Monumental buildings stretched into the city, slowly lowering back into the cityscape as they got further from the center.

As they drove closer, they began to pass wide strips of farmland, shadowed crops spread across the fields.

The closer they got to the city, the more signs of habitation John began to see. The car light glared off the passing rows of stalks until they emerged to see the city in its full glory. John was awed at just how much the city expanded outward, stretching out past sight. Compared to the City of Lights, it was far brighter if less varied in colors than the city at night.

As they drove, a tall watchtower like building stood by the road, illuminating the area around for thousands of meters, and as they hit the edge of the light, John saw figures piling out of the tower standing in the road.

"Karat—"

"I see them." Karat had stepped up and was looking over his shoulder. They came to a stop around 10 meters away, so close that John could see a single figure had stepped out in front of the others waiting for them.

Zayne was already stepping out of his transport, followed by the other adventurers.

Karat spoke, "Guess we should follow them."

They popped their back hatch and went around, joining Zayne's group as they walked up to the line of people that John could now see under the tower's light. They were armed with swords and bows, none readied; but there was a tension in the line.

The single figure turned out to be a woman with slate grey hair dressed in a lightly armored navy-blue outfit similar to the rest of the people behind her. She spoke once they crossed to about two meters in front of her. "What is your business here?"

Zayne replied, "We're here to bring an urgent message from the City of Lights and the Mountain Hold. Both cities are under occupation by hostile forces. We are requesting help as according to the treaties between the cities."

If the woman was surprised by the information, she did not show it.

"The Seventh Federation's Council will hear your plea as representatives of its allies. We'll transfer you to living quarters in the city."

The soldiers immediately started moving, and they were ushered into another transport shaped in a longer rectangle than their previous ones. The car was streamlined and smooth, and the interior had multiple rows of seats to the back. John settled himself in the midrow, finding himself next to Trajan. The driver and a couple of guards piled on after them, their navy-blue outfits blending in somewhat with the dark interior.

The car started with a rumble, and then they were off. The city lights were even more brilliant through the windows as they got closer, with tall glimmering buildings taking up a large piece of the skyline.

They reached far better paved streets, and continued for a while. John found himself surprised by the buildings' sizes compared to the City of Lights and even the Mountain Hold. They were far taller. Some seemed to be entirely constructed of glass. A tram track that weaved its way in and out overhead was one of the only similarities that John could compare to his home.

They came to a stop eventually at a tall building, which they were ushered into by a man in a navy-blue uniform.

As they walked through the doorway, they were greeted by a large atrium with tables and stuffed chairs arrayed about the room. The man guiding them went to a desk on the far side of the room where a bored-looking clerk sat, and after a hushed exchange between the two of them, he returned with three keys that he handed over to Zayne.

"These will be your room keys. You have rooms 1203, 1204, and 1205. Rooms 1203 and 1204 are divided into two rooms connected in the middle. Someone will be by tomorrow morning to tell you when your meeting with the Council is."

The man walked away; as he exited the building, Zayne spoke, "Well, it looks like we'll be bunking down for the night. I'll take Martin, John, and Lon in 1203."

"I'll have room 1204 with Karat, Aysel, and Silvia," Marcila said.

"Which means Trajan and Seven will have the third room." Zayne handed the keycards out.

They walked back into the hallways and found their rooms with little trouble, guarded by a varnished wooden door. The room John and Martin found themselves in was relatively small with a center door on the far wall leading to Zayne and Lon's room. Their room contained two beds and a bathroom. John waited till after Martin took his shower to take his.

Washing away the accumulated detritus from the days felt nice but did little to distract him from the seemingly ever-present grimness of their situation. He and Martin were in the same room, and it was quiet as he settled down in his bed except for the whisper of Martin's breath as he lay on the other bed.

It felt strange to be there, John decided, so far from his home. He wondered if Bernard was going to be safe. He wondered how the rest of the people in the City of Lights were doing. Were the Baron's soldiers searching for them right now?

It was these worries that sat with John until he eventually succumbed to sleep.

INTERLUDE 4
WHEN TWO ENEMIES MEET

It was frustrating, Captain Fromir reflected, that even when one had complete control of a city, things still slipped through the cracks. Some dead soldiers and two missing cars had greeted him when he woke up that morning, and the bad news wasn't done, it seemed. He had been ordered to send an expeditionary force to the Mountain Hold to determine their next steps in that regard.

Unfortunately, the tram had not returned.

This meant that there would not be peace. The Red Baron did not suffer attacks upon its troops lightly, so he would be putting together a task force to begin the subjugation of the Mountain Hold.

He sighed as he signed another requisition form for supplies.

They were lucky that their supply lines had held up as well as they did for the course of their campaign. While fighting other Barons had been well and suitable for their overall goals, capturing the City of Lights would provide an adequate, stable outpost to begin amassing for their next attack, that is, after they had dealt with the Mountain Hold.

To do so, they would need to expand their supply base, and the City of Lights would be critical as their usual main supply lines were required to direct materials to other parts of their forces. They needed repair work on some of their heavy equipment and general repair for their forces' weapons and armor.

Captain Fromir's finger traced the map, glancing over the various businesses that his men had identified, names inscribed in small print. Most would be used for smaller arms and supplies, but he needed a shop with an existing sizable workforce.

His finger paused on one, checking the data gathered on it. A sizeable workforce already had high-quality materials.

He nodded.

The Western Workshop would be an excellent choice.

CHAPTER 13

A MEETING WITH THE COUNCIL

John was woken early the next morning to the sound of Zayne knocking on the door. They showered quickly and then assembled themselves with Zayne and Lon outside their room, leaving their weapons behind before heading out the door. A guard stood there dressed in navy blue same as the other guards last night.

A couple of minutes later, they were joined by Marcila, Karat, Aysel, and Silvia. They, in turn, were followed shortly by Trajan and Seven. The guard led them away from the rooms and back outside, where they waited for a car. They were driven a short distance, ending up at a massive circular building with soaring pillars spaced out. The building was a clean marble white that stood out distinctly from the other buildings. They walked up the stairs to the entrance of two shining steel doors that were already opened.

As the group stepped in, their feet met the marble floor of

the large atrium. They were led to the lobby and up a series of stairs. At the top, the guard stopped in front of a door. He reached into his pocket, pulling out a key and turned it in the lock to open the door into a small room furnished with fluffy chairs and a low table.

"You will wait here," the guard said and then turned, walking out with clipped steps and shutting the door behind him.

Zayne shrugged to himself and, after a moment, turned to the rest of them. "Make yourselves comfortable, I suppose."

They did so, and John found himself sitting in a chair with nothing to do but look around the small room. It had dark maroon wallpaper that contrasted sharply with the marble floor. There were two doors set into the room, opposite each other. The other members of the group had also seated themselves in varying states of contemplation or low discussion.

They waited a while, before the second door opened, and a somewhat stooped figure walked in, a long sword clasped at his side. He had brilliant white hair swept back around his shoulders and was clean-shaven.

He spoke, "My name is Elio Way, the Sergeant of Arms for the Council; follow me, if you please."

Elio turned smartly on his heels and began walking away. Zayne, Marcila, and Karat followed with the rest of the group. John found himself bringing up the rear. They entered a large chamber filled with seats and desks that looked down at the floor where there was another desk with three chairs at the bottom. About half the seats were filled with people in black suits. At the front, a female dwarf with black hair and red eyes sat at the center seat, flanked by an elf on her left with blonde hair and blue eyes and a clockwork made of silver metal lined with gold accents and bright green eyes.

"We bring this Chamber together to hear from the representatives of the City of Lights and its sister city, the Mountain Hold," belted out the dwarf.

The room was quiet as Zayne walked a little further forward till he was at the center of the floor.

"Thank you for hearing us today. The City of Lights has been attacked by the Red Baron, who now holds the city under occupation. Furthermore, the Mountain Hold has also been conquered by a separate force which we were unable to identify."

There was a slight stir among the assembled people, but nothing else occurred.

"We are here on behalf of both cities; we ask that you send a force to liberate them, as according to the treaties."

There was a moment of silence before the dwarf spoke again, "Thank you. The Sergeant of Arms will now escort you back to your lodgings as we deliberate."

That was it. The Sergeant of Arms came to retrieve them, and they were brought back out of the Council Chamber and walked out of the building, finally being returned to the car, which made its way back to the hotel. A single guard stood in front of them. "You may travel about the city as you please while the Council deliberates. When they reach their decision, you will be notified. Do you have any questions?"

Zayne glanced about the group before he responded, "No, thank you."

The guard nodded and walked away, leaving them outside the building.

"That's it?" Lon's face was twisted into a frown.

Marcila sighed. "It's probably the best we could have hoped for, all things considered."

"The best?" Trajan was also frowning. "They didn't say they'd do anything."

"They at least listened to us," Marcila responded. "They could have very well completely ignored us."

"So, what do we do now?" Martin asked.

"We'll wait and see," Zayne sighed heavily. "Enjoy what time you can in the City. We could all use a break."

With various assents, they split up until only John, Martin, Silvia, and Aysel remained.

"So, what do you guys want to do?" Silvia mustered a wan smile.

"I've never been to the Seventh Federation before," Aysel stated. "I wouldn't mind trying some of the food."

John nodded, feeling the protests of his stomach as he realized he hadn't eaten anything. Martin and Silvia agreed, so they set off down the street, passing by the various assorted businesses. From crafters to restaurants, to wholesale stores, John realized that the Seventh Federation was far more densely populated than the City of Lights. They eventually stopped at a restaurant called "Wan's Eats." They entered to find a bustling but cozy establishment. After taking a table in the back and receiving their menus from a cheerful waiter, there were a couple of silent minutes as they decided what to eat. John settled on a dish with some stir-fried noodles as something that probably wouldn't be horrible, and after the others chose their meals, they had nothing to do but wait.

Martin was balancing his fork over the tip of his forefinger. After a moment, he said, "So what do you guys think the Council is going to do? Do you think they'll help us?"

"The treaties they signed should hold them accountable, right?" Silvia said.

John frowned in thought, rolling over the event in his mind. "I'm not so sure."

Three sets of eyes locked onto him, and he had to resist the urge to fiddle with his utensils uncomfortably. "It's just… if they don't honor the treaties, there's no real consequence to them. If they do honor the treaties, they'll have to commit their forces and resources to wage war. They could just dismiss us and start trading with the Barons as if nothing happened."

"Do you think that?" Aysel asked, eyes piercing into him.

John nodded.

"You may be right." Martin looked contemplative. "Is there any actual reason for them to hold to the treaties in such circumstances? Removing the Baron's army from the City of Lights would require a large application of their forces, not to mention the Mountain Hold as well. It would likely be incredibly costly both in terms of soldiers and resources."

Silvia frowned as she weighed their words. "If they abandoned us, what would it show to their other allies? Wouldn't that mean other cities or nations would be wary of keeping on trusting the Seventh Federation?"

John shrugged, nodding to acquiesce the point. Still, the second part of his point hadn't sunk in. "Yes, they may be less trusted, but the Seventh Federation is probably the biggest nation aside from the Baronies on the Northern continents. How many cities could afford to make their distrust known in any meaningful way? Even the Mountain Hold and City of Lights, which were largely self-sufficient, needed trade with the Seventh Federation for our economy."

"What about the Amelion Imperium? They value honor and are big enough to cause a trade issue," Aysel pointed out.

"I thought they were in the middle of a Civil War?" Martin questioned.

Aysel made an odd noise but shook her head when attention fell on her. "Sorry, I thought the Civil War was winding down."

Silvia shook her head. "Not from what I've read on the Mountain Hold System. The succession line was broken when the Empress-elect was assassinated during the first months of her tenure. There hasn't been another election, and instead, two factions are fighting it out to determine who they will put on the throne."

Their conversation paused as their food came. A steaming bowl of noodles was placed in front of John. He carefully spooned up a portion, blowing to cool the temperature slightly before tipping the spoon back. It was delicious, if a little spicy, and he dug in a little more, his companions following suit. The conversation was put on hold for some minutes. As John looked about the restaurant in the silence, an odd thought occurred to him. It felt like someone was looking at him. He could not see a single person not focused on their meals and conversation, but he couldn't shake the feeling. He went back to his food, trying to check out of his vision peripherals to try and catch any glances at them.

Nothing happened. Maybe John had imagined it? Though he guessed that even if he wasn't imagining it, the chances of spotting a spy was minimal at best. John spooned another mouthful of noodles into his mouth, trying to dismiss the odd sensation. His eyes wandered the ceiling for a moment, an odd couple of marks catching his attention. There wasn't anything inherently suspicious about them, he supposed, but the marks were strange compared to the smooth tile surrounding it. They were black and looked like two parallel lines marked across by various others almost haphazardly.

He tried to focus once more on his food, but the lines kept catching his eyes every time he so much as looked up from his food.

Martin noticed. "Hey John is something bothering you?"

John gave a small, stretched smile, shaking his head. "It's nothing, it's just…" he shook his head. It was stupid. It was just a strange mark; it didn't mean anything.

"It's just what?" Martin prompted.

John struggled for the words before he finally said. "Isn't that kind of a strange mark on the ceiling?"

"What?"

Martin looked up, furrowing his brow as he gazed at the mark. "That is kinda strange looking, but what about it?" he turned back to look at John.

Now Aysel and Silvia were also looking at him.

"I—"

A sensation like a current ran through him, trailing down his senses, submerging them in a strange heat. John raised his hand, magic springing outward just as a cacophonous sound rang out and a bright flash of green light ripped outward, blinding his eyes for a moment. As his vision recovered, all he could see was a cloud of dust surrounding him, and he choked on the air as he tried to inhale. Slowly the dust began to clear, and he saw Aysel, Martin, and Silvia all around them, coughing just as he was.

He felt drained. Silvia moved her hands, and the air began to stir around them, dispersing the remains dust cloud, and he was now able to see that the section of the roof had disappeared entirely with small pieces of rubble scattered about.

His conjured blue shield of magic hung above their heads, cracked in parts from the force of the explosion, and he let it fade, wincing at how drained his reserves now felt. Dust fell from where the shield had stopped it.

"What was that?" Aysel's voice caused him to turn to her. She looked stunned and was covered in dust, just the same as he was. Martin and Silvia also were lined with a covering of grey dust.

He realized that other patrons in the restaurant had panicked, and he could see that a number had fled with others sitting frozen in their booths.

John was too stunned to move for a moment before his scrambled mind chose a course of action. "We need to get out of here."

There were no disagreements as they removed themselves from the booth as quickly as they could, Silvia taking the lead out of the restaurant. A crowd had gathered outside, trying to look in to see what had happened. John heard various jumbled words.

"What happened?"

"Is everyone okay?"

"We need to call the fire department!"

He made his way through the crowd and emerged on the other side, closely followed by Aysel, Martin, and Silvia.

They paused after making their way through the crowd, now on the outskirts of it. John turned back to look at the building. The exterior of Wan's Eats looked mostly intact except for the top, which no longer had a sloping roof over a section, just a gaping hole.

"What was that?" Martin murmured, his face drawn and pale.

John shook his head mutely. He had no idea.

"Did anyone else get caught in the blast?" Silvia murmured.

John's heart sank as he tried to recall who had surrounded them. Had the seats been occupied? His mind blanked.

"How did you know, John?" Aysel asked.

Aysel's words dragged John back from his thoughts enough to see that the group's attention was focused on him.

"I—" How *had* he known? One moment he had been sitting there, looking at the strange marking. The next, he had reacted without conscious thought. There had been a sensation, he recalled, something he didn't quite have the words to describe.

John shook his head. "I don't know. I saw a mark on the ceiling, and I just reacted."

The discussion was tabled as they heard a piercing wail and saw that fire cars were traveling down the street; firefighters were rushing out to enter the building while also herding the crowd back.

"We should check on the rest of our group." Silvia's words seemed like the most sensible course of action, so they began to head back through the streets.

They arrived back at their lodging and, within moments, spotted Zayne and Marcila in discussion by the doorway. The debate broke as Marcila's eyes landed upon them.

"Zayne, they're back," Marcila said, and Zayne turned, and his expression relaxed from its deep frown.

"You're all okay. Good." Zayne smiled in a somewhat strained manner. "You weren't caught up in whatever's going on in the city, were you?."

It must've shown in their expressions because Zayne's smile faded slightly. "You were?"

"Unfortunately, we were," Aysel replied.

"What happened?" Marcila asked with a solemn expression on her face.

"We went out to lunch," Aysel took the lead. "We were eating, and John noticed a mark on the ceiling right before the entire roof exploded."

"A mark?" Marcila questioned, turning to John.

John nodded, feeling somewhat uneasy under her intense stare. "It looked like two parallel lines, but there were other marks in between."

Marcila, looking somewhat disquieted, said, "That sounds like a rune and could have been on purpose. Zayne, we need to check on the rest of the group."

"Agreed; we should split up to cover more ground."

"I'll take Aysel and John," Marcila said.

Zayne nodded. "Alright, Martin and Silvia with me."

Zayne strode off quickly, followed by Martin and Silvia, leaving Marcila standing with Aysel and John.

"I believe Seven and Trajan went this way to search for food," Marcila said and turned to walk the opposite way down the street, leaving John and Aysel to catch up in her wake. They continued down the road at a fast pace looking about for any sign of Seven or Trajan.

The streets still had the regular traffic from the day, the news of the explosion seemingly not having carried over to this section of the city yet. They continued down the street, passing by restaurants searching for a glimpse of their wayward companions. Minutes passed as they continued down the road, occasionally stepping into restaurants and shops, searching for them.

A familiar sound ripped through the air, and a building a little way down the street erupted into a plume of smoke and dust pulled from the ground. People screamed, running away. Some ran forward, an action mirrored by Marcila, Aysel, and John.

The building that erupted had been another restaurant, and some people emerged from the smoke coughing raggedly. Marcila led the way in, covering her face with her sleeve, mirrored by Aysel and John as they foraged their way in. There was far more smoke in this building

John lost track of Marcila and Aysel. His foot hit something on the ground, and he bent down to find what felt like a body. He lifted the body and staggered to where he thought the entrance had been. The smoke lightened, and light peek through as he adjusted his course to the light. He stepped forward out into fresh air and moved farther away to lay the person he had found on the ground. He glanced down to see the face of a young woman with bright blonde hair.

It wasn't Seven or Trajan.

He turned back to the building and saw that some of the smoke had cleared slightly. Another person stepped through the smoke, and he saw Aysel carrying another body. She spotted him and moved towards him, laying her burden down, a dwarven woman.

Marcila emerged another minute later, carrying nothing, and she looked around, spotting John and Aysel. She approached them.

"I couldn't find anyone else in there, but with the dust and smoke, who knows who else could be in there?"

A piercing wail grew cacophonous as firetrucks raced down the street, stopping by, and firefighters emerged, rushing into the building equipped with face-covering masks and thick yellow clothes. One came over to them, bending down to look at the unconscious bodies on the ground. "Did you pull them from the building?"

"Yes," Aysel said hoarsely, something John could understand as he felt his own throat feel dry and cracked just from being inside the dust-filled building.

"Good job," the firemen said, calling over another, and together they started to check over the people.

John, Aysel, and Marcila stood back as the firemen began to conjure streams of water, dousing the building and then the inside.

"We need to keep looking," Marcila's words spurred them onward, and they continued down the street even as more people came out to look at the fire. They continued for some time, spotting two other buildings with smoke coming out of them. Firefighters had already arrived on the scene, so they carried on.

"I think that's them," Aysel's voice caused John and Marcila to turn, spotting Seven and Trajan outside of a smoking building that was partially crumbled.

"Trajan! Seven!" Marcila called out. "What happened?"

The pair turned, spotting them and walking over. "We don't know," Trajan responded. "We were still deciding on a place to eat, and then this happened. One moment we were walking by, the next—" he gestured at the smoking destruction.

“Aysel, John, Silvia, and Martin were caught up inside one of the buildings.” Trajan’s mouth, already set in a severe frown, deepened further.

“You don’t think this was targeted, do you?” he asked in a hushed voice.

Marcila grimaced. “I don’t know, but we should meet up with the others. We don’t want to be blamed given that we’ve just entered the city.”

Seven’s metallic voice said, “Agreed.”

They moved back through the streets that had become significantly less congested as it seemed that people had hidden inside. They passed by their lodgings. As they walked, John could see the smoke plumes that filled the air; he counted five of them, two from where they had come—one, obviously having belonged to the restaurant—and two more in the direction they were moving.

They passed by a blown out store, which seemed to have suffered even more damage than the previous buildings to the point where its front-facing façade had collapsed entirely. Firefighters were dousing the building, and some were lifting large pieces of debris out of the way, their bodies shimmering with different colors of magic.

They continued past it after verifying none of their companions were about and headed on their way to the second fire till they spotted Zayne, Martin, Silvia, Karat, and Lon. They were standing a distance from the smoking building with ash settled in the hair and clothing of Karat and Lon.

They walked over, catching the tail end of what Lon was saying, "—Karat shielded us, but I have no doubt that if she hadn't, that blast would have been the end of us."

Zayne nodded at them in acknowledgment. "I'm glad to see you're all alright. I assume the same thing happened to you, Karat and Lon?"

Karat nodded. "We were about to enter the shop just as the blast happened."

"What in the blazes is happening?" Lon's mustache twitched. "This can't be a coincidence that every building we were in was hit."

John couldn't help but internally agree with Lon. Still, what about the other buildings that were hit? Maybe this was just a coincidence? But nothing had been a coincidence for quite a while, a small voice in his head reminded him. They had fled an occupation. Could agents from the Baron have infiltrated the Seventh Federation? If so, what did that mean for them?

"We need to move," Karat said. "This isn't a place any of us want to be. We should go back to where we were staying."

"If we're being targeted, is that safe?" Marcila pointed out, and Karat nodded, acknowledging the point.

"Soldiers were guarding our lodgings, weren't there?" Lon stated. "That's certainly likely safer than staying out on the open streets."

"We'll be careful," Zayne said. "But we should at least get off the open streets."

There was a grudging agreement, and so they began to head back down the street. People were milling about or hurrying away as emergency responders surrounded the sites of smoke. The air felt sharp and anxious, and John realized he was sweating, cold liquid trailing over his body.

He shivered despite the warmth of the sun beating down on them. They continued forward, passing by businesses and turning down the street of their lodgings. The building still stood, and as they stepped inside the lobby, John tensed, looking around the ceiling, but nothing was there.

They continued to their rooms, and they cautiously went in, checking about for any strange markings. They found nothing, and so they sat down in Zayne's room as a group. There was some small discussion, but it was uneasy, a tension hanging in the air.

There was a loud knock at the door, causing John to flinch, startled. Zayne got up and went to the door, opening it to a guard similar to those earlier that day.

"I'm here to check if your group is all right?"

"We're fine," Zayne responded. "What's going on? We saw explosions—"

"Everything is under control," the guard assured Zayne in what was supposed to be a calming voice. "Just a magical accident; nothing to worry about. The Council is asking everyone to stay inside. You may go to the hotel dining area, but we ask that you do not leave the building."

The guard walked away, and Zayne closed the door, giving a deep sigh.

"They're lying to us."

The words, "but why," went unspoken.

CHAPTER 14

THE KNIGHTS OF THE DAWN

It was some hours later that another emissary of the Council came to talk to the group. They had allowed the group the freedom to move about outside. However, they hadn't taken the opportunity, preferring to stay inside. They had only emerged to retrieve food. John and Aysel had been designated to retrieve food for the rest of the group.

Despite the time John had spent with Aysel, he still felt the flush of embarrassment and anxiety when they were alone. They walked down the street, having retrieved food from a place that dealt in eastern cuisines. As they walked, they did not talk to each other until Aysel broke the silence.

"I didn't expect this," she said.

"What do you mean?" John questioned.

"I thought it would be a relatively simple mission into the mountain to find that something strange had intercepted or held up the previous adventurers. I didn't expect for us to end up here of all places." Aysel's lips were twisted in a small smile.

"How many places have you been?" he asked.

"I've been to the far side of the world," Aysel quietly replied as she gazed outward into space. "I've seen all kinds of magic: the Universities of the High Mages; the towns by the ocean with their simple magic that they use to fish. Marcila has taken me everywhere to explore the world and its wonders."

John was awed. He hadn't been anywhere except the City of Lights in all his years, and to hear from someone who had so extensively traveled was strange. John smiled, not able to quench the jealousy in his gut. "Anywhere that you felt like staying?"

Aysel shook her head. "The closest was the Forests of the Forever Woods. elves live there in numbers like my homeland Alvion. It's... peaceful there in a way it's hard to describe. While cities such as here and the City of Lights bustle with life, Alvion flows. It's a place I've never seen the like of. The homes are crafted from massive trees where the wood is sung together to form homes."

"Where exactly are you from?" John couldn't help but ask.

Aysel's soft smile turned slightly. "The City of the Queens. I grew up there for most of my childhood until," she paused for a moment, seeming to consider her words, "Marcila took me into her care. She's taught me all I know of adventuring."

A moment passed before Aysel spoke again. "So what of you, John? Where do you come from?"

John was surprised for a moment, but he responded just the same. "I've lived in the City of Lights for as long I've known. Bernard raised me and taught me how to forge and to fight. I honestly considered becoming a forge master, but—" John trailed off.

"Yes?" Aysel looked at him, and he turned slightly from her intense gaze.

"I couldn't imagine spending the rest of my life in the same place. I just…" John searched for the words. "I couldn't just see the world through Bernard's stories. Bernard traveled a lot, and he's seen a lot, and I guess I wanted to see some of that for myself."

"I understand," Aysel responded. "My sister, who's some years older than me became an adventurer as well. When she came back, she said that the experiences changed her view on everything. I… want that."

Silence spread between them for a moment. They were approaching their lodgings now, the gleaming lights from the building shining on their faces, illuminating in a strange contrast of light and shadows. They walked through the lobby and arrived back at their rooms. They entered the first door to see that the rest of their group had gathered around a table. Greetings were exchanged, and they distributed the food. There was only small talk as they ate, carefully centered away from the discussion of current events. The more experienced adventurers like Trajan talked about past battles. Marcila engaged Aysel in a debate on Alvion, which John found himself engaging in along with Martin.

The talk continued late into the night, and it was only at midnight that they broke to go to bed. As John laid in bed that night, his thoughts raced. He worried over what had happened that day. His thoughts slowly became replaced with his conversation with Aysel, and his mind became distracted. Aysel was so incredibly beautiful that his thoughts became filled with her smile as he slowly fell asleep. Light filtered through John's eyelids, and he struggled against it as he woke up. Half-remembered dreams faded as Martin continued snoring.

As John readied himself for the day, he tried to remember the occurrences of his dreams, but nothing came to mind except for faded memories of large crowds and a strange scent in the air. As he went through his morning rituals, he couldn't help but try and remember his dreams. Nothing came to mind as he scrubbed his hair and dressed. The morning was spent with the rest of the group as they discussed the events of yesterday. They didn't come to a conclusion as some of the group, like Lon, believed the events were coincidence. At the same time, Zayne and some others were worried that they had been targeted for their recent contact with the city's representatives.

These discussions were broken for breakfast, this time served by the hotel, and as John sat in the dining area, he observed the rest of the occupants. For the most part, they seemed like tourists discussing where they would go next during the day.

A man in a dark grey suit was talking to his neighbor about the explosions yesterday. His neighbor assured him that "there won't be any more of that. I've heard that the Council has things well in hand."

What the Council had "well in hand," no one seemed to know, and it put John more on edge than he had been before.

He poked at the eggs on his plate, piling them onto a half piece of palm bread, a thick bread without crust with grill marks on its face. He ate solemnly with the rest of the group around him. The conversation was muted among the table, the tension in the air hanging over all of them. As they sat around the table eating their food, John's thoughts turned to yesterday, wondering what exactly had occurred with the explosions. Could adventurers have been the targets given that other buildings had exploded that they hadn't been near? Or was that just some sort of cover-up to cloak the real intentions of the perpetrator?

John took a bite of his food, taking the chance to look around the room, surveying the other people. They wore clothing that looked significantly lighter than that typically worn in the City of Lights. Perhaps because he had noticed, the Seventh Federation's temperature was considerably warmer than up in the mountains.

As his thoughts chased around in his head, Aysel's voice brought him back to the present.

"Is there nothing we can do to help?" she was asking Zayne.

"The Seventh Federation's Council likely has the matter handled, and to offer our help when we have our mission may be counterproductive," Zayne said.

"Why is that?" Lon asked.

Zayne replied, "We have little to go off, and given that we are recent guests in the city, they may suspect us of being the cause of the attacks."

"For now," Marcila spoke. "It will be in our best interest to leave the Federation to deal with its issues. They no doubt have many people already working on the issue with far more to go off of than we do."

They broke from breakfast a short while later, leaving to go back to their rooms or other leisure areas at their lodgings. John found himself with Silvia, Martin, and Aysel in a recreation room empty of other occupants. Some short bookshelves lined the wall, along with a couple of terminals that had access to the city's network. At the center of the room resided a broad table where they sat a deck of cards between them.

"Zayne seems worried." Martin frowned. "I can't say I blame him, with all that's going on. I can't help but think that someone doesn't want us to talk to the Council." He placed a card down showing two knights dueling.

Silvia nodded. "I normally wouldn't agree, but it all seems rather convenient that just when we brought our case to the Council, this happened." She laid down a card with a rampaging dragon.

"I just wish there was something we could do," Aysel said, slamming her card with a grand castle. "It's so frustrating to be trapped in here."

John couldn't help but agree. Down in the mountains, their goals had seemed clear: to get their companions and then escape. Now here in the Seventh Federation, there didn't seem to be a clear path forward whatsoever. He placed down his card, a unicorn that pranced across an open field. "What can we do?" he asked, looking at the others. "Wouldn't going outside lead to some suspicion on us or worse we could get attacked again, and we wouldn't escape?"

Aysel grudgingly nodded. "You're not wrong, but it still feels like we're letting down the people of the Mountain Hold and the City of Lights."

The cards were compared, and Silvia's hand was found to have the superior value, so they reset and began again with another round. So, they played for a while, trying to turn the topic to something lighter regarding some childhood misadventures. Martin was describing a harrowing encounter with an unfriendly troll when John glanced outside the recreation room's door to spot a guard garbed in the same armor as the Seventh Federation's soldiers rushing past the room. Another second later, and another guard flashed past. And another, and another.

John stood up, walking to the door, slightly opening it to look outside and down the hallways. A troop of guards was running down the hallway in an assemblage of clinking armor.

"John, what are you looking at?" Aysel's voice caused him to turn to the rest of the group.

"There's a group of guards running down the hallway," he said and was quickly joined by the rest of the companions peeking out the door as the soldiers vanished from sight around a bend.

They looked at each other before Aysel said firmly, "I think we should follow them."

"Won't that make them suspicious?" replied Silvia worrying her bottom lip with her teeth.

"Wouldn't it be more suspicious if we didn't follow a strange occurrence going on?" Martin's face was set.

Their eyes turned to John, who shrugged. "I guess we should."

All their inputs settled; they exited the room, traveling at a fast walk down the hallway. They turned a corner back into the dining area to see some other patrons gathered around the guards who stood in a semi-circle in the center of a room.

A healer dressed in green robes had his hand raised over a man lying on the floor. The man's hair was thinning and grey as he laid unnaturally still under the attention of the room.

After a moment's silence, the healer rose, turning to the guards. "He's dead. We will need to move him."

There were gasps about the room. The guards spread about, trying to dismiss the crowd, including them, and as John found himself ushered from the room by a guard along with Aysel, Silvia, and Martin, he spotted something silver embedded in the side of the man's neck.

In the first of their rooms, they turned to each other; their companions occupied the additional space.

"What happened to him?" Martin looked slightly unsteady and sat down in a chair.

Aysel responded somewhat hesitantly, "He was dead, right?"

An uncomfortable moment of silence settled in the room.

Silvia hesitantly spoke, "Do you think that it was whoever destroyed the buildings?"

"But wouldn't they have targeted one of our group?" Martin pointed out.

"Either way, it shows that even being inside under guard isn't going to keep us safe necessarily." There was a murmuring of agreement with Aysel's words.

John let loose the burning question that had been inside him. "So what do we do then? We can't just sit back and let whoever this is keep on taking shots. They eventually won't miss."

Martin responded with a grimace. "I'm not saying I like it, but if we do something, won't that look suspicious to the people guarding us? We've already been so close to each incident."

John sighed, nodding. He had a solid point, but that didn't make waiting any better.

"I agree with John," Aysel said, and the group turned to her. She continued, "While Martin is right, that could make things worse by acting. By not acting, we encourage whoever this is. Every time they miss, there's more collateral damage. It's not just for our sakes. People near us are going to get hurt if we don't do something."

John blinked, processing Aysel's words. She was right. This wasn't just about them. All the buildings that were destroyed had been occupied by other people who had been hurt.

"I also agree with Aysel and John," Silvia said softly, tucking her red hair behind her ear.

They turned to look at Martin, who winced, tapping his fingers against his knee rapidly. "All right," he said. "But don't say I didn't warn you."

They stayed in their rooms for the remainder of the day, some guards coming by and giving them clearance to leave but providing no other information. No other group members left except to retrieve meals. The older members, meaning everyone aside, John, Aysel, Martin, and Silvia barricaded themselves in Zayne's room likely to discuss a plan. This arrangement suited them just fine, and allowed them to make their plan for their later outing.

It was late, and the outside was illuminated by lanterns down the street as John, Aysel, Martin, and Silvia snuck out after silently leaving their room. The night air was surprisingly warm as they walked out, and in the light of the streetlights, they could still see people moving about the city.

They traveled down the sidewalks moving back into the city where they had been only yesterday, stopping by the building that had been destroyed. It was rubble now with safety lines surrounding the area. Thankfully there were no people near the site, so after a glance around, they bypassed the lines, stepping in the rubble.

Some of the walls were still standing. John tried to walk to the area where they had been seated before looking around for something, anything they could have missed. The broken rock and stone gave no answers. As he made to turn away to another section of the building, a flash of steel caught his eye.

He frowned, walking over to a large rock that was crushing the steel, which seemed to be reflecting far more light than it should be able to, giving off a soft blue glow.

It couldn't be…

He bent down, and this close, he could see the tell-tale striations of Hart Steel.

"John?"

John was startled, flinching as Aysel's voice unexpectedly came up from behind him. He turned to see her looking over his shoulder. "What's that?" she asked softly.

"Hart Steel," he whispered.

"Hart Steel? But I thought that that kind of steel was used for devices, not construction."

John nodded just as perplexed. "It is."

He reached out to the piece of steel, grasping it and lifting only to find the piece stuck by the massive weight of the rock on top of it. Flaring his magic through his arms, John's blue glow lit up the area slightly as he pushed the rock off, this time with ease, pulling loose a rod of Hart Steel.

As he lifted it, he felt along its soft edges under his grip. "Aysel, can you give me some light?"

Silver light glowed over them, and he was able to see the rod was marked entirely by an innumerable series of runes. The marks wrapped around almost looking like writing but a type with no space between the letters and words.

It tickled something at the back of his memory as he ran his hands over it. It was almost like he had seen this kind of device before—a faint memory when he was young, watching and learning from Bernard as he forged yet another order. Long rods just like this one that he marked to be sold to…

Who?

"I recognize this," he whispered to Aysel, who looked up from her examination, directly in his eyes.

"Where?"

"At the workshop where I grew up. Bernard forged rods exactly like this," John replied.

"For what?"

John strained his memory, trying to recall just what Bernard had said while forging these rods. What had it been? It wasn't a standard order. It had been for some miners, hadn't it?

After a moment, he shook his head. "I can't remember. I think it could have been for miners."

Aysel frowned. "Should we bring it back to see if anyone else recognizes it?"

John was about to reply before a soft crunch brought his attention up to the shadows not touched by the streetlight or Aysel's silver light.

The darkness shifted, and a foot was struck forward into the light, followed by a tall, gaunt looking man. He had silver hair trimmed neatly about his head and carried a long cane in his left hand. He was dressed in a fine black suit. A rose was peeking out of his front pocket. A long, tense moment emerged between the two parties, and John found himself slowly edging his hand to his sword.

"Good evening," he said in a confident, even-toned voice that carried to them. "What might a pair of adventurers be doing here at this hour?"

John exchanged glances with Aysel, worry visible in her eyes. Aysel turned back to the man and said, "Our business is our own."

The man chuckled. "So it is. I couldn't help but also notice that you seem to have found something in the rubble there." He gestured at the rod in John's hands.

John looked down at the rod then looked back up. "Yes?" he said cautiously, "Do you know what it is?"

The man stepped a little bit forward and looked over the rod, "I do believe it's a blasting rod."

A blasting rod. The memory came back like a wave to John; these rods were used in the mines to clear rock.

"This rod caused the explosion," John murmured.

The man solemnly nodded, "Indeed it did."

"But who would have done this?"

"Ah, the more important question." The old man nodded. "To answer that question, you would need to know what situation you have found yourselves in."

"And what situation is that?" John asked, eyes narrowed at the man.

"One that you and your companions are wholly unprepared for," the man replied calmly. "The agents of the Barons are already here. They have convinced some of the legislators to not act in favor of the City of Lights. At the same time, they are already acting to deal with your adventuring group."

"And what's your angle in this?" Aysel questioned.

"My angle is my duty," the man replied. "I am a Knight of the Dawn."

A Knight of the Dawn. Hadn't Treemor mentioned them?

"What is a Knight of the Dawn?" John couldn't help but ask.

"We used to be the guardians of the land," the man replied. "We were formed to prevent the forces of the Six Kings from destroying the peoples of the Thirteen Realms. That is before the Thirteen Realms became the seven that you know."

John nodded. There was that mention of Thirteen Realms again, and that this man was Knight of the Dawn, apparently the organization that Treemor had mentioned. This man had to know what Treemor was talking about. He was about to question the man further before the man raised his hand. "Please, I know you have questions, but I would recommend that we leave first. It is not safe for these discussions to be held on the open streets."

John hesitated to look at Aysel, who said, "May as well. Nothing more that we can find here."

Aysel turned, calling out, "Martin, Silvia!" Footsteps emerged from over the stone heap, and Martin and Silvia appeared, hesitating as they spotted the man who stood across from them.

"He's a friend," Aysel assured them, and they somewhat reluctantly continued forward.

"Now we should move before your enemies find you," the man said, and he headed off over the heap and onto the street. They followed him through the lit streets, onto a street with residential buildings.

The houses lined the street on both sides, some with a light on their door, while others appeared dark. They continued their path through the streets, walking by the houses without disturbance. They eventually paused at a house set back from the street slightly with a stone path that meandered its way through several tall trees up to a door. The man walked down the path, and they followed him up to the door, which he opened with a small key, gesturing them to step inside.

They did so and were greeted by a room of dark shapes before the man closed the door and, with a small click, illuminated the entryway where they found themselves. A bench was arrayed by a coat rack, which the man passed by, hanging his coat upon it.

He walked deeper into the house, where, with more clicks of switches, the area was illuminated to show a well-set kitchen and circular dining room table with six chairs around it.

As they walked in, the man gestured at the seats. "Do sit down," he said. "I'll grab some tea from the kitchen."

The man proceeded to busy himself about the kitchen, filling and placing a kettle on the stove.

John, Aysel, Martin, and Silvia sat down around the table.

John couldn't help but feel ill at ease in this mysterious person's house, and he had to remind himself that not only did he have a sword, but the rest of his companions sitting around the table were armed too. After some minutes, the man returned to the table with the kettle and five cups he placed and filled around the table before taking his seat.

"Now, I presume the lot of you have some questions for me, and I will endeavor to answer them.

John looked to Aysel, Martin, and Silvia, and for a moment, there was hesitation as they each waited for the others to go first. Finally, Aysel took the lead, turning to the man. "What did you mean when you said there were Thirteen Realms?"

"There were once Thirteen Realms instead of the seven that you now know. It was the Six Kings who stole the Lost Six Realms from us, using magic and ritual to dominate those once free Realms. The only reason they didn't take over all of them is the Grand Mage Lano, who created a barrier to protect us from them."

"Why have we never heard of this?" Martin asked.

"You've never heard of this because it was erased from our history," the man replied. "It was thought that even the acknowledgment of the King's evil would lead to the temptation to contact them to seek favor."

"Then how do you know?" John asked, examining the man sitting in front of them.

"Because I was there four hundred years ago," he replied.

"You were there!" Martin said, shocked. "But most humans live at most a hundred and fifty years; even those with strong magic rarely live over three hundred years."

"I am no longer human." An intense weariness passed over his face.

"How old are you?" Martin asked.

"Thousands of years have passed me by," the man replied. "I have stopped counting."

"And why are you telling us this?" Aysel questioned. "You said that Lano sealed the Kings."

"Because the seal is only impenetrable from their side," the man replied. "With enough effort from this side of the seal, it can be breached. Something that I fear is all too close to happening if what I have been told of the Mountain Hold is true."

"What have you been told?" Aysel asked, a slight edge in her voice. "We haven't mentioned anything."

"Your companions should be more careful who they are speaking in front of. I have heard of the construction taking place in the Mountain Hold. It sounds all too familiar to the portals that were constructed for the gateways of the invasions of the Kings."

"So, someone is creating a gateway for the Kings to invade," John said with a calmness in his voice that he did not feel.

The man nodded. "I fear that it is so."

A long moment of silence passed. Silvia was the first to speak, "So what do we do? We can't just let this happen."

"You must stop the completion of the gateway," the man said solemnly. "If you do not, the Kings will be able to send their armies through, and this realm and all the others will be lost."

"But how?" John's frustration bled through his voice. "We weren't a match for them when we were in the Cold Mountains, and even if we were, the City of Light outside of it is occupied by the Barons."

"This is something that can be dealt with," the man said.

Martin shook his head. "But even if we did, there's still an entire army in the Cold Mountains. We can't hope to fight them all. We would need an army."

"Then get one," said the man. "There is still an army to be found in these lands. The Knights of the Dawn are disbanded, but if you managed to gain an Index, a captain could send out the call to reassemble."

"A Captain?" Silvia's dismay was evident on her face. "We don't even know where one is!"

"Incorrect," the man said. "I'm sorry for not introducing myself sooner. I am Captain Grant of the Knights of the Dawn, and I need your aid."

"Aid?" questioned John, "to find the other captains you mean?"

Grant nodded. "Yes. I can't do it alone, and you're the group most likely to trust me given what you've seen."

"Where would we even start?" Martin asked. "It's not like there's a map to this.. 'the Index', you said?"

"Well, in a way, there is," Grant said, and at their questioning looks, he continued, "I know the location of the Dawn Index."

"This 'Index' isn't just available right?" Martin said, prodding for more information.

Grant shook his head. "Unfortunately, it is not; it's located in one of the abandoned castles we used to hold back when the Knights were still a going concern."

"And where is this 'abandoned castle?'" Aysel asked, eyebrows furrowed.

"Thankfully, not far from here. Only some leagues," Grant said.

"If you know where it is, why haven't you gone yourself?" Aysel pointed out.

"Other than the fact I just learned of this threat from your companions?" Grant raised an eyebrow. "Because, without the aid of a group of adventurers, I fear the current defense system would fatally obstruct my way."

"What do you mean 'defense system?'" Silvia asked.

"The defenses as they are now will not recognize anyone other than a registered Knight at that Citadel as a non-hostile target. Given that the last time the defenses were updated was some hundreds of years ago, very few possible persons could still be alive to pass the defenses safely."

"What makes you think we can get past the defenses?" Martin pressed.

"You're adventurers. Breaking into old dangerous ruins is one of your past times, isn't it?" Grant cocked an eyebrow.

A moment of silence passed as John, Aysel, Martin, and Silvia looked at each other to respond to the question. John spoke up first, somewhat hesitantly, "Well, this is my first adventure, to be honest, and Martin and Silvia aren't adventurers," he gestured to the others. "Only Aysel has been an adventurer for any actual length of time."

Grant hummed and nodded. "Ah, I'm sorry for assuming. Do you believe your compatriots would be willing to assist?"

"If they believed you, sure," Aysel said. "The issue is that while we," she looked at John, Martin, and Silvia, "somewhat believe you as what you've said has contained details you could not have known unless you knew something, our leader has the final say in what we do."

Grant nodded. "I see how that would be a problem. I don't presume attempting to hire them would work."

"We're still on a mission." Aysel shook her head. "I doubt Zayne would be willing to let us divert to accomplish this task unless you were able to convince him of what you said."

"Well, I guess that means I'll be meeting with them tomorrow," Grant responded.

"You're just going to tell them all this?" gaped Martin.

"Well... yes." Grant shrugged. "While this information is something only to be carefully shared, your group has already encountered the machinations of the Kings. Filling them in on their situation would only be the right thing to do. Could you arrange a meeting with your leader, Zayne, I believe you said, for me?"

They all looked at each other.

"I believe we could do that," Aysel said.

CHAPTER 15

THE FORTRESS OF THE KNIGHTS OF THE DAWN

For adventurers, it is a given that the Party Leader must be obeyed. This is a must. Without the Party Leaders, there is no hope for the adventurers to make any headway. Centralized decision making is essential not just for speed but because there is no room for debate.

That is not to say the Party Leader should unilaterally decide everything. Input from other members of the party provides differing perspectives and increases the party's problem-solving capability. More than that, the party must work as a team. If the Party Leader abuses their authority, they will quickly find they have few friends indeed.

(Excerpt Zayne Dallard's,
Encyclopedia Adventuria Volumes 1–3:
Never Say Die Edition)

As they walked back to the hotel, having left Grant back at his house, John's thoughts buzzed in his head like angry hornets. They now had the full picture of the situation in which they had found themselves. A benefit, at least John hoped so. The fact that their position was so dire carried with it a mind-numbing terror that he still had yet to figure out how to deal with.

Things had been wrong.

Things had been terrible.

The City of Lights was invaded; the Mountain Hold was under control by a hostile force. With the full picture of everything, John couldn't help but wonder if the situation was hopeless.

The Six Kings—at first, John had been inclined to disbelieve Grant. The very idea sounded preposterous. A chapter of history wiped from the record out of fear? Beings so powerful they could rule entire Realms by themselves. The Realms were incredibly vast spaces only separated by the Blue Expanse that surrounded all of them. Transportation between them was difficult and had to be guarded from all sorts of attack. If not from the creatures that inhabited the deep waters than the pirates who maneuvered freely about the expanse.

On the other hand, Grant's explanation was the only one John could fit in with what he had seen; with Treemor's strange words about the giant construction that had been taking place in the Mountain Hold. If what Grant said was right, the danger they were all in was nothing compared to what they thought the threat had been before.

So, John followed Martin's lead through the streets as they walked back to the hotel. Lights from the inky blue darkness above shown down without care upon the world below and the two pale glowing orbs that were the moons.

It worried him that they would now be dependent on the rest of the adventurers in their party believing them. The mission they had gone to accomplish had strayed and taken them so far that he worried that adventurers' contract or not, this would be the point where they quit. Or worse, they wouldn't be believed. John was still having trouble believing, and a part of him somewhat feverishly hoped that they were being lied to; that the situation was not as bad as it seemed.

They arrived outside the hotel and walked in, passing the desk operated by a bored-looking clerk who was leaning on their palm as they stared out blankly over their desk. The lobby's lights were dimmed due to the time at night, and as the group arrived in the hallway outside their doors, they paused, looking at each other.

"Well, I guess we'll deal with this tomorrow," Aysel said softly. "Night."

Murmured assents were given, and John followed Martin into their room. They took turns taking showers, but as John laid in bed, he found that sleep was the furthest thing from his mind. The new worries from the night paraded about in his head. It was only as the light of the sunrise began to peek through the window that he fell into a restless sleep.

John woke in the morning feeling like he had gotten no sleep at all, and he dragged through his morning routine. Martin also seemed to be doing the same, and as John sat on his bed waiting for Martin to finish, he tried to reframe the events from yesterday the way Bernard would have thought of them.

If Captain Grant was to be believed, the real threat was the portal being constructed. If completed, there would be an open passageway between the barrier that currently separated the seven "Free Realms" and the six ruled by the Kings.

On the other hand, that just made him even more worried. Martin exited the bathroom dressed, and together they walked outside their hotel room.

They looked at each other.

"Think we should wait for Aysel and Silvia before we try to talk to the rest?" Martin asked.

John hesitated before he nodded. "Yeah, I guess."

Marcila poked her head out of her doorway, "Oh, there you all are. Come in. We're being brought breakfast given the current situation with the food."

Oh yeah. John had nearly forgotten *that* piece of the issue.

They entered, sitting around in the various chairs that had been arrayed about the room. Most looked to have been pulled from the other rooms. There was already a discussion going on, so they waited for it to finish by unspoken collective agreement.

"We can't just stay locked up in here," Lon was saying. "Both the cities are depending on us."

"And what would you have us do, Lon?" Trajan asked. "The Seventh Federation will move at its own pace regardless of anything we could attempt to move it forward."

"Are there any alternatives, Marcila?" Zayne asked heavily.

Wasn't this the perfect moment to speak? John was about to interject when Aysel began to say, "Actually," she began and the rest of the group turned to her. "We were contacted by a man yesterday who called himself Grant and claimed to be a Captain of the Knights of the Dawn."

John noticed she left out how and where they were when they were contacted.

"He said that if we met with him, he could help us find and procure an item called an 'Index,' that would, in turn, allow us to find two other Captains and with them summon a force that could help us retake the City of Lights and the Mountain Hold."

"A Knight of the Dawn?" Zayne stroked his chin thoughtfully. "I haven't heard of one of those in years. I've never met one, as far as I know. They were long before my time. You say that he wants to help us with this 'Index'?"

Aysel nodded. "He does, and he seemed genuine."

Zayne looked about the group. "Well, what do the rest of you think. Should we see if this Grant can help us?"

"Given our current situation, it's a reasonable alternative," Marcila said.

"It seems suspicious to me," Lon said. "But on the other hand, it's not like we're exactly flush with options."

Karat said, "Any option that would allow us to save the City of Lights and the Mountain hold deserves to be explored regardless of how wary we still should be.

A consensus formed; the rest of the group agreed.

"So how would we meet with him?" Zayne asked.

"At his home," Aysel responded. "I think any time would work with him."

"No sense delaying then," Lon said. "Let's go talk to him."

Marcila nodded, and the group stood up, exiting out the room's door down the hallway and then out the door of the hotel. They walked through streets that should have contained far more people in the early morning but perhaps due to yesterday's circumstances, were only occupied by them.

Aysel led them back to the Captain's house, which was far more visible in the daylight, looking quite homey set behind its copse of trees. Aysel knocked on the door, and they waited a bit before the sound of footsteps became apparent, and the door opened to reveal Grant.

"I'm glad to see all of you here," he said. "Please come in, and I will tell you what I know about the Index and its location."

They followed him inside his house, and since there were not enough seats around his table, most of them stood while Zayne, Marcila, Karat, and Trajan sat.

"I presume you are here, of course, to learn about the Index?" Grant said.

Zayne nodded, "Yes, if it can provide us the ability to assemble a force that could deal with the occupiers of the City of Light and the Mountain Hold. It can do so, correct?"

Grant smiled a grim smile. "The Index can do many things. Among them is raising an army of Knights."

"Where exactly can we find this Index," Marcila asked.

"The Index is the culmination of all the collected knowledge of the Knights of the Dawn. It is contained within a large diamond that sits at the library's center of the abandoned fortress. It is easily removable from its plinth, but the challenge will be in the fortress. It's guarded by golems and interwoven spells that will not easily let a trespasser go," Grant said with the air of one reciting knowledge that they had long ago committed to memory.

"So what do you recommend we do?" asked Zayne.

"You will need to infiltrate the fortress, something I can assist in."

"Why do we need to infiltrate it? Shouldn't you as a Knight of the Dawn still have access to the fortress?" asked Marcila.

"That would normally be the case except that in the centuries the fortress has lain vacant, the data has been internally corrupted. I entered the fortress myself some years ago only to find that the defenses were very much active and perfectly willing to attack me."

"So how would you recommend that we get past these defenses?" Marcila questioned.

"You will have to be as quiet as possible; active as the defenses are, they are not all-seeing, and there will be at least some degradation after so long," Grant said.

"Why should we trust that you're telling the truth?" Karat asked. "We know that we already have enemies in the city."

"You can't trust me, at least completely," Grant replied. "For all you know, I could be one of your enemies. The fact remains, though, that you have few other options. The

Seventh Federation's government is slow to act during the best of times, and you have given them a reason to drag their heels. They will not rush to fight the Barons if they can help it, so you need help from another source. The Knights of the Dawn are your best hope."

Silence fell over the room for a moment as it seemed that Zayne, Marcila, and Karat tried to gauge the man in front of them. After another moment, Zayne nodded. "All right, we'll do this. In exchange, you must promise us that you will call the Knights to help us."

Grant gave a half-smile. "The Knights must deal with such dangers. They will answer the call."

He said no more on the matter, and the discussion turned instead to how they would transport themselves to the fortress. It was determined that they would need to get access to two cars, which they would then use to travel out to the fortress' location. To do so, Grant offered his resources to rent the transport for the day to drive out to the fortress. Once they got there, though, they would have to deal with actually infiltrating it.

For quite some time, the discussion continued, and John found himself slightly tuned out as they discussed the possible entrances and automated sentinels that still roamed the halls. Instead, his attention shifted to another thought: his worries about his home, specifically the man they had left behind. Bernard was more capable of a fighter than he had ever met, which, even including his limited experience, still meant he judged Zayne to be somewhat below Bernard's skill level. From an individual perspective, he knew this made sense, and Bernard had been around for a long time, living longer than most people with magic did. With this age came experience and ability that was still far more than John had seen in someone else, even if it had dulled over time.

Yet Bernard had not done anything when the City of Lights had been invaded. He had not fought the Baron's soldiers whatsoever. In the end, he was only one man, so the Baron's forces could have eventually worn him down, but not before massive losses. It was disconcerting, he realized, to think of Bernard surrendering to anything, even unwinnable odds. In a way, he was thankful. He knew that Bernard had always seemed like he could die just like any other living being despite his invincible force.

Shaking his mind from the dark path it had trailed down, John refocused on the conversation.

The discussion had shifted to the minutiae of procuring a transport, something that Grant claimed would be no trouble for him, leaving the question of when.

"I can procure the car whenever you feel your group is ready," Grant said.

Zayne looked at the rest of the group. "I feel that it would be best to leave as soon as possible, given that no one can think of any preparations we should make beforehand."

The group looked among itself for a moment, trying to determine if anyone had any thoughts.

"I agree," Marcila said.

Karat nodded. "The sooner, the better."

Murmured agreements came from the rest of the group.

Grant stood up. "Then let's go." He walked out towards his door and the adventurers stood from their chairs to follow. They exited the house and walked further towards the outskirts of the city. Sometime later, they arrived at a large building that Grant led them into where they found several cars, not unlike those they had abducted sitting in the bay.

Grant spoke to the clerk behind the round counter by the entryway, and after a quick exchange which included the passing of coin, Grant came back.

"You have the cars at the far corner," he said, pointing to tan two tan cars that were sleeker looking than the cars that they had commandeered.

Zayne nodded. "Thank you."

"No," Grant replied. "Thank you. I am glad to see that even without the Knights of the Dawn, there still are those willing to do what is necessary."

The exchange was over, and they parted from Grant and walked to the car.

Zayne turned to them. "All right, I'll take the lead in the first car. Karat will pilot the second one. Each car seats six, so divide yourselves as you wish between the cars."

He stepped into the first one, and Karat walked into the second. The adventurers split from each other, and John followed Karat into the second ship along with Aysel, Martin, and Silvia. They seated themselves, and John was struck by déjà vu as their seating arrangements mirrored their last journey in the car they had taken from the City of Lights.

The car hummed to life with Karat's coaxing, and they followed Zayne's car out, crossing onto the plains that surrounded the city. The gently rolling fields passed by as they moved towards a tall rock-like formation in the distance.

As time passed, the formation became clearer and morphed into the shape of a massive fortress. The walls were a slate grey, and the structure looked like a castle John had once seen in a book.

As they drew nearer, John got a new sense of how truly massive the fortress was, perched on the mesa that towered over the surrounding area while the fortress looked just as tall as the mesa.

Sometime later, the mesa encompassed their entire view, and a road carved in the side of the rock became visible that Zayne's car took and started to climb upward into the sky. Karat followed him, and they swept up the side of the mesa, switching back every so often as they climbed higher and higher.

As they breached the top, John saw it was a fair distance to the closed gate that stood in front of the fortress. Grant said the gate could be opened by accessing one of the gate towers that stood on either side.

Zayne's car stopped a short distance from the gate, and Karat positioned herself next to the other car. They exited, observing the dusty piece of rock they stood on. Zayne was gazing at the two watchtowers and finally turned to Marcila.

"Think we should just scale the wall?" he asked.

Marcila didn't respond for a moment before she turned back to Zayne. "Yes, I think that would be for the best. No need to open the gate to bring in the car. She strode over to the wall and flicked her hands, purple magic flaring out into spiked projections. She slammed her hand into the wall finding purchase and drawing herself upward and driving her other spike into the wall.

Quickly she ascended the wall. Zayne looked over at the younger members and asked, "Comfortable making solid projections?"

Silvia, Martin, and Aysel nodded, as did John, not at all comfortable with the process but not willing to single himself out before he at least tried. He walked up to the wall and focused on the vertical surface made of smooth grey stone.

He looked down at his hands and focused on channeling his magic to them, forcing the energy to elongate into sharp claws that stretched out of his fingertips. He double-checked out of the corner of his eye and saw Aysel having done the same, sinking her claws onto the wall and beginning to pull herself upward.

He looked at the wall section in front of him, cautiously put his hand forward, and felt the energy sink cleanly through the stone. He put his other hand further upward and sunk his claws into the rock. Then he withdrew and pulled his bodyweight upward, magic fueling his strength, allowing him to complete the move with ease as he moved up the wall.

His feet left the ground, and he began to slowly but surely pull himself up the wall. Up, up, he climbed, stretching his arms slowly, fearing that if he rushed he wouldn't find accurate purchase and fall.

John glanced up, finding himself halfway. To his side, Aysel had already mostly completed her climb, and he saw that Martin, while not as far as Aysel, was still above him. Silvia was about even with him, which gave him a little bit of comfort as perhaps he wasn't the only one who had never done such a task before.

He refocused, pulling his body upward arm after arm.

Finally, he caught the edge and pulled his body entirely up and over the wall, joining the rest of the adventurers. Peering around, he was stunned for a moment at how high up they were from the ground. The courtyard below was overgrown with plants having stretched from their former basins and now cracking through the pathway's stone.

The doors to the castle were locked behind a dull steel gate that rust had seemingly crept through.

Marcila stepped close to the gate and waved her hand, causing purple light to shimmer outward, passing over the gate. She turned back to the group. "No enchantments on this piece. They must have faded."

Zayne nodded in acknowledgment. "Seven, Lon, try and lift the gate."

Seven and Lon stepped forward and gripped the metal. They lifted their arms, shimmering with green and yellow magic, respectively. With a long groaning creak, the gate shifted upward, rising as high as they could lift it. Zayne stepped forward under the portico and pushed against one of the double doors.

It didn't budge.

Orange magic shimmered around Zayne's arm, and he grunted, pushing harder.

Crack!

Something gave way, and the door swung in. Suddenly Zayne was almost unbalanced but caught himself. He stepped in through the gap and disappeared for a moment. He stepped back out. "Clear inside; let's go."

The rest of the group followed him, stepping under the gate that Seven and Lon let down behind them. They walked past the door and were greeted by a massive hallway lit by the orange light Zayne was holding.

Unlit bulbs lined the ceiling above, and as they walked through the hallways, no sign of any life appeared. No insects or rodents skittered, contributing to a silence only broken by their footsteps. They passed hallways that stretched out around them, some transforming into stairs leading up; some converted into stairs that led down. John felt like he was in the middle of a maze, and that if he were one step away from the main hallway they were traveling down, he would be lost forever.

They passed by doors embedded into the walls and would check each one, finding multiple dining areas, a kitchen, and presumed storage rooms filled with empty, dusty crates. As they checked another room only to find racks that presumably had been used to store equipment open, Martin commented, "Did the Knights take everything with them when they left?"

John shrugged, looking about the room lit by the multicolored magic lights they held, given that the interior otherwise was pitch black. John examined the wooden racks, noting the elegant craftsmanship that had been used even for something so simple.

The group moved back out into the corridor, where Zayne stopped moving, looking at the group. "If we keep moving like this, it's going to take the rest of the day to find what we're looking for. We need to split up. I'll take one group, Marcila will take the second, and Karat will take the third."

They split up, and John found himself walking behind Marcila with Aysel. Karat was leading Martin and Silvia, and Zayne leading the remaining, Seven, Lon, and Trajan. Marcila led them up a stairway and onto another floor filled with hallways similar to the one below. They moved down the corridor, opening doors to find empty and mostly empty rooms.

The floors clicked with the passage of their feet as they trudged through the dusty halls. The double doors up ahead caught John's attention for no reason other than every door they had passed until then had been a single door. These were made of similar wood, and after checking the last room before them, Marcila attempted to open the room.

"Locked," she murmured. Marcila drew out the long, elegant blade at her side, which glowed purple before she slashed it across the center of the doors, creating a gash from top to bottom. She pushed, the doors came apart, and she stepped into the room.

John and Aysel followed her. John was immediately struck by the massive number of shelves that lined the space. The second thing that struck him was that every bookshelf was filled to the brim with actual books. Every other area they had passed through was emptied of its contents.

The library was also extensive to the point where looking down the aisles of bookshelves just seemed to lead to more aisles of bookshelves. The room was only lit by the lights they held, and they passed through the aisles, illuminating books as they passed. John took the time to glance at some of the covers: *Monsters and Mayhem*, *Caves of the Deep*, *Wildlife in the Eighth Realm.*

The last title caught his attention.

John paused and glanced back to see that Aysel and Marcila had spread out into the shelves out of sight. He turned around and grabbed the book from the shelf, taking it down to look at the cover. In gold embossed letters, it read simply, *Wildlife in the Eighth Realm* by Dan Remberant.

He opened to about the middle of the book and was struck by a page containing a sizeable quadrupedal creature covered in dark grey fur with four tusks. "Tundra Mammoth, an animal native to the Eighth Realms it—" John refocused his attention on the creature which he was sure he had never seen the like of in any of the books he had read much less seen. He flipped through the pages, witnessing all manner of creatures with wings, flippers. Some were coated in a shell of crystal, others small and fuzzy.

Some he recognized but others he had never heard of, and after a couple of minutes, he closed the book and placed it back on the shelf. He scanned the rest of the shelf, trying to locate others that might have something to do with the Eighth Realm. Nothing immediately popped out, and he continued down the row observing the books closely. Further and further he went into the library, turning corners at random, caught between two objectives. He searched for more books on the Eighth Realm and the Index that they had come there for.

Shelf after shelf passed by, the books covered with dust as he walked through the library. It was quickly becoming apparent that this library stored more information than John had seen in one place ever before. Not even the City of Lights City System likely contained the sheer wealth of knowledge found in this Library.

John found himself in a section where the shelves opened up, and a large rectangular space was set with a pedestal in the center. A huge, pale green diamond-shaped crystal sat on it. John was caught off guard for a moment. Was this what they were searching for?

He turned back, looking to see if he could spot Aysel or Marcila. They weren't in sight. John made to call out, but stopped himself. Hadn't Grant said that there would be protections? Given that they hadn't encountered any so far, John was almost willing to think that maybe there weren't any or at least that they had worn out over time.

He hesitated for a couple of seconds before he softly called out, "Aysel; Marcila."

There wasn't an audible response. John had to shake himself physically. Of course there wasn't. This library was extensive, and he had called out in a voice barely above-normal volume.

He called out again. "Aysel! Marcila!"

His voice echoed through the library.

He waited. Then waited some more. He looked through the bookshelves around him for anything interesting to pass the time. Nothing. Boredom set in quickly, and John found a chair to sit on, and a book, which he propped open on his lap.

Metallurgy of the Twin Kingdoms proved to be a dull read. The author had focused on the different forging techniques used for weapons, armor, and sundry items; as he was reading a paragraph on the makeup of ancient candlesticks, he heard a thud.

John looked up, searching for the source of the noise. Nothing came into view, causing him to stand up to look around. There wasn't anything nearby that he could see, or so he thought, till he spotted another book that had fallen from its shelf. He walked over to it and picked it up. The title read *The Legendary Swords of the Thirteen Realms.*

John opened it up and was greeted by a picture of a curved sword labeled "The Cursed Sword of the Giant." He flipped through the pages, finding similar blades: long, short, curved, straight. He continued flipping through the pages until he stopped dead as he spotted a blade that looked familiar.

Quickly he looked down at his sword, drawing the blade in one hand and examining his book in the other. They looked identical down to a pale blue steel diamond of metal in the center of the hilt. He read the entry underneath the sword:

"The Blade of Knights: Forged by Lano Grand Mage of the Eighth Realm with Bernard the Blade Master's assistance. This sword was created for the Slayer."

The Slayer? What was the Slayer? John flipped to the next page, which continued about a trident. He flipped another page: an axe. Each had far longer entries than the previous one.

John closed the book, wanting to curse in frustration. He looked at his sword. Maybe it wasn't the blade in the book? But it looked so much like it. John sighed, realizing that there was no real way to confirm the name, but regardless he kept a hold of the book. He turned back to the rest of the library, and he sighed again, seeing no sign of Aysel and Marcila.

INTERLUDE 5
MATTERS OF DESTINY

Aysel walked alongside Marcila in silence as they observed the library around them. It was unnerving to be inside a Stronghold that had once housed so much life; it now laid empty and abandoned. It was as if with every step, she half expected for some sound of life to pierce the air to signify the place was not entirely as abandoned as it seemed.

"I worry that we are getting too distracted from our mission," Marcila suddenly said, catching Aysel off guard.

"Doesn't this have everything to do with our mission?" Aysel asked, already not liking where this line of questioning was going.

Marcila looked at Aysel, a frown stealing across her face. "I mean our real mission."

The real mission. Aysel didn't like where this was going.

"We didn't sign the Adventures Contract for a reason," Marcila continued. "Zayne has enough adventurers to deal with whatever the occurrence is beneath the Cold Mountains. With the assistance of the Knights of the Dawn, of course."

"We can't just leave them!" Aysel protested loudly, her voice echoing slightly.

"We can." Marcila's face had hardened into stone. "Your destiny is our priority."

"Then why did we even accept this mission?" Aysel questioned, trying her best to keep her frustration from her tone.

"We needed the money. This was supposed to be much shorter than this has turned out to be, as you well know." Marcila was examining her with a piercing gaze. "Why do you protest? You know what we must do better than anyone?"

"What about Silvia and Martin's home?" Aysel fired back. "What about John's home?"

"They will gain it back, or they won't," Marcila replied. "You must think about your duty."

"And what about the Kings?" Aysel furiously questioned. She had told Marcila in private of the full details that Grant had told them, unsure as the rest of them had been at voicing the whole story to the rest of the group, fearing disbelief.

"I do not believe the Kings can break through the barrier, even with the construction that we saw. That barrier was created by the greatest mage that ever lived, and you are of his blood. You would know if the barrier was in real danger. I am sure of it," Marcila dismissed seemingly offhandedly, and Aysel couldn't help but gape.

"Even after all we've seen?" Aysel asked softly, then in a stronger voice, she continued, "We're not leaving them. What does my 'destiny' matter if the Kings free themselves?"

Marcila looked ready to protest, but Aysel had already drawn herself up to her full height. "We're staying."

Marcila deflated. "If that is what you decide. I will follow your lead."

Aysel winced but nodded all the same. They continued down the bookshelves in silence for a while longer.

Aysel realized that they hadn't seen John since they had entered the library. John, who had already almost died once before, a fact that bothered her in a way that she couldn't honestly describe and didn't want to think about.

She turned her thoughts purposely away and examined the aisle around her. These books looked to be in rather good condition despite how old they were supposed to be. What kind of magic could keep the books so pristine?

What magic was set in the Fortress around them waiting to deal with intruders?

CHAPTER 16

ROCKING THE HOUSE

Maybe he should just try and take what was probably the Index from the pedestal. John moved towards the pedestal with slow, cautious steps. He reached out for the pale green crystal, slowly expecting something to happen at any moment. His hand clasped the cool crystal, and he pulled it loose from the pedestal quickly. He hesitated, holding the crystal and looking about. No suddenly appearing spikes. No instant magical blast. Was it that easy?

The pedestal clicked, and a grinding sound emerged as the pedestal slid down into the floor. The floor began to shake, and John backpedaled.

The stone broke free from the floor, and a massive stone golem rose, oddly comparable to Treemor. This golem shared none of Treemor's affability as inset ruby eyes glittered down at John. Raising a stone fist, the golem slashed down with a speed that John was barely able to stumble back from. The floor where John had been standing erupted in a plume of dust. The stone cracked and crumbled under the force of the strike.

John sprinted away from the golem, which began to chase him,its first ponderous step forward, followed by another quicker step as it gained speed, charging directly at him. John swung himself around a bookshelf as the golem barreled right past him, obliterating a wall turning it into rubble. The golem paused and slowly turned itself around, centering its eyes on him.

John turned, the rumble of footsteps behind him, giving him ample motivation to pick up his speed dodging through the shelves the sound of crashing chasing him. Even out of sight, the golem continued to move towards him, the deep pounding of its footstep reverberating through John's ears.

This wasn't good.

John spun around another corner, hearing the crash of the golem obliterating a bookshelf behind him. The pounding footsteps started up again, and John heard the crashing and breaking of the bookshelves behind him. John forced magic into his legs, increasing his speed even more as he barreled through the shelves looking for the exit desperately. The crashing grew louder again, and John threw himself to the side as he exited the aisle, watching the massive golem barrel past him, obliterating another bookshelf. It was like the golem wasn't even trying to catch him; instead, it was focused on smushing him underneath its feet.

Not wanting to be smushed, John turned, continuing his sprint away. He cursed himself for not paying more attention when he came in as he ran through the shelves. Every way he turned, it seemed, all he saw were more bookshelves.

When he had walked through, the library seemed like a maze. Now, the maze felt turned against him and the way out. As he passed through the bookshelves, John found himself less appreciative of the knowledge contained within. Each aisle looked the same, with hundreds of texts lined up on each side.

John split into another offshoot of the bookshelves and felt the rustle of the air as the golem ran past him, steps already coming to a ponderous halt.

He needed a new plan because this one was going to end up with him smushed sooner rather than later. Running down the aisle of books, he burst out only to face a rather shocked looking Aysel and Marcila. They stared at him, and he stared back. John was about to speak before the pounding of footsteps revised what he would say. "RUN!"

He sprinted away as he heard the pounding of large footsteps begin their path toward him again. He knew the golem must not be following him with vision, not that he could do anything with that information. He turned another corner, almost running headlong into Aysel, who had diverged from Marcila. She turned, spotting both him and his pursuer, and she also turned on her heel, joining him in his headlong flight.

"What did you do?!" Aysel shouted as they made a series of turns among the bookshelves.

Despite himself, John couldn't help grinning sheepishly. "I picked up the glowing crystal."

He raised his hand carrying the probable Index.

They made a sharp turn around the corner of a bookshelf, letting the golem barrel on past them.

Aysel spared him a blank glance. "You didn't."

Under her gaze, John winced. "It seemed like a good idea at the time."

"Every time I lose track of you, you get yourself into more trouble," Aysel said.

John wanted to protest but decided to remain silent as he couldn't contest the point. The golem was gaining on them again; its far larger strides were giving it a significant advantage, at least when it didn't have to turn. They spun around another corner, but this time the golem managed to slow its speed enough to turn to crash into the bookshelf on the left side of the aisle as it did so.

Aysel and John ran as fast they could to the end of the aisle, turning instantly into another. Across them, John spotted the entrance they had come in and immediately changed his direction. He and Aysel sprinted out of the doorway and down the hallway before the horrible crash and breaking of stone came from behind them. John spared a glance and gaped as he saw the golem, too big for the doorway, rip its path through the top of it.

It stood in the hallway and howled a stone shaking roar. The walls seemed to shift and grind away, revealing alcoves of smaller stone figures as tall as an average human stepping out as one of the statues turned and began to run towards them.

Needing no further encouragement, Aysel and John continuing their flight down the hallway, dipping under the reaching arms of the statues that came from ahead of them, reaching out to grasp them. John ducked under one pair of arms and, tucking the Index under his left arm, drew his sword, channeling his magic through the blade and slashing at another statue obliterating the stone under the force.

He didn't stop his headlong run, slashing at any statue that drew close mirrored by Aysel as she slashed her blade through the oncoming stone taking out two with a single strike. Out of the library doorway, Marcila emerged behind the golem who was now charging at them. She flew forward, dodging around the golem, and managed to overtake them despite their pace. They raced down the corridor and took the stairs at a run.

The other Adventurers were already grouped up and fighting the statues and were slashing away at the statues as the statues attempted to surround the adventurers. Upon spotting Marcila, Aysel, and John. Zayne shouted out, "What's going on?"

"They came from the walls!"

John waved the crystal, and Zayne looked taken aback. "You found it?"

He ducked around the swing of a statue, driving his foot into the ground to send the stone floor flying up to obliterate it. "I guess that explains it," he said almost to himself.

"Let's go!" he shouted. The adventurers broke off from their engagements and raced to the gate, followed closely by Marcila, Aysel, and John. Seven and Lon gripped the bottom of the gate and lifted allowing for the rest of the adventures to duck underneath before Seven and Lon followed behind.

They ran to the walls, which they began to scale with far more haste than they had done when entering.

The distant pounding of stone footsteps from inside the castle motivated John even further, and he ran to the wall. Hesitating a moment, he tossed the Index over, hoping that it was at least some level of durable before slamming magic spikes from his hands into the wall. He began to climb up to the top of the wall.

He risked a glance backward to see that the golem had smashed through the gate and the statues were beginning to spill out of the entrance, but they seemed somewhat unsure how to handle the new challenge that the wall presented in getting to their quarry.

He pulled himself over the top of the wall and dropped to the ground, cushioning the impact by forcing magic through his legs.

They piled against the gate as the group continued their flight to the car, filing inside. Karat took the controls, and the car roared to life, behind Zayne's, which had begun the traversal down the ramps. As they drew distance from the fortress, John calmed down, as did the rest of the people in the vehicle with him. Aysel, Marcila, and Trajan were silent.

John glanced down at the crystal in his hands, unsure of what to do with it besides hold it.

The journey back took a while and was made mostly in silence. As they came upon the city, they diverted to the garage they had come from. They drove through the entryway, parking in the garage, and were met at the exit ramp by a worker that checked in the cars for them.

They exited the garage, walking through the city which was now lit by artificial light as it was now late into the evening. They walked through the streets, making their way back to Grant's home. Zayne went to the door and knocked. A couple of moments passed before John heard footsteps, and then the door swung open, revealing Grant, who looked at them for a moment before his eyes fell upon the crystal that John had tucked away under his arm.

"I haven't laid eyes upon that crystal in well over a century," Grant said. He gestured for them to come in, and they followed him inside back to his now somewhat familiar kitchen.

They sat around the table before Zayne said somewhat unnecessarily, "We got the Index." He gestured to John, who placed the Index on the table.

Grant reached across and grabbed the Index. The moment he touched the pale green crystal, it began to glow, and Grant's eyes turned blank and lit up, matching the crystal's shade.

A minute passed. Grant stayed in the same position, hand outstretched, touching the crystal.

Then the glow faded from his eyes, and he withdrew his hand.

"The Knights have been summoned," Grant intoned. "They will begin arriving in the coming days. Come here again three days from now, and you will have your army."

There was little more that needed to be said. They went back to the hotel, ate, and went to bed. John found himself lying awake that night, thinking over the events of the day.

The fear he had felt while in mortal danger this time had been dulled somewhat and John wondered if perhaps he was getting used to the threat he kept finding himself in. What had indeed struck him as strange in retrospect was they had all made it through unscathed, which had happened through every situation that they had been through so far.

Maybe in the case of their most recent adventure, that had made sense as while the statues had been dangerous, they hadn't been intelligent. On the other hand, in their escape from the City of Lights and the Mountain Hold, they had been against intelligent guards, whom he had cut down.

John tried to divert his mind, but now he could not push the thoughts out. It was something that he hadn't thought about when he had dreamed about being an adventurer while he worked and trained at the Western workshop.

He had thought about the places he would see, the people he met, and the quests he would participate in, but he had utterly sidestepped what it would mean when he raised his sword and used magic in something besides his training. Martin's breathing was still light and shallow. John glanced over and saw in the dim light coming in through the window that Martin's eyes were still open.

"Martin?" he said hesitantly, softly, not sure if he was awake.

A couple of moments passed. "Yeah?" Martin said in a low voice.

"Sorry, I didn't want to wake you," John said, already feeling bad for possibly having woken him up.

"You didn't," Martin replied. "You all right?"

"I..." John hesitated, unsure of how to voice his thoughts, "I'm not sure. I was thinking, about well, everything."

"I know what you mean," Martin said. "This isn't close to anything I ever expected to see. In the Mountain Hold, I worked every day thinking about what I wouldn't give to be somewhere else. Now all I can think is how I wish things would return to normal and I could go home."

"Yeah," John replied. "I know what you mean."

"Do you think that we'll be able to take back our homes?" Martin asked.

"I hope so," John said. "With the Barons and soldiers inside the Mountain Hold, though, I don't know how we're going to be able to match them even with the Knights."

"The Knights have an army, though, right? They'll be able to help," Martin said with feeling.

"Will they?" John questioned, and he heard Martin shift in his bed.

"What do you mean?" Martin asked.

John replied, choosing his words carefully. "Well, I mean Grant said they would help us. I wonder if they'll be able to. How many will come to answer his call?"

Martin shifted in his bed, rustling the sheets. "I don't know. How many Knights do you even think there still are?"

John sighed. "Probably some but that could easily be far less than the size of the army we need."

They fell into a grim silence before Martin broke it, asking, "So that Bernard guy back in the City of Lights, he raised you right?"

"Yeah," John responded, somewhat caught off guard by the change in topic. "Since I was young. He took me in after I was found in the wreckage of a caravan attack."

"I guess that makes you an orphan like me," Martin said, a strange note in his voice.

"You're an orphan?" John asked.

"Yeah, my parents got caught up in a hunt with a couple of wyrms when I was younger. They were Hunters who dealt with the various creatures that attacked towns and cities, and they were contracted to deal with wyrms who had been attacking towns. They went out fought wyrms managed to take them down but died from their poison after," Martin said.

"I'm sorry," John said.

"It happened a long time ago," Martin responded. "I don't think about it much, especially because I was young when it happened. I mean, I wish it hadn't happened. Obviously, it's just life goes on, you know?"

John nodded even though he knew Martin couldn't see him. "Yeah, I know. So then you became a scout in the mines?"

"Yeah," Martin said. "I did it as preparation to become a Hunter but now…"

Martin trailed off.

"Now?" John urged.

"I think I want to be an adventurer," Martin said softly.

"Oh?" John looked at Martin's indistinct face in the opposite bed. "I thought given everything that's happened, you wouldn't mind settling back down after this?"

"You'd think that wouldn't you," Martin chuckled. "It would make sense, but with everything I've experienced now, I couldn't imagine spending the rest of my life in the Mountain Hold. Would you want to go back to the Western Workshop after this?"

From that perspective, it made sense, John realized. Even after everything that had occurred, the danger, the stress, he still wanted to see more. "I guess I know what you mean. Even though this isn't what I expected as an adventurer, I wouldn't want to stop now. There's still so much I want to see."

They talked until the weak early morning light began to filter through the window. They broke off to fall asleep, John's heart feeling lighter than it had in a while.

They woke late the next day, and John experienced a moment of confusion when he realized that neither Zayne or Lon had awakened them. As Martin was still asleep, John showered first, rinsing himself with the hot steaming water, which helped wake him up. He dressed and woke Martin before walking to the door that separated them and Zayne and Lon.

He knocked on it a couple of times and waited.

"Come in," he heard Zayne call out, and John opened the door to see Zayne and Lon sitting around a table, broken from a discussion.

"Morning, John," Lon said.

"Good Morning," John replied. "What's our task for today?" he asked.

Zayne shrugged. "We're waiting, so it's up to you what you'll do with your time. I'll remind you to be careful as we still don't know the circumstances behind the attacks near us."

John nodded in acknowledgment. He turned, heading back to the room he shared with Martin. He sat in a chair and waited until Martin was finished with his morning rituals.

After explaining that they had no objective set today, they headed to the dining area. Picking food up from the buffet-style breakfast, John assembled a meal with hot bread, eggs, brown beans, and a drink of red-colored juice. Martin assembled his breakfast, and they ate in companionable silence.

It was nice, John reflected. He had been unable to share something with anyone besides Bernard at the workshop, and this was with a genuine … friend. As they continued to eat, John saw Aysel and Silvia walk into the room, fetching their breakfast before looking around for a seat.

Silvia spotted them and the pair walked over to the table.

"We're on our own for today," Silvia said.

John nodded. "Yeah, Zayne told us."

"Do we want to do anything?" Silvia asked the group, and John shrugged at her and looked at Aysel and Martin. "I don't know; what about you guys?"

"We could try eating out again?" Martin half-joked half-questioned. Silvia gave him a quelling glare.

"Or we could not," Martin retracted his statement.

Aysel looked contemplative. "What about we walk around the city and see what there is to see?

"I wouldn't be opposed," Martin said.

"Neither would I," John said. "It would at least help us decompress."

Silvia nodded decisively, "So it's settled then. We'll go for a walk after we finish breakfast."

After dropping off their dishes, they finished up and left the hotel, choosing a random direction to walk down the street. As it was the late morning, hundreds of people were walking all around them, heading to their jobs or other orders of business. Street vendors were selling food and various items showcasing their wares, the smell of spices filling the air.

They continued through the streets, passing buildings advertising various wares and services. They continued walking through the streets, staying in the commercial area but were somewhat wary about entering any buildings.

A part of John wondered if this was maybe not the best idea given they still had no idea what the cause or the aim of the attacks had been, but on the other hand, the poisoning at the hotel had proven that they weren't necessarily safer at their lodgings either. Who could be behind the attacks, though, John wondered? Could it be the Barons? It wasn't like the Seventh Federation seemed particularly willing to help them in the first place.

They had left and come back to the city without any trouble from possible attacks, which made John wonder if they had even been the targets in the first place. On the other hand, if they weren't the targets, who were?

As they continued their way through the street, the people became sparser until they arrived at a park area. As they entered, John spotted a sign that said, "Welcome to Green Park." The park was filled with large trees whose circumferences were bigger than John could wrap his arms around. They walked down a path under trees and arrived at a pond area where they settled down, sitting on the grass a small distance away from the edge of the placid water.

As they sat on the edge of the lake, they conversed quietly with no particular topic. John stared at the water smooth as glass without a ripple to budge its surface. He could almost feel his thoughts slipping beneath the surface of the lake, a feeling of calm passing over him as he looked outwards over the water.

John was so caught up in his thoughts he almost didn't hear the footsteps coming up behind them, tramping through the grass. He turned to see five figures dressed in black cloaks that went down to their knees. Their faces were shadowed from their hoods, and what little was visible was covered by black cloth masks.

John stood up, stepping in front of the other group members, a tension starting to sing in his gut. They stopped a short distance from their group. The one in the middle spoke, "If you surrender now, we'll only imprison the lot of you. Resist and meet your end."

Aysel, Silvia, and Martin stood up behind him.

"Why?" Martin questioned. "What have we done?"

"Surrender," repeated the middle figure, and his hand grasped the sword hilt at his waist.

The air was thick with tension as the groups faced off. The tension snapped.

The middle person in the group of black cloaks lunged forward with his sword streaking towards John.

Instinctively, John drew his blade from his side, blocking the malicious attack and sending his opponent's blade skittering to the side.

John spun his blade into the attacker to strike back, but the attacker leaped about smoothly, dodging John's strike. Attempting to take advantage of John's attack, both people at his side jumped forward, launching their swords at him, giving him a split second to leap back from the one on his left and to parry the one coming from his right.

John danced backward, parrying their attacks as they pressed him before Aysel leaped forward, bringing her sword to bear on the cloaked person attacking John on his left. The other attackers drew their swords to engage, and Silvia drew her two long daggers while Martin drew a sword, leaving his bow strapped behind his back.

An opposing group of two black cloaks pushed back against Silvia and Martin's charge into the fight and brought their steel to bear. Blades flashed back and forth before Martin drew his back, the air flashing red around him before he got his sword down, unleashing red magic against his attacker.

The air ripped, and Martin's magic lanced outward, lashing his opponent backward, tossing him some meters away. In response, the black-cloaked figure next to him lashed his fist forward, causing red fire to spill outwards in a scorching wave that Martin was unable to shield himself from, causing him to shout in pain as the fire drained his personal magic shield.

Silvia ran forward, slamming a kick into Martin's attacker, launching him backward while she attacked with her daggers to keep the other attackers back.

Aysel retreated under a dual attack by two of them, causing John to slam his sword blade into his opponent, driving him back and his green magic shield to crack. John didn't have the time to take advantage, though, and joined Aysel, protecting her from a slash to the side while she drove her opponent back with a series of blows that glanced off their shield.

Rallying together, they continued to drive their opponents back as their magic shields splintered before John's former opponent joined in, attempting a sneak attack on John which he barely dodged. He could not dodge the second slice, which ripped across his torso, causing a heavy drain on his reserves.

John and Aysel squared off against three of their opponents fighting back and forth, gaining and losing ground alternatively as each did their best to drain the others shields. Their opponents were good, much better than the Hemlock Guards they had fought within the Mountain Hold.

John pushed the attack on two of them, putting every ounce of what Bernard had taught him to the test, slashing with sweeping strikes enhancing his muscles to the max with his magic. One of his opponents wasn't able to properly deflect the force of his blow, sending his sword flying and allowing John to direct a hard slice, which broke through his opponent's hastily reinforced shield and cutting him down.

The other person he was fighting roared in anger and attacked furiously, driving John back a couple of steps and causing him to take a substantial blow to the stomach, which drained his magic reserves to around half of what they had been.

John rallied, deflecting his opponent's sword to the side and driving his free hand forward, sending a blast of magic outward, catapulting his enemy skyward in a plume of blue magic.

His other opponent attempted to take advantage of John's focus and sliced his blade towards John's stomach. John, out of position from his attack, was unable to block. He braced himself only for Aysel's edge to intercept, blocking the attack. She raised her hand, ripping it sharply upward, creating a silver river of magic that ran streamed from her fingertips and swept up the water in the lake behind them, bringing it down in a raging current that slammed into their two other attackers.

Their attackers were sent flying in the current of water, into two trees before Aysel gestured sharply down, and the water froze solid, imprisoning them in solid ice. John and Aysel turned towards the other attackers to see that Martin and Silvia stood over them, their weapons at the ready.

Their eyes met, and slowly they relaxed a little bit, the threat for now dealt with.

"What was that about?" Martin said, eyeing the bodies scattered about the clearing.

"I don't know," Silvia said. "They didn't hesitate at all."

Aysel's face was twisted in a deep frown. "It must be related to the previous attacks."

Martin looked about at the fallen figures. "We should find some guards."

"I don't think we should stick around for that," Aysel said. "Who knows when they'll wake up, and there could be far more of them around."

There was a long moment of silence.

"What about the others?" Silvia said slowly, and they all turned to look at each other before they immediately turned and started running.

They ran through the streets, passing around groups of people who would turn their heads to follow them along with curses if they got too close. They arrived at the hotel and slowed their run to a fast walk, passing through the lobby.

They came into their rooms and opened the first door to see their group sitting down conversing. They turned to look at them, and John breathed a sigh of relief that got caught in his throat as he realized something.

Lon, Seven, and Trajan weren't there.

CHAPTER 17

LOST FRIENDS

They quickly explained what happened on their walk. Zayne acted quickly and directed them to split up to search, dividing into two groups, with Zayne leading the first and Marcila the second. Karat was with Zayne along with Martin and Silvia. Marcila led Aysel and John. They divided from the hotel, and John followed Marcila as she led them through the slowly darkening streets.

They only had the vaguest directions on where to search as Lon, Seven, and Trajan had said they were going to look for a workshop for weapon upkeep along with getting a tool that Seven needed for maintenance. They moved down the streets, looking around for any possible workshops.

It was some distance down the street before the group found a workshop. They stepped inside, and the bell chimed as they walked through the door. An older man stood by the counter. The man had silvery grey hair and brown eyes; he was fiddling with an orb and a screwdriver. He looked up from his work, and seeing them, he set it down. "Ah, what can I do to help you?"

Marcila replied, "We're looking for colleagues of ours, an older dwarf with greying hair, an adult dwarf, and a clockwork with green eyes. Their names would have been Trajan, Lon, and Seven."

The man nodded, crossing his arms and stroking his chin. "Yes, I do believe I saw some people matching your description. They came in not too long ago and bought some items from me, then they left."

"Thank you," Marcila said, and they turned around and walked back out of the store. She turned, looking back and forth down the street before seemingly choosing and continuing down the road.

The streets were still somewhat crowded even in the evening, people trailing in and out of stores and restaurants. Chatter, laughter, and life, but John saw no sign of their companions. They continued walking down the streets, dodging the errant passerby.

John tried not to think about the worry settling in his gut as they went further down the street, sometimes looking through the windows of stores to see if perhaps they might catch a glimpse of their errant companions. An hour after sunset, they stopped, having double backed through the main streets.

"They're not anywhere near here," Marcila sighed. "We should head back and see if anyone else has had luck."

They began to walk back to their lodgings, a pit of worry settling into John's gut as he continued looking about, hoping to spot some sign of them. If only they had phones connected to the local network, he cursed inwardly, but that wasn't realistic. They had only been in the city for a short time, and regardless John had barely used his phone back when he had one in the City of Lights. Those were the consequences of having approximately zero friends.

They arrived at their lodgings, sitting in one of their rooms as they waited for the rest of their group to return. Some minutes later, Zayne walked in but still no Lon, Seven, and Trajan.

"No luck?" Zayne questioned Marcila. She shook her head. "Nothing. We found a shop where they might have been, but they were long gone from that area."

Zayne sighed, nodding grimly. "We had even less luck; no mention or sight of them where we went."

A grim silence settled over them.

Zayne spoke again, "I guess we'll have to wait and see if they return. If they don't come back by tomorrow, we'll try and contact the local authorities to see if they can help."

There were murmurings of assent, and they broke off to eat dinner together with an air of tension. As John went to sleep that night, he kept his sheathed sword by his side in the bed, unable to sleep without the blade within arm's reach. By the way Martin shifted, John could tell he was also having trouble sleeping. It was only as the sky outside the shaded window began to lighten that John found himself tired enough to fall asleep.

John woke to a morning that saw no return of Lon, Seven, or Trajan. Zayne contacted their liaison in the Seventh Federation, who promised to alert the local authorities of their disappearance. Still, John couldn't help but think that the likelihood of their friends being located without an extensive search was minimal at best. Given the extent the Seventh Federation had moved so far, that wasn't a great sign. They had breakfast together quietly.

The party, aside from Marcila, was ordered to stay together within the hotel premises, where there was still a minimal presence of guards. Waiting was painful, John soon came to realize; having spent so long in the midst of the action, having nothing to do except wait edged at his mind.

Aysel and Silvia had joined John and Martin in their room, where they sat around on the beds and the scattered chairs with only a few words exchanged between them.

The tension between them was almost tangible.

"Do you guys think they got attacked and captured by the same organization that tried to do the same to us?" Martin asked.

"I mean, it must have been, right?" Silvia's face was set in a deep frown as she drew and sheathed her dagger over and over again.

Aysel's looked similar. "I'm not sure if we can know that for certain."

The attention of the room centered on her, and she elaborated, "I mean, what about Zayne, Marcila, or Karat? Why wasn't any attempt made on them?"

"Because they're probably the strongest," John said almost without thought. The room's attention was centered on him and he felt obliged to explain his thought process. "I mean they are. I've seen them fight and even fought Zayne myself. They're so much stronger it's barely even a contest."

Martin nodded. "That makes sense, but it also still leaves the question of why exactly? We've done plenty of stuff to kick the hornet's nest, but we don't know what specifically their motive is."

"I mean, wouldn't the biggest thing be that we're rom the City of Lights and the Mountain Hold?" Silvia said. "That would mean they might be trying to prevent us from succeeding in retrieving help."

"The Seventh Federation isn't even close to helping us, though." Aysel shook her head. "The only person who is doing something to help us is…", she trailed off an expression of dawning comprehension taking over her face.

"What about Grant?" Aysel asked.

"You don't think he would have betrayed us, do you?" Silvia's expression darkened.

Aysel shrugged. "How much do we know about him? He knew just as much as the Seventh Federation's Council. What if his intentions weren't to help?"

Martin looked conflicted, intermeshing his hands. "I'm not saying that I don't think it's possible, but how could we turn this from speculation to actual knowledge? Wouldn't we have to get him to admit to something? I don't think it would be that easy?"

"We could at least ask for his help locating the others," Silvia replied. "That itself wouldn't look suspicious, that is, if he is working against us."

"I guess that could work." Martin nodded.

Aysel looked conflicted before she sighed, nodding. "It's at least not a bad place to start, but we'll have to be careful, and we should tell Zayne and Marcila before we leave."

John nodded, not sure of the course of action but needing to do something instead of wait.

Getting permission from Zayne and Marcila wasn't as difficult as John expected. They had no more than said that they wanted to see Grant to request his help than both had both agreed. They now found themselves walking down the streets in the late afternoon, heading to Grant's home. John felt incredibly twitchy, almost jumping at shadows and by unexpected appearances of people who seemed just to be going about their daily business in reality.

They arrived on Grant's doorstep, and Aysel knocked on the door. They waited, and a minute later, they heard footsteps behind the door before it swung open to reveal Grant. He looked strangely tired, almost drooping with fatigue.

"Ah, you're back. How can I help you? I've been continuing to contact the Knights through the Index, and hopefully, in the coming days, they should begin to come and assemble in the city," Grant said.

Aysel nodded in acknowledgment. "Actually, we came to ask about something else. Some of our companions disappeared yesterday evening and haven't come back. We were also attacked by a group of people who attacked us after we refused to surrender to them. We think the two are connected and are wondering if we could ask for your help?"

Grant blinked tiredly, slowly processing their words. "That's not good." He murmured and then turned, gesturing for them to follow him into his home. He led them back to the kitchen area, where, set on the table was the Index and other open books, a pen laying askew to the side.

He sat down and gestured for them to do the same. They did so, and Grant began to speak, "I can only think of one group that would act like this. In truth, I had thought they disappeared and died out a long time ago. Unfortunately, they seem to have survived these centuries."

"Who are they?" Martin asked.

"They are the Knights of the Dusk," Grant said. "They exist in opposition to the Knights of the Dawn as they believe the Kings are a force that can be bargained and reasoned with in exchange for powers."

"How many of them are there?" Silvia looked horrified at the thought.

"I doubt anyone, but their leader knows." Grant sighed heavily, looking old in a way that reminded John of Bernard. "I will do what I can to help. Finding them will not be easy, I fear."

"But you do know a way, right?" Martin pressed a determined expression on his face. "We can't just leave them."

Grant furrowed his brow in thought and tapped his fingers on the table rhythmically. After a long moment, he spoke, "I suppose the best way, or at least the best way I can think of, would be to contact one of the Knights who has already shown up. I know her from way back, and she was the best tracker that I've ever met."

"When could we meet her?" Aysel questioned.

"Now," a feminine voice from behind them caused John to spin around along with the rest of them. A woman stood at the base of the stairs in the corner of the house. She was dressed in dark clothing and had black hair and black eyes; her skin was a shade of almond, and a long sword hung at her side.

She approached and took an empty seat at the table. "Sorry for interrupting. My name is Sela, and I'm a Knight, same as Grant here. Now, where was the last time that you saw these adventurers?"

Aysel was the first to recover from the interruption and replied, "They had went out yesterday by themselves. The last time any of us saw them was at our hotel. Then we tracked them to a local workshop where they had been seen but that was as far as we could track them."

"That's not much to go on." Sela frowned. "The Seventh Federation's capital is a big place, and there's plenty of places to get lost in. Narrowing the search field is going to be necessary if we're going to find them. Where did you guys get attacked?"

Aysel replied, "Green Park. It's some distance from here."

"Ah." Grant nodded. "I've been there. It's in the downtown district of the City," he said to Sela.

"Well, that's a location," Sela said. "Anything you could describe about the appearances of those who attacked you?"

"They wore cloaks," Martin said, brow furrowed. "There wasn't much else we could see besides the weapons they carried."

"Did you report the attack to anyone and ensure they were arrested?" Sela further questioned.

Aysel shook her head. "We got out of the area. We didn't know if there were more of them around and didn't want to take the chance that the next group would be more than we could handle. Plus, given what we're here for, I'm not sure extra attention on us would be a wise idea."

Grant frowned. "I understand, and you're likely righter than you know. Whoever this group is, if they're attacking you in broad daylight, they likely have people in the force that would deal with you if you reported it to the local authorities."

Sela shrugged. "You know the Federation better than I do. I'll trust your judgment," she said to Grant before turning back to Aysel. "If we can't rely on any of the city officials to help, we'll need to figure out a different way to track down your missing party members. Are any of you experienced with scrying?"

John looked at Aysel, Martin, and Silvia, who blankly looked back at him. Silvia turned around to Sela. "No, I don't think any of us are."

"It's a ritual which allows objects and people to be located. Grant, could you get us some chalk?" Grant nodded, stood up from the table, and walked out of the room. Sela assembled them in a circle on the floor, positioning them carefully at certain spots till they formed a diamond-like shape.

Grant walked back in and handed a chalk piece to Sela, who began to draw lines between them, joining them in the center of the circle. She drew four lines to the center where she sat and placed one of her hands on the lines while in the other, she held a metal ball she had pulled out from a pouch on her belt.

"I'm going to need all of you to concentrate on all three of your missing companions and channel a small amount of magic through your bodies."

John focused inward, drawing his magic to the surface, and saw a blue glow that began to permeate his body. Aysel began to glow silver, Martin began to glow red, and Silvia began to glow green. The energy ran along the lines of chalk, lighting up the center with multicolored light.

The air began to hum with the sound of magic that John was familiar with from the workshop. Sela's eyes were closed, and her palms were up projecting the multicolored charm around her with an added, swirling yellow.

Minutes passed as they remained like this, Sela not moving an inch or saying a word, focused on something that they could not see. The drain suddenly increased on John's magic, and he gritted his teeth before it suddenly stopped, and Sela opened her eyes. She opened her palm and held up the metal ball in her hand. It was pulsing slightly with a yellow light before it dimmed.

"If you carry this ball, it will pull in the direction that your companions are when you push magic into it," Sela said.

Aysel reached out, taking the ball from Sela's hand, and after glancing around at the rest of them, looked at the ball, which began to glow silver and shifted, rolling slightly in her hand backward before she grasped it firmly.

"Thank you," she said to Sela, who nodded and said, "You're welcome. Good luck."

They said their goodbyes to Grant and Sela and walked outside, where Aysel took the lead, holding the ball in her hand; she began to walk down the street before turning right at the next corner. John, Martin, and Silvia quickly followed her as she began to make her way through the streets.

The sun continued to dip in the sky as they walked through the streets at a fair pace. Aysel led the way, holding her hand out slightly in front of her and choosing each road with careful deliberation.

Further and further they walked, twisting out of the residential streets and into a district filled with large warehouse-like buildings. Aysel kept leading the way with her hand outstretched. She continued to walk forward past the lights that lit the streets into the near darkness surrounding the warehouses. Martin raised his hand slightly, and red light sprung to light their surroundings, making the buildings near them distinct forms that revealed little else. The light itself made John nervous, worry running through the back of his head of the target they were making themselves by holding the light.

Their steps made soft, scratching thuds on the ground as they moved down the row of warehouses. The buildings were large and box-shaped, and as they passed by the large doors that led into them, John found himself wondering what could be contained within. It wasn't what they were there for, though, and John made sure to stay with the group as they moved deeper into the warehouse district.

They passed a building where Aysel then turned right, walking in between the aisles now. Then they twisted around another building, walking past it, then twisting around another warehouse, which she walked past and then stopped turning back to it. They circled the building before Aysel nodded and turned to the rest of them. She whispered in a soft voice, "This is it. Has to be."

Martin responded, "So what do we do now? Do we just break-in?"

They all looked at each other, unsure of how to proceed. It wasn't like any of them had done this before.

Silvia spoke up, "I suppose so?" She said in a questioning manner.

John looked at the building. "So how do we enter? Not through the main door, right?"

Aysel hummed, looking over the building with a critical eye. She eventually pointed at a window a distance above them. "Let's go through there."

Aysel took the lead using the magic technique from the fortress, again sinking her magic through the wall as she climbed, followed closely by Silvia, Martin, and John. John reached the window and found that Aysel had popped the lock with magic manipulation from the outside, allowing the window to swing in.

John entered through the gap and slid his feet as silently as possible onto the floor below. He looked around only to see empty hallways illuminated by the green light Silvia held. Aysel held the metal ball in front of her, and as it glowed with silver light, it directed them forward down the hallway.

They walked down the hall, doing their best to pass quietly by door after door on each side until they reached the end of the hall. The group stood in front of a door that the ball indicated to go through.

They looked at each other, and from a silent, collective agreement, Aysel reached for the door handle and turned it with a small click. She opened the door to reveal…an empty room without a trace of any item or person. Aysel walked to the center and looked around before channeling magic through the ball that gave a small hop out of her palm. She blinked then looked upward. She motioned them back out of the room, and they began looking for a stairway around the floor, finally locating one at the end of the hallway. They cautiously walked up the stairwell and opened the door softly. Silvia peeked out to get their bearings before she motioned them forward.

The next floor was much like the floor below, even in a similar design layout. They walked down the hallway following Aysel's lead before they approached the mirror of the door below. Aysel reached out then hesitated before grabbing the doorknob.

She looked back at them and shook her head silently before holding out her palm where a silver mist emerged, floating forward and then, just when it was about to reach the door, a mist of shining purple magic appeared.

Aysel looked back at them. In a voice barely above a whisper, she said, "There's a current running through this door. I think it's a trap."

John hesitated, feeling entirely out of his depth. "What do we do?"

Aysel shook her head. "I don't know. I haven't learned much about traps or how to deal with them. I can just identify them."

"Isn't it just like a magic that continuously runs at a low level?" Silvia said, "Let me try. I've worked with magic like that before." Aysel stepped back, and Silvia stepped forward, cautiously putting out her hand and closing her eyes. Green sparks began to emit from her fingers, traveling over the door but not quite touching it. Minutes passed before a green crack emerged over the door, spreading into a spiderweb before dissipating into sparks. Silvia reached forward and turned the door handle, opening it up to reveal three figures, two laying on the floor unbound and unmoving, and the third leaned up against the wall just as still.

They were too late. The adventurers were dead.

John unwilling walked forward to get a closer look. He saw Seven's body in the far corner; his eyes were no longer glowing, slumped over in on himself. Lon and Trajan lay side-by-side without any weapons and were all too pale under Silvia's green light.

Seeing Lon as he was now turned something inside John to ice. To think that the dwarf that had comforted him on the night before they had set off to the Mountain Hold was gone was … incomprehensible.

John moved back to the doorway, averting his eyes from the crumpled forms of his companions. He felt lightheaded, unable to concentrate on anything. Silvia, Martin, and Aysel remained in the room, looking about and checking over their companions.

"Who could have done this?" Martin choked out.

"I…," Aysel seemed lost for words.

Something was building up inside John's gut, something that pierced through the pit and began to burn. John gritted his teeth. Through the blood pulsing in his head, he heard something faint … footsteps, he realized. He looked outside the door and saw a figure armored from head to toe, hand clasped on the sword at his side.

Not a thought passed through John's head as he launched himself forward, drawing and slashing his blade, aiming for the armored man's guts. His sword slammed into the metal, ripping through it before colliding with a flash of orange light against the man's shields.

The man fell backward, rolling to his feet and drawing his blade from his side and launching forward at John in a blistering flurry of blows.

John deflected each strike in the hail before spinning a kick, flaring with his blue magic, which collided against the man's armor, denting the metal and sending the man flying backward into a wall, colliding with a resounding crunch against the stone.

Aysel, Martin, and Silvia rushed out from the door behind him and halted, staring down at John's opponent.

"He was just outside," John said through teeth that were still clenching.

"So this is one of the people who—" Martin was about to storm forward before Silvia placed her hand on his shoulder.

"Wait, Martin; we need to find out why," Silvia said urgently.

Martin paused and looked torn between taking his sword and running the man through or listening to Silvia. Better sense won out, and he took his hand off his blade but still unshouldered his bow and prepared an arrow.

They surrounded the downed man, and John walked forward, wrenching the helmet off the man with an application of magic and arm strength. The man was an elf who had been knocked unconscious from his magic zeroing out.

"We should tie him down and see what we can get out of him," Aysel said and took one of the elf's arms. Martin stepped forward, taking the other arm, and they dragged him down the corridor. Martin exited out the window, first dropping down to the ground below, catching the man as Aysel tossed him through the window after him.

The rest of them climbed out the window and made it to the ground below. They moved further into the buildings, dragging their captive with them until they had made some distance between them and the warehouse. They placed him against a wall and stood back with weapons drawn, waiting for the man's magic to recover enough for him to wake.

Long minutes passed by as John found himself having to cap the seething fire burning in his gut. They had left their companions' bodies in the building, something that made him more than uncomfortable, but there was nothing more they could do for them.

The man awoke, startling at the sight of them and reaching for the weapon they had already relieved him of.

"Don't move," Martin snarled.

The man stopped searching for his weapon and looked between them. "It's you, the adventurers they warned us about. What do you want with me?"

"Why'd you kill our friends?" Silvia said in a voice that could have been mistaken for gentle if the iron edge wasn't clear in her tone.

The man hesitated, looking between them. "They were supposed to be bargaining chips, but they resisted too much," he said.

"Bargaining chips? For what?" Martin snarled, an arrow resting loosely on his bow, ready to be drawn back at a moment's notice.

"To stop your group from continuing to testify before the Seventh Federation's Council."

John's anger bubbled even higher, "On whose orders?"

The man shook his head. "I won't tell you. Nothing you do will make me."

They all looked at each other. Martin's hand was edging toward his quiver. Silvia's face had hardened as her hands rested on her daggers. Aysel looked conflicted, eyes flicking back and forth between the man and the rest of them.

John's head was filling with heat, and he rested his hand on his sword hilt. Like a bucket of ice water, the anger was swept away, and he was left with a feeling of emptiness.

"Not this way," he said, and the rest of the group's eyes turned towards him.

"What do you mean not this way," Martin hissed. "They killed them! He deserves it."

John flinched at the anger, but something in him refused to bend. "It's not the right way. I can't let us fall to that level."

Their eyes focused on him, and he could feel the air filled with tension. A long moment passed. The tension drained away, and Martin, Silvia, and Aysel's postures relaxed.

"You're right," Aysel said in a soft voice. "We'll turn him in to the authorities."

Martin's face, formerly in a rictus of anger, had relaxed if only slightly, and his hand was no longer straying towards an arrow. Silvia was frowning, though it didn't look directed at them; she was looking down at her hand that clenched her dagger.

John looked down at the man in front of them. "Come on. We're turning you in."

INTERLUDE 4
WHERE ANGER LEADS

Passing the man they had captured off to the police was liberating in a way that Aysel couldn't describe. They had been interviewed for hours, and when they had been released, Zayne, Marcila, and Karat had been there waiting. Aysel had been ready for Marcila's reprimanding but not for the gentle hug she had been pulled into.

Zayne had given them a pained half-smile and thanked them for finding the others. He seemed lost in thought as they sat around in John and Martins room at the hotel.

Few words were said. The twisting fire in her gut had vanished to be replaced with a hole.

They were all clutching mugs of warm liquid that Aysel had yet to taste. The silence seemed to be pressing down on her ears. John was sitting next to her, and she saw he was focused on his hands, twisting them slightly as he gazed down at them. Aysel found herself intensely grateful to him. She had been ready to kill the man, or at least she wasn't going to stop it, but now she felt revolted at the thought.

She had killed before, not often, but sometimes amid a fight. This wouldn't have been a battle, though. The man had been beaten, and she had been willing to strike him down where he was.

That wasn't how she should act. They were supposed to be rational, thoughtful, and compassionate. She had felt none of those traits at that moment, just cold, burning anger. She shook her thoughts free from her head and refocused on the present, taking a sip from her mug, which she discovered to be tea.

"I think it would be best for you all to head to bed," Zayne said softly.

There was a murmuring of assents as they split off and walked back to their rooms. Aysel walked with Silvia into her room, and they individually got ready for bed before turning off the lights and allowing the darkness from outside to sweep in.

Minutes passed, but Aysel felt no closer to sleep than she had when she had laid down. Whenever she closed her eyes, she was back in that moment, ready to strike the man down, or she in that horrible room with the remains of their—

"Aysel? You still awake?" Silvia's voice broke her from her thoughts, and Aysel turned in her bed to look at her even though she couldn't see much of anything in the darkness.

"Yeah," Aysel said, hesitating a moment before asking in return, "You can't sleep either?"

"I can't keep my mind quiet," Silvia responded softly. "It's … horrible."

"It is," Aysel whispered back.

The silence spread between them for a while as they laid in their beds, staring into the darkness. It was somewhat comforting, though, to know that she wasn't the only one unable to sleep.

"I've never been so angry," Aysel finally said into the darkness.

"Me neither," Silvia replied. "I mean, they just … killed them. Like it was nothing."

"There's still more of them," Aysel whispered. "Just waiting to attack, waiting for us to split apart and take advantage."

"We'll need to talk to Grant tomorrow," Silvia said. "We should tell him what happened so he at least can be on his guard."

"Yeah," Aysel replied.

The silence grew again at the end of their words, and Aysel realized she desperately didn't want it to return and be left to her thoughts.

"So you lived in the Mountain Hold doing work on the City System, right?" Aysel found a topic to inquire on.

"Yeah, it was nice. I generally just worked to help people find books, movies, or any data they had trouble finding,"

Silvia responded. "I didn't want to do that kind of stuff forever, though. That's why I started learning how to use my daggers. I thought in a few years, I would apply to one of the Guilds and become a full-fledged adventurer. I guess things went a little differently than how I planned."

Aysel shifted slightly, looking at the space that she knew Silvia occupied. "Do you still plan on becoming an adventurer?"

It wasn't like becoming an adventurer had been much of a choice for Aysel. It had been the best way to stay on the move and still make money. As someone in exile, there wasn't a normal job she could do while still working towards freeing her people one day.

Silvia paused for a while before she responded, "I think so. It's been so dangerous, and so many awful things have occurred, but I still can't help thinking it's better than spending the remainder of my days upkeeping the City System. This has been the farthest I've ever been from my home, and it's so amazing seeing everything here."

Aysel smiled at Silvia's answer even though she knew Silvia couldn't see it. She admired Silvia's conviction, wishing she had some of that.

"For what it's worth, Silvia, I think you would make an excellent adventurer."

Even though she couldn't see Silvia's face, Aysel had the feeling that Silvia was smiling too. "Thanks. Maybe we could go on another adventure together after all this?"

"I would like that," Aysel said.

CHAPTER 18

THE TRIALS AND TRIBULATIONS OF BATTLE

The loss of party members is a sadly not an uncommon occurrence in the course of an Adventure. Magic provides a shield of protection, but even the strongest protections can be pierced. Even if the party members are not close, the burden can weigh heavily on the hearts of even the most experienced adventurers.

Even with all my years of experience, the only advice I can provide in such circumstances is thus: You must Carry On.

Else the weight will crush you.

(Excerpt from Zayne Dallard's
Encyclopedia Adventuria
Volumes 1–3: Never Say Die Edition)

A month had passed since their encounter with Knights of the Dusk. They had checked in with the Council twice since then with no sign of any movement to help the City of Lights and the Mountain Hold. They had stayed together, rarely leaving their lodgings.

They had been together almost always; something that had worn on all of them, but the knowledge of what would happen should they be isolated and attacked had maintained their discipline. During the time, John had spent most of his time with Aysel, Martin, and Silvia, making the days bearable. They had played card games. They had talked. Sometimes they had just spent the time browsing on a terminal hooked into the City System, reading and watching whatever they came across.

It remained still in the back of John's mind: the knowledge of his home's capture and what might be happening there now, but he tried not to dwell on it. Zayne had located a sparring area not far from the hotel and would take them all out a couple of times a week to spar and prevent their skills rusting.

Zayne had even personally worked with John to show him how to use his magic for general manipulation of his surroundings, such as the stone chunk Zayne had pulled up during their spar that felt already so long ago.

John was glad to keep his mind busy as it prevented him from overthinking about their … former companions. He couldn't quantify his emotions as that felt like a disservice to their memory to pretend he had known them in any personal way. Yet, at the same time, he couldn't help but keenly notice their loss and the gap it had left in their group.

He chose not to share these thoughts with the others as he had no way to explain himself in words. It seemed Martin shared this, and it was in their spars that John took some solace as when he fought blade to blade with Martin, he could forget the complexities that had entered his life.

He had also sparred with Aysel and Silvia, whom he couldn't help but notice seemed closer than they had been before though that could have also been because of his inability to read people.

Aysel had been another topic that he found coming to his mind far more often, and he had found himself wanting to spend time with her and avoid her at the same time. The more he got to know her, the more he got anxious in her presence. He had pushed it to the side for the most part and tried to act as naturally as possible. Still, there were times when he noticed that she didn't seem quite there, as if she was thinking about something far away.

As the morning light began to peek through the curtains, a knock came at Martin and John's door.

"We're meeting with Grant! Get ready," came Marcila's voice.

Martin and John stirred from their beds groggily, alternating turns in the shower before they got dressed and went outside. Zayne, Marcila, and Karat were standing there and greeted them with low hellos. Minutes later, Aysel and Silvia exited their room and joined them.

Zayne looked about them for a moment. "This is it. We're going to be heading back to the City of Lights, and chances are it's going to be rough. This mission has extended far beyond the original scope assigned to it, and I'm glad that all of you have stayed with us. This isn't about the mission anymore. It's about the freedom of two cities which most of us called home. This is the last chance to back out. You can take a transport away from Seventh Federation and be on your way with no hard feelings."

Zayne paused, looking around the group. John didn't flinch under his gaze. His home was at stake. He realized that he couldn't leave Aysel, Silvia, and Martin to face this alone.

No one said anything, and Zayne nodded after a long silence. "All right, let's move out."

They followed Zayne from the hotel, carrying everything they had taken in, not that they had brought much to begin with. They exited the hotel and started walking down the street, passing building after building that were just now being touched with the early morning sun.

They traveled until they reached the city's outskirts, where they had first entered, stopping at a large squat rectangular building whose doors were rolled up, allowing them to see the sight of cars arranged in neat rows inside. People moved about, clad in glinting steel armor that, as they drew closer, John realized carried a shoulder design of a pale sun rising above ocean waves.

They moved about with rigid efficiency, loading containers into the cars or caught in low conversations with each other. Looking across the area floor, John spotted Grant, who was clad in armor similar to the rest of the people. He was currently in the middle of a discussion with two other people. The first was a human woman whose face was slightly wrinkled with age and had hard brown eyes and dark red hair. The other was an elven woman who had short purple hair cut around her ears and pale grey eyes.

Grant greeted them, "I'm glad to see that you're here. We'll be joined by the other segments of our forces further out as they've set up camp a distance from the City. If you'll all load into that transport," he pointed at a car some meters away from him, "we'll be heading off shortly."

Zayne nodded. "Alright."

He turned, and they followed him to the car, piling in after him and settling themselves down in the seats after Zayne took the controls. It was reminiscent of their flight from the City of Lights. John realized only that they now lacked three of their number and could fit into one car, albeit slightly larger than the ones they had previously confiscated.

Forcefully, John steered his mind away from those thoughts and focused on the front viewport as the car hummed to life under Zayne's coaxing. They rolled out of the hangar, and John saw out of the side viewports that other cars were coming to life too and following their lead.

Other squat buildings to the side of theirs opened their doors, disgorging their contents till what must have been at least fifty cars rolling outward across the plains. They kept a wide berth from the other few buildings that resided outside of the City, including the tower where they had been stopped.

John wondered how much communication there had been precisely with the Seventh Federation's Council but ended up dismissing the thought as unimportant with no small amount of vindictiveness. Even though they were in a treaty with the City of Lights and the Mountain Hold, they had still not come to uphold them.

They rolled across the smooth plains until they eventually came to the forests, where they dispersed through the trees, going into single file lines along the few roads that stretched through them.

Further and further they traveled and eventually, the hum of the engine and the passing of trees became mere afterthoughts in John's brain as he gazed out the viewport unseeingly. They were headed back at last, and the worries he had kept at bay bubbled underneath the surface of his mind.

Would they be able to free the cities? The forces around them were not close to as large as the forces he had seen about his home. There were supposed to be more but would that even be enough? Worse, he worried for Bernard. He had been trapped in the City of Lights for well over a month now, and John couldn't help but worry about what could have happened to him.

They traveled through the forest for some time as the sun made its path, the sky above them passing midday and starting its descent into evening. Still, the car rolled onward across the road that continued forward through the forest. They were in single file behind another car, so there was little to look at or observe. John found himself wishing he had brought a book, given that there was no terminal, phone, or even the requisite network to browse. John entertained himself by watching the trees pass by the car, amazed at their incredibly broad trunk sizes. The leaves shaded their path high in the sky as they were, but John still saw glimmers of evening light pass through them.

The hum of the car moving beneath them slowly lulled John into a drowsy state as he continued gazing out the window. In this pleasant haze, their journey continued, till eventually, he realized that all light had faded from the sky, and the lights of the car were now the only way to see the path ahead of them.

The car rolled to a halt, startling John into full awareness. Zayne exited the car, followed by the rest of the group. John could see others in the light cast off by the magic around them, moving about in their armor to ready campsites.

John was directed to gather firewood with Martin, so they tramped into the forest, grabbing loose branches from the ground and finding a fallen tree. They split off a couple of great chunks with their swords. Gathering their wood, they walked back toward the main road, passing by other Knights doing the same.

They emerged from the forest and saw that their group was sitting directly by their car, organizing the packaged meals they were to eat. They set their wood down in the relative center, piling their wood together before Martin ignited the wood with a click of his fingers, sending a bright red spark off, catching the wood alight.

They tended to the branches until they had an actual fire going, crackling cheerfully.

John could see other campsites flaring with fire, light scattering off the armor of the Knights that surrounded them.

Zayne distributed the packaged meals, which after heating over the fire, they began to eat. John had to forcibly stop his face from twisting in disgust at the rations he was chewing on. He forced down bite after bite until finally he had completed his meal and was able to toss his packaging into the fire, watching it catch light after a couple of minutes of direct exposure to the flame.

The box burned, dissolving into nothing as he watched, soon joined by the packages the other members of the group had eaten from. It felt strange, he thought, to be sitting in this forest again just as they had done when they had three more of their members. John grimaced, thinking about it and focused his thoughts on relaxing and drifting as he stared into the fire.

Throughout the encampment, he could hear a low murmur as the Knights talked to each other. Sporadically the sound of music would break out from squat rectangular boxes by their campfires. The music would conglomerate into a low undercurrent of noise that scratched at John's ears, but he tried to ignore it.

He noticed that Zayne, who sat across the fire from him, had a grim look on his face as he stared at the fire. He realized with a start that he still knew so little about Zayne along with Marcila and Karat, though he had technically met Karat previously.

They all sat seemingly lost in their thoughts as they looked at the fire, and John wondered if any of them had been in a real battle like the one they were likely about to march into.

"We'll arrive outside of the City of Lights tomorrow," Zayne said, breaking the silence and causing everyone's attention to fall upon him. "When we do, we'll begin splitting into groups to begin preparations for the assault."

He looked around the group, meeting everyone's eyes before focusing on John, Aysel, Martin, and Silvia.

"You four will join Marcila in whatever your group is designated to do. You'll be getting your orders from Grant, so you'll want to find him the moment we halt. In recognition that we may not all meet again, I would like to say it has been my honor and pleasure to serve as your party leader. I hope we may all travel together again someday under better circumstances."

"It's been my pleasure as well, Zayne," Marcila said.

"Thank you for your efforts to free our home." Karat nodded grimly.

"I second that," Martin said softly. Silvia nodded. "Thank you."

Aysel smiled wanly. "It's been an adventure I won't forget as long as I live."

"Thank you," John said. "Even if my first adventure is my last, it was worthwhile." He smiled faintly at Zayne. This was the moment of truth, not at all what he thought his first adventure would be. John glanced at the members of his party, focusing on Aysel, Martin, and Silvia.

These were people he knew that he could call friends. If he died, at least it would have been after he had finally found people he could call as such. The next morning dawned, and John woke to Aysel nudging him awake. They ate and piled into the car; there was a tension in the air that John could feel. As Karat took the controls, the rest of the cabin was quiet; everyone seemed wrapped up in their thoughts.

The cars began to form up and roll out, and Karat joined the procession, easily sliding into a gap. Another car took up space beside them and most of what view they could have seen. They rolled across the ground, the cars quickly traversing over any rocks or holes in the path.

The cars had dull grey metallic hulls that reflected little light and made for a tedious view as they rolled along. John winced, chastising himself for the thought as being bored shouldn't exactly be of utmost priority in his thoughts.

They rolled onward, and the hours slipped past. John found himself blankly staring into space, which as it just so happened, contained Aysel's face. Realizing he had been staring but not wanting Aysel to realize it, he maintained his gaze.

Aysel's face seemed to be carefully neutral, and John could not tell what was going on underneath her pale silver eyes.

The rumbling onward continued for some time. Karat would occasionally speak into the headset she wore, which allowed for communication between the transports.

The forest became sparser, and John looked out the front window to see a familiar mountain and his home glinting in the sunlight. Distant as they were, John could still spot cannons that spouted along the walls sparkling in the sunlight. As they emerged farther onto the field, they crossed into the land where the former encampment housed the Baron's armies. There were still signs of them in the torn and ruffled ground and the pathways worn into the soil.

They did not stop and continued their advancement forward until a loud boom sounded from the wall, and in a flash of green light and a small plume of smoke, something was hurled across the gap, slamming into one of the cars ahead of them and causing a moment of purple glow as the car rocked at the hit.

More cannons erupted, sending their contents into the car, causing plumes of dirt and alternately flashes of multicolored light as they impacted. The loud report of the batteries blasted through John's eardrums, and he flinched as a plume of dirt erupted in front of them, obscuring their view momentarily.

Their car continued to roll forward, dipping as it tracked into the trench dug into the dirt but continuing its path forward. A car directly to their left was not so lucky, taking a direct hit that dented the red shield flaring over it horribly. It slowed to a halt before a green shield sprung over it, and the car roared back to life, continuing its path forward.

They hit the road going up to the city, and traveled upward to the wall, the cannon fire dying down slightly as it focused on the car behind them. Their path continued upward to one of the large gates set about the city, and John saw one of the vehicles that had a sizeable mounted cannon on top take the lead.

The end of the cannon glowed, and then with a roar, opened fire blasting a shot at the gate, which shook at the impact. That was not the end of it, though, as another car that had cannons on top opened fire, blasting into the gate.

The blasts seemed to merge into a multicolored splendor erupting on the gate, which, under the flares of light, John was unable to see the condition of.

The cannons continued to roar as they trekked up further and further on the road.

Another flurry of salvos slammed upon the gate, and with the wrenching of broken steel, it collapsed, revealing the interior of the city where soldiers of the Red Baron were. They surged forward, magic shining brilliantly, sending a wave of earthen chunks ripping forward, upending some of the approaching cars.

Knights poured out from the upended cars and surged forward, launching a hail of arrows over a sizeable multicolored shield. The arrows hailed down, exploding in plumes of stone, scattering the Baron's soldiers, who were then pierced by the hail of arrows.

The Baron's soldiers attempted to rally together. Six of them stood together, raising their hands, ripping a chunk of stone from the ground, which they hurled forward, barreling into a Knight transport in front of them, crunching through its shield and stopping its progress.

"Everybody out!" Zayne roared, taking the lead, opening the door at the back of the transport, and running out, followed by Karat, Marcila, and then the rest of them. John found himself just behind Karat as they charged up what remained of the slope.

The cars were still firing inward, scattering the soldiers that remained, but some had advanced to try and destroy the vehicle up close. Zayne hit them full-on, raising a hand sharply, causing the earth to erupt, and sending the soldiers flying into the air.

They continued running past another car that had been tumbled over onto its side and where Knights were spilling out from. Soldiers were scattering back into the streets, and the car that remained intact began to move through while squads of Knights began to run, scattering throughout the city.

As they passed by the city gates, they found themselves accosted by soldiers running to defend the gap. For a moment, both sides seemed surprised before they launched themselves at each other. John found himself face to face with three soldiers who drew their swords and ran forward, attempting to run him through. For an instant, he froze before his right hand that held his sword seemed to flare with heat, and he instinctively lashed his hand downward, sending a wave of magic forward, ripping into the approaching soldiers, scattering them and sending them flying.

One remained standing from the onslaught, and John met him blade to blade; they danced back and forth. John parried and swiped. He stepped back from the soldier's blast of magic that ripped past him by a hair's breadth.

Taking advantage, he swiped his sword hard into the soldier's gut, ripping clean through his magic barrier, which must have been weakened from his level of magic. John's blade ripped quickly through the metal, felling the man, and John grimaced, stepping over the man and coming face to face with the recently risen soldiers who had sprinted back towards him.

John fell back under the onslaught of blades, weaving the best defense he could against them. Still, he was driven back before one of them swung his hand forward, and red light erupted, sending John's gut-twisting as he was launched into the air.

For a moment, he felt as if he was weightless before he slammed against one of the buildings that stood to the side of the gate. His body dropped to the ground, and John barely had a moment to get his bearings before the second soldier stabbed down, attempting to impale him.

John rolled across the ground before springing to his feet, bringing his blade back up to fend off his opponents, who advanced on him. His opponents worked incredibly well together as they pressed the attack, each one covering any gaps in the other's defense as they took turns attacking, sending flashing steel toward John, which he would barely manage to parry to the side.

A blade slipped past his defense, cutting across his stomach, and John groaned as a chunk of magic slipped from his reserves to absorb the hit. They continued their advance, and worry began to seep into John's thoughts as he backpedaled, desperately defending against the onslaught.

Further and further, he was driven back until another blade came lashing towards his face, and John winced instinctively at a strike he knew he couldn't parry before—

CLANG!

A loud ring of metal sounded directly into John's eardrum as another blade intercepted his attacker's sword. John glanced to the side to see Martin taking up a position, flashing him a wild grin.

Martin moved forward, letting loose a flurry of attacks, raining strike after strike down. The other soldier attempted to take advantage of Martin's single-minded focus, drawing his blade back, but John leaped forward, deflecting the blow to the side and pressing his attack on the man.

Together, John and Martin fought side by side against their opponents, driving them back, landing glancing blows that caused their shields to flicker. John ducked underneath a wild swing and pushed his hand forward, channeling his magic, and sending a blue wave launching outward; his opponent flew to crash against a building, his shield shattering on impact.

John turned to help Martin, but Martin was already driving his sword through his opponent's plate, his shield already drained.

The soldier collapsed, and John and Martin looked at each other for a moment before they turned to survey how the rest of the battle was faring. The Knights were driving the soldiers back, and now most of the square was cleared, the isolated pockets of fighting turning in favor of the Knights as they joined together, striking down the soldiers that remained.

They spotted Zayne, Marcila, and Karat talking with a Knight who had stopped in front of them. John and Martin moved to join them, Aysel and Silvia coming over and reuniting the group temporarily.

"—need some of you deeper in the city. They're blockading themselves in Leonardo's District."

John was surprised for a moment, recalling Gargoyle Tavern, where arguably the start of this current journey had begun.

Zayne nodded and looked at the rest of them. "John, Aysel, Martin, Silvia head to the Gargoyle Tavern we'll push deeper into the City." He began jogging through the streets the rest of the group followed in his wake.

John, Aysel, Martin, and Silvia took another street pushing deeper into the City of Lights. John could see signs of the fighting all around him from the sprawled armored forms. Knights looked to be merely lightly wounded and rested against walls, their magic visibly recovering, sealing their wounds and reinforcing their shields.

Others were gone beyond other help, and John had to turn his head away, forcibly focusing forward on their current mission. They passed by broken buildings, and sometimes they would hear the roar of magic and the clang of weaponry, but their immediate surroundings remained clear of the Red Baron's forces.

They forged further onward, jogging past buildings that John recognized and remembered. One of the building's entire fronts was crumbled inward from what must have been a massive magical blast with some glinting red armor shining out of the rubble. John winced internally. These were people's homes and livelihoods. He hoped that by liberating the city, they were not destroying the lives of the residents.

They turned onto a familiar road, and John saw that multiple Knights of the Dawn were crouched about the street, some behind shimmering magical shields and others only behind stone rubble.

They were faced off against the Gargoyle Tavern's front, whose front door seemed to be sealed tight against intrusion. From the windows, arrows would fire out, occasionally glancing off magical barriers in showers of bright sparks. One of the arrows hit a building and exploded, sending stone to the ground and forcing the Knight underneath to hurry back to avoid being hit by the falling chunks of debris.

John took cover behind a pile of rubble where three Knights had already taken cover. Aysel slid into place next to him while Martin and Silvia joined some other Knights behind a building wall.

John took a peek over the rubble he was crouched behind. He could see archers ducking in and out, launching arrows at the people in the Gargoyle Tavern windows.

A figure stepped into the window to fire another arrow, only for a red-lit arrow to fly in a blur toward them and explode, sending the armored figure reeling back out of sight. John risked a glance behind him to see that Martin was drawing another arrow to his bow.

Martin leaned out again, having to quickly draw back as an arrow flew past him, blasting a chunk of the ground out. John grimaced, looking back.

With how things were going, they weren't going to make any progress, and they couldn't just leave the Baron's soldiers holed up here as they would only attack passing troops and further disrupting their ability to move further into the city.

Strangely, his mind was dragged toward one question that he always seemed to ask himself, "What would Bernard do?"

It was ridiculous, he knew. Bernard was a smith, fighting capability aside, yet the question remained embedded in his mind.

John looked around the street, observing his surroundings, his mind frantically working. His eyes fell on the large pile of rubble directly in front of him. He reached out and, channeling his magic through his arm, lifted a stone from the pile with ease.

He peeked his head out over the rubble once more. Trying to get a fair judgment of the window, he ducked back down, turning over the piece of rubble in his hands. It wasn't a blasting rod and thus wouldn't conduct a substantial quantity of magic.

He might be able to channel some in, though. How did Bernard do it? Recalling his lessons, John dragged his finger roughly over the rock, engraving rough-looking runes on the stone. It took multiple minutes as he tuned out the warfare going on around him, focusing single-mindedly on the task at hand. As he carved the last rune, he looked up from his work. No progress had been made on breaking through.

He mustered his courage and quickly shot his head up to see over the rubble and flushed as much magic as he could into the chunk of stone he held. He knew the runes delaying the ignition wouldn't have long, so he threw them as hard as he could at the window.

The stone streaked through the air, going through the open window. John ducked down again, immediately preparing himself for the explosion.

Any moment now.

Nothing happened. No explosion of sound and light. Nothing. Had he done it wrong? John cursed himself; he must have forgotten something. He felt so stup—

KABOOM!

An explosion of blue light erupted above.

John blinked away the spots in his vision and cautiously peeked back over their cover. The front portion of the building's wall had disappeared, leaving a gaping hole in its place. The explosion seemed mostly contained to the second floor that the Baron's soldiers had been shooting out of.

The street was silent without the fire from the building, and the Knights around John cautiously slipped out of cover to observe the results of John's makeshift blasting rod. Next to him, the Knight, a female human with short cut dark hair and dark skin, flashed him a grim smile. "Nice work, kid. Thought we were going to have to wait for some reinforcements with the heavier ordnance."

She clapped him on the back, standing up, and cautiously made her way forward with the rest of the Knights into the building. Some flashes of light erupted out of the hole, but then John saw some Knights dragging out the armored bodies of the Red Baron's soldiers, some still conscious, hands raised in surrender, others completely limp, drained of magic or worse.

John swallowed the rising bile in his throat, forcing his mind away from what exactly was worse. There would be time enough to think about that when this battle was over. For now, he needed to stay focused on the goal.

Aysel, Silvia, and Martin rejoined him from where they had hidden, looking over the destruction John had just inflicted.

"That was something John," Martin murmured. "Didn't know you knew how to do that?"

John shrugged, forcing a smile that he knew must have looked somewhat pained. "It was mostly guesswork. I've never made a blasting rod without the proper materials before."

Martin nodded. "Well, I'm glad you did."

They waited a moment, watching the Knights capture more of the Red Baron's soldiers.

"We should keep moving," Aysel said.

There was a round of agreements, and Aysel took the lead through the streets. They followed her, jogging through the streets, passing more Knights who were holding groups of the Red Baron's soldiers prisoner.

They continued through the streets. Some buildings to the side were collapsed, and the roads would occasionally have large chunks of stone ripped from them. They ran further, the sound of yells, the clang of metal, and explosions seemingly an ever-present companion.

John was feeling the burn of the constant magic flowing through his system and trickles of sweat trailing down his back. They came into another portion of the street where several Knights had assembled. Sela stood at the head of them, directing them into groups, after which they would start jogging down the road to where they were directed.

Sela turned and caught sight of them, beckoning them over. She finished giving orders to a squad of five Knights who turned and began jogging down another street.

"Glad to see you four are still doing alright," she said. "I need your help provided your magic reserves are still relatively high."

She paused, waiting for them to give a sign to the contrary. Aysel glanced back at all of them before turning around. "I think our reserves are still in the green."

Sela gave a smile that John could tell she didn't feel at all. "Good. There's some trouble going on near the Mountain Tram station. Some of the Baron's forces have holed up there and are taking a shot at anyone who comes near."

"All right, we'll take care of it." Aysel turned back to the rest of them. "John can you lead us? You've probably got a better sense of the city streets than any of us."

John nodded and took a moment to orient himself, looking about the streets, trying to determine which way they should head. He selected the street to their left, which would take them towards the tram station; he beckoned at the rest of them. "Come on."

John took off at a light jog through the streets, passing through what had been fighting zones judging by the destroyed building fronts and armored bodies. He took a left down a side street that exited onto the main road that he was almost positive was closer to their objective. They continued running for some time, the sounds of explosions, cries, and shouts growing fainter as they traveled up the road.

The further they traveled, the more on edge John became, expecting a group of attackers to leap out. They continued their pace until John caught sight of a familiar sign which had remained intact: "A Knight's Rest."

This was likely because the battle had yet to get this deep into the city proper. As they stepped a little further in, John saw a flash of light from on top of the tram station, and an arrow slammed seconds later into his head, sending him stumbling as his magic flared brightly at the damage.

Aysel grabbed his arm and dragged him to cover in an alleyway directly by the street. John saw Martin and Silvia ducking into an alleyway on the opposite side of the road as an arrow flashed past them, missing but only just as it exploded into a ball of crimson light on the wall behind them.

John saw Martin prep an arrow on his bow, lean out, and fire it toward where John could only assume their attackers were located. An explosion ripped through the air, but Martin had to duck as an arrow flashed past him, exploding on the building behind where he had been.

Arrows were exchanged back and forth, and it seemed that despite how many Martin had fired, he still was unable to create an opening for them to get through. John gritted his teeth, feeling completely useless. If he made it out of this, he was going to learn how to shoot arrows.

Still, that didn't solve their problem at the moment. John tried to think of a plan. Creating another makeshift explosive with a rock was possible, but he didn't know how far he needed to throw it. Plus, if he stepped out, he would make a far easier target for the archers.

Still, at least they were behind a building. A building.

John looked up at the stone wall they had hidden behind. What if they scaled it?

"Aysel," he whispered.

Aysel turned from looking at Martin's fight and looked at him. "What?" she whispered back.

"What if we climbed the building?" She stared at him for a moment before she nodded. "All right."

She turned towards the building, and John mirrored her actions, readying his hands and focusing for a moment. He watched as glowing blue claws emerged from his fingertips. He reached up, catching hold of the sheer rock. He dragged a hand upward; then the other. His feet left the ground, and he slowly began climbing up the wall. Hand after hand, Aysel was mirroring his actions at his side.

Together they kept climbing up. They reached the edge of the roof, and John peeked over, trying to catch sight of any of the Baron's soldiers that could spot them.

Red armored figures moved with bows about the top of the tram station, focused on hitting Martin, whose dodges were becoming more and more narrow. No one was looking up to their height.

John pulled himself over, Aysel followed him. They crouched on top of the roof together, looking down on the platform below. John and Aysel weren't too much higher than Baron's soldiers, and John judged that they could probably jump the gap. It wouldn't be that much larger than the one that he had jumped while escaping from the Mountain Hold.

John glanced at Aysel. "Jump on three?" he asked.

Aysel examined the gap for a moment before she slowly nodded. "All right."

They slowly stood up, positioning themselves on the roof a little further from each other.

"One."

John shook his legs loose. He could do this.

"Two."

He could definitely do this.

"Three."

He really hoped that he could do this.

He broke into a sprint with Aysel. They sped towards the far edge of the roof, crossing the top with giant loping steps and coming to the edge startlingly quickly. John leaped, pumping magic through his legs, sending him flying into the air. He soared through the sky, feeling weightless.

The soldiers below looked up, probably seeing the light that they had generated from their leap.

One was faster when drawing an arrow, then the others followed, flicking through the air toward him in a blur. John tried to brace his magic for the blow.

"JOHN!" A harsh, grinding, metallic voice echoed through his head, and suddenly his sword was drawn in his hands, spinning in a slash that cut the arrow from the air.

John landed, rolling across the ground to bleed momentum. He spun, cutting down two of the archers that stood beside him, their shields not going up in time to block the slashes laying them across the ground. The two other archers on the platform's far side raised their bows only for Aysel to cut one of their bows in half while kicking the other person over the edge. She pointed her sword at the remaining soldier's throat, who, after a moment of hesitation, raised his hands. "I surrender."

CHAPTER 19

TO SAVE A HOME

They handed off their prisoners to the first detachment of Knights that made their way to them. The Baron's soldiers had been led back by five Knights who looked ready to spring at the first wrong move.

They had waited on top of the tram platform for their reserves to recharge slowly. In the meantime, they made somewhat stilted conversation as they sat leaned against the low stone walls of the forum.

Knights passed through the streets, audible below them from the clank of their metal armor. The exhaustion John felt was bone-deep and only tangentially related to the magic he had been pumping out. He had carefully focused his mind away from what had happened in the city.

This wasn't something he had ever prepared himself for. He had wanted to be an adventurer, but that didn't mean he wanted to fight a war. He could hear and even see flashes of light in the distance as the fight raged further into the city. To an extent, it seemed the sound and light had died down somewhat, which he hoped meant that the majority of the Baron's forces had been dealt with.

Martin had his bow laid on his knees in front of him and seemed to be focused on it to the exclusion of the world around him. Silvia was flicking one of her long daggers around her hand, causing the blade to flash and flicker in the midday light. Aysel's sword was sheathed, and she sat hugging her knees, playing with a small spark of silver magic over her fingertips.

John checked his reserves and felt that they were about three quarters of the way to full, which meant that the others likely were at least above half; the actual recovery rates of person magic he knew varied widely.

Still looking at them, he found it hard to muster the words to ask them to keep moving. They probably felt something similar. But he had to. They should at least report to Grant and see where they were needed next.

John made to speak until he suddenly realized how dry his throat was. He fumbled around at his belt until he found a water canteen. He pulled the container out and took a swig of the tepid water, swallowing carefully. It wasn't refreshing, but it at least helped the dryness in his throat.

John tried to speak again, and this time the words did not get caught in his throat. "We should report back to Grant."

The other three turned to him and stared at him for a moment before Aysel responded, "Yeah, you're right."

Silvia sheathed her dagger and rose to her feet. "All right," she said.

"Which way do you think we should try?" Martin asked as he rose to his feet as well, keeping his bow in his hand.

John and Aysel stood as well, and John shrugged. "No idea. Maybe we should try back the way we came."

Aysel didn't respond for a moment as she looked back down the street where they had come from before turning to look the other way. "There doesn't look to be any Knights around here as far as I can see. I guess we should go with your plan, John."

They walked down the station platform steps and through the city, encountering signs of the fight every so often carved and blasted into the buildings and the street. They continued further down the road around the gouges until they passed into a square where some Knights sat around resting, leaning against buildings, quietly eating, drinking, and talking.

They looked around for a moment. Aysel walked up to a group of Knights leaning against a broken pillar that had once connected to the ruined building behind them.

They looked up at her approach, and Aysel asked, "Can any of you tell us where Captain Grant is?"

They paused in their quiet conversation, and a human woman with dark skin and dark eyes turned to Aysel. "He should be just a little further into the city. I heard he was in the former Council Chambers and is directing things from there."

Aysel nodded. "Thanks."

The woman waved her off. "If you get any orders for the rest of us, let me know, and I'll get this lot moving. If I'm not here, ask one of the Knights for Sergeant Dalia."

"I will," Aysel replied and turned back to them, looking at John. "Do you know where the Council's Chamber are?"

"Yeah," John replied. "It's not too far from here, follow me."

John took the lead, taking a street on the opposite side they had come from; the streets of what he knew to be his former home didn't feel much like it. He led them through, passing by another broken building before they came out onto a wider road.

At the end of the street, a large pale grey building with high arches and long columns held the roof up, and several steps led up to it. In truth, John had not been here very often as he had little reason to see the seat of government for the city.

As they approached the building, the large bronze metal doors swung open, releasing the Knights' group onto the street. The Knights passed their group as they continued to the doors. Silvia opened the one on the right, and they walked across the threshold.

The group stepped into an entry hall paneled with dark brown wood and clean white marble floors. They continued their path forward and passed a couple of stairwells. Eventually, they arrived at a set of double doors that opened; many Knights were moving about the chamber, with some sitting at terminals and others surrounding a table at the center where a three-dimensional web of white light hovered.

John realized after a moment of staring at the light that it was a three-dimensional map of the city, on which red and green dots hovered. Every so often, one of the Knights who surrounded the diagram would gesture with his hand, and a dot would flicker and disappear, either reappearing somewhere else or disappearing in its entirety.

Grant stood at the head of the table. The tall, gaunt man seemed in his element. He gave orders to the Knights, causing some to head to the door and others to move merely to another part of the table and rotate a part of the map.

As they approached, Grant looked up, spotting them. He beckoned them over, and they moved to join him.

With no preamble, Grant began to talk, "The battle is progressing well, and even now, the Baron's troops are still being forced to retreat from the emplacements they've set up within the city. The battle is mostly over already, and we should be able to advance into the Mountain Hold. Still, it's going to take some more effort to keep them on the retreat. They have some soldiers who've holed up in a place called the Western Workshop."

John wasn't able to suppress the startled exclamation that came from his mouth. Grant turned to look at him. "You know the place?" he questioned.

John nodded, something hot and smoky igniting in his gut. "I lived there most of my life. If you're putting together a detachment of Knights to deal with it, I would like to be included."

John tried desperately to not sound pushy even though he knew if Grant didn't send him, he would go by himself anyway. It was not just for Bernard but also for the other people he had known growing up for most of his life. To think that he had wanted to leave so badly and now at hearing that the Red Baron's forces were attempting to hold out there made him furious.

Grant eyed him for a moment, a solemn expression on his face, before he spoke, "The Knights that were sent to deal with it are likely already nearing the workshop. You'll need to leave now."

John nodded and was about to turn and leave before Aysel spoke up, "Can we go as well?" she asked Grant.

John felt a rush of warm feelings for Aysel.

"Yes," Grant said. "Join up with the rest of the Knights once you're done. They have orders on what to do after."

They left the building.

"You're the lead, John," Aysel said. "You'll know how to get there better than any of us."

John nodded briefly in acknowledgment, taking the lead and breaking into a jog. Through the twisting city streets he led them, every so often passing by a group of Knights, some escorting the Baron's soldiers and some jogging in their direction.

John had to consciously not direct too much magic into his legs as he ran through the streets. They passed broken buildings that gradually grew more familiar as they got closer and closer to their destination.

John turned onto a street, which he recognized as the main street where the Western Workshop was located. Up ahead, he spotted a group of Knights in their steel armor that looked significantly worse for wear than the Knight's armor he had seen at the beginning of the battle. It was dented and scratched. Some pieces were even torn off entirely.

The group turned as they approached, some of them raising their weapons before lowering them as they realized they didn't wear the double-headed red axe of the Red Baron's forces.

As John and his companions got within a reasonable speaking distance, one of the Knights called out, "Are you our reinforcements?"

Aysel called back as they slowed down to a walk as they came up to the group. "Yes, Captain Grant sent us," she said.

"Glad he did," the Knight replied. "We have no idea how many of them are holed up in there."

"So, what's the plan?" Aysel asked.

"We're going to approach the building from the front side and see if they start taking shots at us. We don't know how many of them are in, and civilians are in there as well. So, we're going to be careful in how we approach this," the Knight said.

They continued down the street for a little while longer until John spotted the place he had called home for most of his life. From the view on the road, it didn't look different than he remembered it. They took cover in the shadow of some of the buildings, and a couple of Knights cautiously made their way to the door.

One stepped forward, and his fist flared with blue light before he slammed it forward into the door, causing the wood to explode inwards. The instant he did so, arrows came flying out, two colliding with his shield in bright flashes of light before he took cover to the side.

The door was breached, but there was no obvious way in as the moment anyone tried to even peek around the corner, arrows came flying out. John grimaced before he realized that they were going about this the wrong way.

Staying out of the view of the door, John headed down an alleyway of the building; he came around to the back of the workshop where they had entered before. He grasped the door handle and flowed his magic through the seven channels, and with a click, the door unbolted. He cautiously opened the door a couple of centimeters and peeked into the courtyard.

It looked deserted, so he slipped his way through the door, closing it behind him. He walked through the courtyard, doing his best to prevent his boots from colliding hard enough to make noise as he treaded over the familiar stone. He approached the back door of the workshop and pulled at the handle lightly.

The door stayed put, locked from the other side. He contemplated, attempting to blast the door down for a moment before he decided against it. The explosion would draw way too much attention, and he would be ridiculously outnumbered. If he grabbed some of the Knights, it would be different, but he didn't want the Baron's soldiers inside to realize something was off.

He looked over the back of the workshop, examining the windows that could give him a way in.

Utilizing the technique he had learned at the fortress, he began to climb up the wall until he was level with one of the windows. Inside was an empty room with a couple of crates piled inside. Gripping the window's base with his magic claws, he pushed upward, and the window slid open easily.

Pulling himself through the window, he closed it behind him and crept his way further into the room. He opened the door at the end a crack and gazed through the narrow gap to see if any of the Baron's soldiers were there.

Seeing none, he slipped around the door, closing it behind him, and began to make his way through the familiar hallways. He heard low muttering behind the doors, guessing that the workers had likely been shunted inside by the Baron's forces once they had taken control of the building.

He arrived at the stairway and began to creep down the steps, the Baron's soldiers' voices on the main floor coming clearly to his ears.

"Even if we hold them, what are we supposed to do? It's not like we can stay in here forever," a loud voice was saying.

Another voice responded harshly, "We'll hold the line here. You gave your oath to the Baron."

"Where are the rest of our forces?" A third voice spoke up. "Are they still inside the mountain?"

John arrived at the main floor and turned slightly around the stairwell's edge, and spotted ten soldiers spread out by the doorway, two of them aiming their bows through it to shoot if any of the Knights tried to come through. John stepped back hiding in the stairwell, his mind pumping through options.

He didn't like the odds of attempting to take them on by himself. Even distracting them from the doorway for the couple moments it would take for the Knights to charge would be dangerous. He looked around the workshop, searching for an idea.

The workstations had piles of materials, and finished products were lined up against the wall—weapons and armor in shining rows.

His eyes caught onto an object that he recognized all too well sitting on top of his former workstation: a blasting rod. Why were they constructing blasting rods? John furiously shoved the idea to the side as unimportant.

His mind caught on—the rods.

John glanced down at the entrance and saw that their attention was still focused on holding off the Knights, who would occasionally peek around the corners.

John crouched down slightly and began creeping his way through the workstations, slowly making his way back to his former workstation. Slowly, he reminded himself, trying to keep himself below the workstations' levels in case any of the Baron's soldiers looked back.

He reached the desk after minutes. He grabbed a rod from the desk, knocking another one loose, and his heart seized as he fumbled, trying to catch the other rod. His free hand bumped into the rod, diverting its fall to the side but unable to catch it, the rod collided with the ground with a dull metallic tone.

John paused, heart frantically beating in his chest, waiting for one of the Baron's soldiers to spin around, to say something. Nothing happened.

John poked his head over a desk and saw that they were still focused on the Knights.

John turned back to the metallic rod in his hand and focused on it. This was an actual device meant for an explosion, unlike his improvised rock from earlier. He channeled his magic through the rod, and the lines lit up blue, glowing softly as he charged more magic into the rod.

He cut the current and peeked his head back up over throwing the rod at the group of the Baron's soldiers beaming it off one of their heads who cried out.

"Ouch! What just hit me?"

The Baron's soldiers turned, looking at the rod.

This wasn't right, John thought. The rod should have gone off. What was the—

Oh! The stone John had used earlier had exploded because it wasn't meant to contain such magic, but the rod was designed for it. He needed to trigger the explosion, but how did he...

John felt desperately through his magic, trying to figure out if there was some connection between him and the rod. Any moment the soldiers would check for him he needed to—

A line of magic was out of place, trailing out of him to the rod. He grabbed the line frantically, and suddenly it snapped.

BOOM!

Blue light ripped forth, sending the soldiers flying through the air away from the doorway. They crumpled to the ground, and after a moment, a Knight peeked his head through the doorway and, seeing no opposition, cautiously stepped in.

John slowly stood up, raising his hands slightly as the Knight spun his bow out, directed towards him.

"Easy, I'm with you guys," John said, with somewhat inadequate words, and the Knight looked around at the Baron's soldiers.

They lowered their weapon and nodded. "Right."

More Knights began to stream in through the doorway, and John spotted Aysel, Martin, and Silvia within their midst.

They found him and joined him in the workshop area.

"I didn't see where you went," Aysel said. "You could have let us in on your plan."

John frowned, nodding.

"I didn't want them to suspect something, so I thought it was best if only one of us disappeared."

Aysel patted him on the back. "Fair enough. Just let one of us know next time."

Soft thuds caused the room's attention to spin to the stairs, where a worker that John recognized by face though not by name was peeking out from the stairs.

On seeing the Knights and the downed soldiers, she turned to look up the stairs and called up, "It's safe."

John heard the click of doors opening, followed by a stream of workers walking down the stairs. In the middle of the crowd, he spotted Bernard, whose eyes also fell upon him.

Bernard made his way through the crowd and walked up to him, and before John could say a word, clasped him in a hug. John blinked, not used to the physical display of affection. He couldn't remember the last time Bernard had hugged him. It was … nice.

"You're all right, John," Bernard murmured and stepped back. "When I sent you off, to tell the truth, I was worried I wasn't going to see you again."

John nodded somewhat mutely before he realized he should respond, "I was more worried about you," he admitted.

Bernard gave him a strained smile, his emotion showing clearer on his face than John had ever seen. "Well, I'm glad to see you've made it back safe."

Bernard looked at the Knights, who were now dragging the Baron's guards out of the building. One of the Knights said to the assembled group at large, "We are the Knights of the Dawn. As of now, we are currently working to liberate your city and ask you to remain indoors so you do not get caught up in the fighting."

The Knights began filing out of the building, taking their prisoners with them, some being dragged unconscious.

John turned back to Bernard. "I need to go."

Bernard nodded, something flashing through his eyes. "I'll join you."

John paused, doing a double-take. "You will?"

Bernard smiled. "I figure I've sat back and done nothing long enough."

"All right." John was still shocked. He knew Bernard could fight, but a part of him worried as he waited for Bernard to head upstairs to grab his equipment.

John looked back at Aysel, Martin, and Silvia, who were waiting right behind him.

Martin shook his head with a half-smile on his face. "Can't say no to more help."

"I guess not," John replied, pushing down the instinct that said to leave now without Bernard.

They waited some minutes, and John's nerves grew more. He was about to tell them to head out when he heard the clunk of steel, and looked up the stairs to see a Knight of the Dawn walking down in burnished plate armor with the stylized insignia of the sun on his shield.

He had grown used to the sight, except that the person in the armor was quite obviously Bernard.

"Bernard?"

Bernard gave him the same grim smile from before.

"There's a lot we haven't talked about, John. After this is over, I promise I'll give you a full explanation about everything."

John nodded dazedly, his mind catching at the end of the statement. What did Bernard mean by everything?

They exited the building and started jogging down the street back toward the Council chambers. It took some time as John led them through, Aysel, Martin, Silvia, and Bernard following along in his wake.

He forced to the side all the questions he now wanted to ask. He knew it would do no good to be distracted right now, not in the middle of a battle.

The sounds of clanging metal and warfare had faded from the city. When they turned a corner, they ran past another Knight group who were jogging in the opposite direction.

They soon arrived at the pale grey building where he saw many Knights talking as they scarfed down quick meals. They made their way past the crowd into the building through the entrance hall and down into the Council Chambers. Grant was still standing giving out orders, and he caught sight of them as he entered.

"Good, I'm glad to see you're back. I've already heard the reports that the raid…"

Grant trailed off as he looked at them. More specifically, John realized he was looking at Bernard.

After a moment, Grant began speaking again. "It's good to see you again, Bernard."

Bernard gave a tired smile. "It's been a long time, Grant."

They approached each other, and John almost thought they were about to begin swinging swords at each other before suddenly they clasped arms.

"I won't say no to another Captain. Come join me," Grant said, turning to walk back to the table where the map was located.

Bernard followed him, and John's mind was set awhirl. Captain?

John saw the questioning looks directed to him from his friends, and he shrugged helplessly. They refocused on the discussion between Grant and Bernard.

Bernard was standing at Grant's side, exchanging brief reports of the city's status.

"As far as we can tell, we've dealt with the majority of the Baron's forces in the City," Grant said. "What I don't understand is where the rest of the army is."

"Caught that, did you?" Bernard questioned before gesturing to the railway station. "That's why. Some number of their forces have been entering the Mountain Hold. They didn't expect a counterattack, especially so soon."

Grant frowned. "The Mountain Hold? Which means that this is far more urgent than I realized. Do you know what's down there?" he asked Bernard.

Bernard shook his head, and John realized he hadn't told him of the metallic structure they had encountered beneath the earth.

"Someone's trying to breach their way past the barrier down there," Grant said, and Bernard's expression dropped.

"Impossible," Bernard murmured. "The magic alone would take a city's worth."

"And what do you think has happened to the Mountain Hold?" Grant grimly replied.

A moment of silence passed between them as the Knights in the room still moved about the map, examining points in the city. John felt a twisting knot in his gut as he glanced at Martin and Silvia, whose faces had turned, it seemed, to stone. Did they mean what John thought they meant: that there had been some type of … sacrifice?

Bernard looked thunderstruck and stared blankly at the map that hovered above the table.

After a couple of moments, Bernard shook himself, looking back at Grant. "Then we'll have to move quickly."

"Indeed." Grant nodded and looked up at John, Aysel, Martin, and Silvia.

"I would recommend you four get some rest, and we'll be moving again in the morning."

They didn't respond for a moment until Aysel took the lead and nodded, "Right."

Aysel led them out of the Council Chambers and back onto the city streets. Temporary shelters were being erected through the streets in the late evening light. They made their way through the encampments, searching for a spot to set themselves down. They walked for some time until a familiar voice interrupted their search, "There they are. Over here!"

They turned to see Karat waving at them next to a hasty pair of tents where Zayne and Marcila were prodding at the food in their bowls. They turned their direction and walked over to their companions, sitting around a large pot where a stew bubbled, giving off an aromatic scent that caused John's stomach to grumble.

He realized that he hadn't eaten for some time and quickly sat down with the rest of his companions, taking an offered bowl, and began to dig in hungrily. It was not the best food he had ever had, but it was hearty and filling, which made it taste divine. Only the sound of spoons and slurping filled the site as they focused on their meals for some time.

Having finished his bowl and thankfully gotten another serving, John slowed down to look at the rest of the adventurers. Their clothing was somewhat torn and dirt covered. Still, John felt the swell in his heart at seeing them alive. Amid the fighting, worry had fled from his mind, but he was glad to see that at least for now, he would not have to mourn more friends.

It was almost funny, John realized. When he had worked at the workshop, he had found himself isolated and alone but in relative peace. Now with his days filled with danger and combat, he had found at least a part of what he had been looking for. Was this what Bernard had experienced when he had traveled the Realms?

Bernard. John couldn't help the frown that crossed over his face. He had, of course, known Bernard was full of secrets, and he thought he had been okay with that. With at least one of Bernard's secrets, John couldn't help the feeling of loneliness that came from it.

How well did he really know Bernard? He had thought he had known the man who was a father figure to him but this…

John took another bite of his food, trying to push away the thoughts that clung like spider webs in his mind. It was not like he didn't know Bernard at all, he told himself, but the words felt hollow.

More than ever, John realized that this city, the Western Workshop, they were not his home. Did he even have a family?

CHAPTER 20

AFTERMATH AND PREPARATIONS

John lost himself in work the next few days. The Baron's soldiers had been imprisoned in camps outside the city. The Knights had made sure to go through the city with a fine-tooth comb to make sure every last one of the soldiers had been found.

The citizens had been surprised at their liberation but in general thankful. The Stone Council that had been imprisoned were now released and back to managing the city. The Council Guard, those who were still alive, had retaken their positions on the city walls. They had been reduced to less than half strength, and the knowledge of that loss of life caused John to grit his teeth. He was thankful that the Red Baron's soldiers' imprisonment had not been left in his hands and the Knights were on rotating guard shifts.

John had instead been working with the Knights to prepare the next stage of their plan. They had opened up the depot and loaded the tram cars that remained with supplies. Given the trams' size, they could not bring any of the vehicles that had provided some of the heavier ordnances they had used to assault the city.

John had not seen Bernard much in those days as he and Grant had hunkered down with other Knights to plan the next attack. The Knights themselves were friendly, though John found it difficult to connect with any of them genuinely.

Though, John thought, that could have been his inherent problem with people.

John still was able to work well, helping roll out the tram carts to be loaded with supplies. It was nice to get lost in the work.

He lifted a large crate to fit into another tram cart when a voice called out, "Are you John Doe?"

John almost dropped the crate in surprise and, after fumbling with it for a few seconds, managed to set it down lightly.

He turned to see a Council Guard walking up to him, clad ina navy cloak over his light steel armor.

John realized that he hadn't responded yet. "Yes, I am. Did you need something?"

"The Council is requesting your presence in the Council Chambers," the Guard said.

"Oh," John said intelligently. "I'll go see them."

The Council Guard nodded and turned to walk away. John picked up the crate again and carried it to the tram, setting it down before beginning his walk to the Council Chambers. A part of him was curious about what they wanted, but it was minimal. After what had happened so far, worrying about simply meeting with the City Council seemed a trifle comparatively.

He walked through the streets where even now, he could see necessary repairs occurring. The city people moved about not as easily as they did before, but there was at least some ordinary life to the streets.

Eventually, John arrived at the Council Chambers, walked up the steps, and through the doors. He was thankful for the reprieve from the sun that had been burning all day.

He walked into the Council Chambers and was struck by the Council's difference occupying the chamber instead of the Knights' makeshift command center. Around thirty members of various peoples of the Realms were present: a female elf of indeterminate age with dark-toned skin, brown eyes, and long dark hair sat at the chamber's relative head.

The setup reminded John of the Seventh Federation even though the number of people was fewer. At the bottom of the chamber, John saw the other adventurers already assembled, with Zayne and Marcila standing at the forefront and Aysel slightly at the back. John noticed that Karat, Martin, and Silvia weren't there, before he had to resist the urge to facepalm when he remembered they weren't technically part of their group. After having spent so long together, John had in truth forgotten the fact.

He went down and stood next to Aysel, and as he did so, the chamber quieted down from the low murmur that had been going about.

"Zayne Dallard, Guild master of the Raven Fallows, we have convened this Council to address the work you and your compatriots have done in the service of the City of Lights," the woman began. "You have gone above and beyond the call, and such service must be rewarded to show our gratitude. The Council is willing to double the agreed-upon payment for the contract you took to discover what occurred in the Mountain Hold. We would do more, but the city's finances are already strained in the construction we will have to undertake to repair our home."

John blinked, taking in the words. He hadn't thought about what the actual rewards would be besides the freeing of the City of Lights and the Mountain Hold since the mission had begun.

"The payment has been deposited in your Guild accounts. We thank you."

Zayne shared a look with Marcila before he spoke, "Thank you. As always, please call upon the services of the Guilds again."

Zayne took the lead out of the room, and once they had exited the building, he turned and looked at all of them.

"This means that as of now, we are released from the adventuring contract. What all of you choose to do next is up to you."

"I'm staying," John said, not hesitating. He knew he couldn't abandon the part of their group that wasn't held under the adventurers' contract. Their home was still at stake.

Zayne nodded and turned to look at Marcila. "What about you, Marcila?"

Zayne looked at Marcila and Aysel, who seemed to be having a conversation with their eyes. Marcila broke away first, and Aysel turned to the rest of the group. "Marcila and I will also stay. We won't stop until the mission is complete in its entirety."

John couldn't shake the feeling that Marcila disagreed with Aysel, and a part of him wondered why, if Marcila was Aysel's mentor, Aysel was the one to make the decision.

"What will you do, Zayne?" Marcila asked.

Zayne gave a half-grin. "Even though we're released from the contract, I feel as if I owe it to Karat and the rest to see this through in its entirety. If that's also how the rest of you feel, I would be honored if we stayed together to the end of this adventure."

Their discussion ended, and John said goodbye and began heading back to the tram station to continue loading supplies. His mind was still caught on the strange interaction between Aysel and Marcila. It was hard to put his finger on what exactly had been so odd, but there was something weird going on between them.

Perhaps since he had grabbed the Index, he could not conclude what exactly the matter was. More than that, he worried that he wasn't reading the situation right, and if he brought it up to Aysel, he would seem at best foolish and at worse that he was prying into her private affairs.

He continued down the streets, taking note of the damage still on the buildings around him that had yet to be repaired. The doors of various shops were opened, and a trickle of traffic walked the road around him.

The City of Lights was unlike he had ever seen it before, and the thought hammered at the discomfort he felt at being at his relative home. These streets that he had walked for his entire lifetime felt alien to him.

Even as he passed by buildings that he had seen a thousand times before, even as he looked up at the mountain face that the City of Lights rested on, he still felt the sense that he did not truly belong here.

Where he did belong … he didn't know.

John shook his head. He could worry about that after they dealt with the immediate threat.

He walked further down the street, making his way back to the tram station. He took his place, helping load more supplies into the waiting trams and thus lost himself there for the rest of the day.

It was as the sun began to set that he broke from his work, making his way through the city to where the encampments had remained set around the Council Chamber's. He took a shower in a nearby building titled "Spacious" that was formerly used for spa treatments and temporarily available to the gathered Knights. Moving through the line took some time but taking a shower was completely worth it. Having rinsed himself down, John found where their group's encampment had been last night. Their sleeping bags were still rolled up to the side, and John found himself wishing he had a book or a terminal to entertain himself.

He realized that technically he could see if he could stay at the Western Workshop in his former room, but the idea didn't sit well. Besides the fact that he would be abandoning the other adventurers to sleep outside while he slept inside, he found the idea of returning to the workshop somewhat discomfiting.

"John!" A voice called out, and he turned to see Martin and Silvia walking up to the encampment. He waved to them as they came to join him in sitting at their makeshift campsite.

"What have you guys been doing all day?" John asked them.

Martin responded. "Silvia's been hunkered down with some of the Knights helping sort things out information-wise with supplies and the like. I've just been scouting with some of the Knights, making sure we didn't miss any pockets of the Baron's soldiers in the city."

"Did you find any?" John couldn't help but ask.

"No." Martin shook his head. "We found nothing, which was good." He hastily amended at a side-eye from Silvia.

Not willing to let the conversation die given that he'd spent most of the day moving equipment, he turned to ask Silvia, "So how are our supplies?"

Silvia shrugged. "We seem to have everything we need. The food rations should be distributed shortly, and we'll have enough for when we move into the Mountain Hold."

She hesitated for a moment, glancing at Martin before she said in a carefully controlled manner, "I heard through the grapevine that the adventurers were given payment today."

John nodded. "Yeah."

He noticed that their expressions seemed to shift somewhat, becoming more tense.

"So, does that mean you guys are done?" Martin asked bluntly, surprising John for a moment.

John shook his head emphatically. "No, we're staying to see this through."

They relaxed immediately, and Martin grinned, scratching the back of his head. "Oh, sorry, we just thought that maybe..."

"We wouldn't leave you guys out to dry," John said, trying to pore his earnestness into his words. "It wouldn't be right, plus—"

John stopped himself, and Martin and Silvia's expressions turned curious as they both leaned forward slightly.

"Plus?" Silvia questioned.

John was unable to stop the flare of embarrassment through his cheeks. Carefully centering his gaze between the two of their heads, he said in a small voice, "Well, you guys are pretty much my first real friends."

There was a tangible moment of silence between them, and John felt the heat in his face flushing to his ears. He shouldn't have called them his friends. That was putting too much pressure on them.

Martin suddenly laughed before stopping himself short at Silvia and John's attention.

"Sorry. I just realized that was a long time coming," Martin said, looking at John seriously, "You're a good friend, John."

Silvia nodded, smiling softly. She tucked a strand of red hair behind her ear. "Thanks, John. It means a lot."

Their talk broke into a lighter discussion, a warm atmosphere falling over the group.

It was some time later that the rest of their group assembled with them. Karat, Marcila, and Zayne had arrived together, and Aysel last. They all sat around their makeshift campsite, and John felt some measure of peace. The food was a step above sawdust, and their sleep was on the cold hard ground, but at least the company was good.

They talked about inconsequential things, and John was able to lose himself in the moment. Not thinking about what tomorrow would bring and what the invasion might cost. For now, in this peaceful moment, he could talk and laugh with people whom he could call friends.

His eyes connected with Aysel's, and on her face, he saw that there was no smile. She had a look of concentration as she stared into the distance as if she was seeing something beyond anyone else's sight. As they went to sleep that night, John couldn't help but have his mind roll repeatedly over why she looked so wistful. The chaos in his mind prevented his sleep, and so he heard the slight shifting across from him of a sleeping bag ruffling.

He cautiously opened his eyes to look and saw a narrow beam of silver light held in front of Aysel as she moved away from the campsite. John felt indecision seize him for a moment before he too crawled out of his sleeping bag as silently as possible.

He followed her through the campsite, feeling strange as he did so. Maybe he should have just headed back. Her path took her from where they rested into the city and through the streets until they arrived on an outcropping overlooking the valley below the City of Lights. Aysel paused and looked out into the night illuminated by a half-moon that shined brightly on the world below. The typical lights of the city were extinguished, making the night sky all the clearer. Aysel extinguished her light and stared out into the night.

John hesitated for a moment. He felt intrusive in the moment. He made to turn away before his foot cracked a loose stone.

Aysel spun around. "Who's there?" she called out.

John immediately raised his hands. "It's just me."

"John?" Aysel said in a softer voice. "What are you doing awake?"

"I couldn't sleep," John said, shrugging, wondering if Aysel could see the action in the dim light. "I didn't mean to disturb you."

"You didn't." In the slight backlight from the night, John saw Aysel shake her head. "I just—"

Aysel cut herself off and turned back to the night. John slowly walked up and joined her at the outcropping, resting his hands on the stone fence between them and the edge.

"You just what?" he asked. "Not that you have to tell me or anything," he quickly followed up.

Aysel didn't speak for a long moment.

John thought he should leave before Aysel spoke again, "It's hard to explain."

"You don't have to," John tried to assure her.

Aysel shook her head again. "I want to. I don't know where to start. Have you heard of the Prophecy of the Fall?"

John ran the title through his mind but came up blank. "No, should I have?"

Aysel shook her head, her hair cascading about her face, "No, probably not. The Augur made it of the Amelion Imperium Mages. A couple of decades ago, they made a prophecy—a prophecy on the day of my birth. I don't even know what the prophecy said, to be honest. Whatever it did say, though made it so for my entire life I've been hunted."

"By whom?" John asked, trying to process her words.

"By the Knights of the Dusk. This isn't the first time I've encountered the Knights of the Dawn and Dusk. Agents on both sides have searched for me. Without Marcila, I don't know what would have happened."

"Why?"

Aysel smiled weakly at him. "Marcila told me it's because they both wanted to use me. For what, I don't know."

"Does Marcila?" John asked.

Aysel shrugged. "I don't think so. She doesn't tell me everything, though…" she trailed off.

John furrowed his brow as he stared up into the night sky.

"I could help." The words came out before he could examine them.

Aysel looked at him, surprised. "Really?" she asked.

John shrugged under her examination, trying desperately to keep the heat from rising to his face. "Yeah. I mean, I don't know what I could do, but we're friends, right?"

A soft smile crossed Aysel's face. "We are."

They stood in a companionable silence, staring up into the night sky, and John noticed that she seemed more relaxed than he'd ever really seen her.

When he had first met her, he had been struck by how pretty she was, but in the moonlight, she looked truly beautiful. John realized that maybe what he felt for Aysel wasn't quite friendship.

CHAPTER 21

BACK INTO THE MOUNTAINS

The days passed as the Knights prepared to enter the Cold Mountains. John found himself without much time to think about anything. He helped with the loading of the tram cars and then found work in the forge's repairing armor.

They were still stuck sleeping in the streets as there simply wasn't room to house the thousands of Knights that had won back the city. John heard that the Baron's soldiers had been disarmed of their weapons and armor and sent back home. It played at his nerves; to think that might come back to bite them; but on the other hand, there was no way to hold them in prison. The Knights had the resources to maintain themselves, and that was pretty much the extent of it.

The time John spent in the forges was mind-numbing, not necessarily in a negative way. When he was working to repair the equipment, there wasn't much to think about except the task at hand. Every move brought him a step forward to completing the current objective, after which he would move onto the next weapon or piece of armor.

He had traversed to the various workshops in the city including the Northern and Southern workshops, and a part of him was thankful that he had not yet had to work at the Western Workshop. It was a blessing in a way, given his nonexistent relationship with the people there, especially because Bernard was in the thick of things helping organize the Knights.

Of course, technically speaking, he didn't have a relationship with the people in the other workshops, but the distance was because he didn't know them, not because he had failed to get to know them. His awkwardness aside, his evenings had been spent in the company of the rest of the adventurers, which was something he couldn't help but enjoy.

Zayne would regale them sometimes with tales of his career as an adventurer. As the Guild Master of the Raven Fallows, John hadn't entirely conceptualized till that point exactly how much experience he had had. He had fought in small skirmishes and even some of the Great Wars. Karat also had a variety of experiences to share, having taken her work in the Mountain Hold as a semi-retirement similar to how it seemed Bernard had spent his time working at the Western Workshop.

She had worked as an expedition leader in the past and had uncovered the old Dwarf Lords' tombs in many Realms. She knew her artifacts better than anyone John had ever met, and the sheer scale of her knowledge was intimidating.

In contrast, Marcila had not shared much of her own life. She had spoken briefly about her work for the Amelion Imperium but never clarified her exact role in the actions she had performed. Since the night John had his conversation with Aysel, he had noticed that sometimes Marcila would eye him with something that approached distaste, though that might not be the word for it.

He had summarily done his best to stay out of her way as best he could. A part of him wondered if perhaps Aysel had told her that she had talked to him, and now she was worried that John would leak Aysel's secret.

The thought of doing so seemed anathema to him. Aysel was his friend, and revealing her secret even to their other friends would be a breach of trust.

Still, they had not talked much since that night, and John almost considered that Marcila was purposely making sure they didn't have the opportunity. Moments during the day that they would meet, Marcila would doggedly be with her and mention something that needed to be addressed.

Perhaps it was just his imagination, John thought. He admittedly wanted to talk with Aysel quite a bit more, but there didn't seem to be the time given everything going on around them.

At their informal campsite that night, Zayne told them that they would be entering the Cold Mountains tomorrow.

The talk that night focused on where they would be positioned in the tram that would go into the mountains. The trams were currently loaded full of supplies, and they would have to go in groups.

They weren't the first going in and were instead in the middle of the tram line. Zayne had already informed Grant of the possible state of disrepair the tram line could be in. It would make sense. After all, why would the tram line be kept intact after they left?

As they weren't the first to go over, John felt some comfort that they wouldn't be repeating the same crash that had happened the first time. Thinking about that had made him wonder how exactly the other members of their group had been captured, given that even directly after the crash, they had seen no sign of them.

When he had asked Zayne about this, he had said that there had been a path out of the bottom of the pit positioned on the cave's far side. When they had emerged, they had thought that Aysel and John had perished in the crash. They exited the cave to attempt to avoid whoever set the trap.

They had then been ambushed by a large group of red armored soldiers who had managed to overpower them with sheer numbers leading to their capture.

John couldn't help but wonder why the soldiers had kept them alive. Was it because whoever was behind the soldiers had planned to turn them into the same puppets just as they had the Mountain Hold people?

They soon would be faced with soldiers again, and John couldn't help but wonder how many would fall before they stopped whoever was behind this. Could their magic over the soldiers be broken to return them to the people of the Mountain Hold they once were? How many would die before that happened?

It was these thoughts that John kept to himself, not wanting to burden the others with them.

He managed to keep the thoughts at bay by keeping busy during the day. The manual labor of loading and preparing the trams was an excellent distraction keeping his mind pleasantly blank. It was only during the nights that the thoughts were the most intrusive.

The day arrived where they would head into the mountains. The camps had been broken down, and the army of Knights was loading into the trams. Only a portion of the Knights would be entering at first due to the limitation of the number of trams.

The adventurers stood amid the crowd of Knights patiently waiting to board a tram. The Knights filed forward to fill a tram, and then it would start rolling out. The next tram would roll forward, and then the crowd would once again surge ahead.

They finally found themselves at the front by the tram, which they filed into, taking their seats, followed by a squad of Knights who filled the rest of the seats until there was standing room only, which they filled as well.

The tram lurched forward, and they were off. By a matter of chance, John found himself sitting on the seat next to the tram's wall and with Aysel seated on the other side. She was uncomfortably close, he thought, but they were all packed into the tram.

To distract himself, he gazed out the window into the darkness, which reminded him of when they had first entered the Cold Mountains though he had been at the front of the tram. A part of him almost expected to see a skeletal tale or a blood-red eye, but the darkness remained unobstructed for now.

Sitting in the silence of the tram was decidedly eerie, John decided. Any discussion he may have instigated with the other adventurers would feel odd in front of another group.

Therefore, he sat silently, focused into space, preparing himself for the coming battle mentally. He knew they would have to somehow destroy the portal that was being constructed, but before that, they would have to push back the forces that whoever was behind this held under his sway.

He grasped his sword's hilt, which lay in his lap as he was unable to sit down with the scabbard attached to his side. On closing his hands around the hilt, he felt a cool sensation flow through his head, stilling his thoughts.

John looked down at his sword. There was something about it he knew he hadn't grasped yet. Yet, he didn't feel like the sword was malicious despite how it was affecting his mind. It didn't put thoughts in his head that tempted rage.

The book held the blade's picture along with a supposed title of "The Blade of Knights" along with another strange title, "The Slayer." In truth, he had put what he read to the side for the most part. It hadn't seemed important compared to everything else going on.

Now with nothing to do but sit in his seat, his mind pondered the little information he had about the blade. He had found it impaled into the stone in a cavern with a stone golem who had insisted the blade was not his.

Despite being impaled into the stone and not being cared for, for who knew how long the blade was still sharp and strong with no sign of wear upon it. The blade possibly had a name, not that the "The Blade of Knights" gave him any real clue to anything else about the sword.

The tram continued to cannon forward through the abyss. John saw a small light approaching through the window and tensed until he saw it was a tram on the opposite track headed back. He relaxed: the first group had likely arrived safely.

They continued forward, passing by another two trams that broke up the darkness outside the windows momentarily.

The tram raced forward, and John saw the track merge into one as they crossed the metal beams that he had forged over the cave water. Perhaps it was just his imagination, but he thought he saw the tram lights reflect on the metallic surface within the water that could have been their last tram. Just as quickly, the sight was yanked away from him as they rolled through another short length of the tunnel before arriving at a tram station where he saw a group of Knights unloading the tram that had gone ahead of them.

They slid to a stop behind the other tram and piled out in an orderly fashion, quickly making their way onto the platform, hauling some of the crates of supplies they had carried with them.

Standing on the platform, John took a deep breath, tasting the air underground and surveying the city's buildings that stretched outward. His vision was limited by the few lights in the city that lit the underground. Along with those lights, he saw the multicolored lights below spreading out as the tram of Knights sounded against his ears.

He pushed past the hesitation to look at the monstrous ring whose center seemed to pulse with liquid red light. The distinct sensation of wrongness once more interceded itself into his senses.

"That's something," a Knight murmured next to him, who was staring at the ring.

John looked away from the ring but even avoiding direct eye contact didn't remove the sensation. He took the stairs down from the platform, flowing with the crowd of Knights, who began running off in small groups.

He looked around, trying to spot Martin, Silvia, Aysel, or any of the rest of his group; he had been separated in the crush of people. He cursed himself for getting distracted as he moved further away from the Knights at a jog.

The lighting wasn't enough to see by, and with no need for stealth, he decided to light up the area. His hand flashed blue and sent light out into the streets as he continued making his path forward.

He could see some Knights ahead of him similarly lighting up the area in a kaleidoscopic array. Behind him, he could hear the tramp of more Knights. He kept swiveling his head about, expecting to catch a glimpse of the full armored Hemlock Guards or even some of the native population clad in chains.

There was nothing. The streets seemed utterly vacant except for the occasional tramp of passing Knights.

John continued forward at a jog, gradually making his way closer to where the ring stood. As he moved further down the streets, he eventually found himself alone. Every corner he turned around, he expected to see some sign of the city's inhabitants, but it was eerily empty.

He came to a stop in the middle of the street, looking about, resting his hand on his sword as he stood there momentarily. He glimpsed a sliver of red-light flash in one of the windows of a nearby building.

This was all he had time to see, before—

"JOHN!" a familiar metallic voice ground out.

His hands moved faster than his brain could command, spinning his blade out and slicing a streak of red light out of the air. A halved arrow clattered to the ground, which he had a second to pay attention to before his hands moved again, slicing another streak of red out of the air.

Red light shot at him, and he backpedaled his sword, moving without his command, dancing in front of him, slicing through each arrow before they could land against his barrier.

Every parry was closer. Suddenly, even with the mysterious force moving his arms, an arrow found its way through a gap, hitting him in the chest, taking a chunk of magic out of his barrier.

He kept backpedaling as a second then a third arrow hit him directly. Each hit tore chunks out of his magic.

He needed to do something. Anything.

But as his magic barrier dipped again, he could feel a gnawing terror edging at his mind. He looked around, desperately searching for a place to take cover. There! In the shadow of one of the buildings! He sprinted towards it, feeling two arrows impact him almost simultaneously as his defense dropped. He made it around the corner just as another arrow slammed into the rock wall, blowing a chunk out of it.

John took a moment to get his bearings. His magic was at around half. The alley he had found himself in ended in the back of a large building that soared overhead. If he tried to climb it, he would be exposed as the other building wall he was hiding behind was far shorter.

Another arrow slammed into the corner of the wall blowing, a chunk clean out of it, and John edged back into the alley.

He looked about, trying to spark an idea in his mind. Maybe he could just wait here for his magic to recharge. It would take a while, but they weren't going to destroy the building only with their arrows; that was unless they relocated to another spot where they could shoot down the alley with impunity. Once again, John looked around before his eyes fell on the building wall blocking him in. Wouldn't Bernard just—

He approached the wall and began to etch runes into it, making them large and as clear as possible. The material wasn't particularly great, but he wasn't looking to do a great piece of work.

He completed the runes and pressed his hand against the wall, focusing on magic passing and lighting up the runes. He backed away down the alley as far as he dared to.

Turning, he shielded his eyes and—

BOOM!

He turned to see a large hole torn into the side of the wall. He jogged towards and went through, entering a building whose business he could not tell. Desks and terminals were laid about, but he ignored them, moving through the somewhat cramped hallways before making it to the other side of the building. He pushed at the door only to find it locked. With a slice of his sword, he cut clean through the lock and pushed the door open, cautiously peering out into the street. The street was clear of any Knights or possible attackers, so he stepped out slowly, ready to duck back in case there was another entrenched position.

Taking the lack of arrows flying at him as a possible good sign be broke into a jog, running parallel to the street he had just come from. He reached the end of the block. A chirrup at his belt alerted him to the one piece of equipment he had been provided for this assault: a radio linked with the rest of the adventurers salvaged from the equipment that had once belonged to the Baron's soldiers.

He cursed himself for having nearly forgotten it but held it up to his face, clicking down to complete the connection to the rest of the radios.

Zayne's voice came through, slightly scratchy. "Encountered ambushers hiding in the buildings; stay wary. Over."

John clicked his handset. "Already met some of them myself. Over."

"Are you alright? Over."

"Magic's down a bit, but I got out of their trap. Over."

"Double back and tell any Knights headed that way. Over," Zayne instructed.

"Will do. Over," John responded.

He began to make his way back through the city, passing through the streets that were only lit by the occasional lamp that still worked, the ever present red glow from the portal, and his blue magic that lit the area around him.

He moved at a jog that ate only slightly at his magic reserves as he moved down the street, searching for any sign of the Knights who he knew should be moving in this direction. He continued for a couple of minutes, his feet colliding with solid thuds against the ground until he spotted a group of multicolored lights ahead of him.

He jogged towards them, and as he got closer, he saw it was a squad of five Knights, their magic casting the shadows of the inadequately lit streets. Their hands strayed immediately to their weapons on his approach, but they seemed to relax as they saw his lack of aggression.

"There's an entrenched group of the Hemlock Guards in the next street over," he told them without delay.

The woman at the front of the group with short black hair and dark eyes nodded.

She pulled out a radio at her belt and clicked it on. "This is Knight Jaeth. I just had a report of the enemy's presence hiding in the buildings. Relay to all other squads."

She released the button and slid the radio back onto her belt.

"You should join with us for now, take a position in the middle of our group," she gestured, and John nodded, falling in with them as Knight Jaeth preceded to lead the group forward. They continued down the streets, the Knights continuing to swivel their heads about, examining each building they passed closely.

They had taken a different street than the one John had come from, filing between the Mountain Hold's abandoned homes. John couldn't help but feel more dread gathering in his stomach as they continued forward as nothing seemed to happen.

Any moment he expected arrows to come flying at him, to trigger some kind of magic trap.

As they turned a corner, the group headed closer to the ring in the city center.

Knight Jaeth halted her run; stopping dead in her tracks, surveying the area around them. John noticed that as she looked around, a green light seemed to fill her eyes, causing the pupils to glow, turning the rest of the eyes dull in comparison.

"As I thought," she said, still looking in front of them. "There's some magic trip lines across the next set of buildings." She pointed ahead of them, and for a moment, John didn't see what she was talking about until he noticed a small distortion in the air, which was mostly unnoticeable in the inadequate lighting unless you were looking for it.

John wanted to ask how she had seen it, but he knew now wasn't the time.

"Eren, up front," she called out, and a woman Knight who was the shortest out of all of them stepped forward. She carried a long wooden staff that was almost as tall as she was. She held it out in front of her.

Brown light spilled forth, running ahead of them before it lanced over what looked like hundreds of formerly invisible strings that ran through the air. The brown highlighted strings ran back and forth from the tops of buildings to the bottom of the street before they went up again.

Knight Eren spoke shortly, "Looks like a basic trigger trap for explosives embedded in the walls and the street. It will take me a moment to disarm it."

Knight Jaeth nodded in acknowledgment. "Do it. The rest of you spread out. This is the perfect place for an ambush."

They did so, and John found himself surveying the way from which they had come. He willed the light in his hand to go outward slightly, so it hovered above his head a few feet in front of him.

Staring down the barely lit street, he rested his hand on his sword, trying to draw what comfort he could from the strange weapon. There was something not normal about it, but for now, the actions it had taken seemed benign if not actively helpful toward his continued survival.

He kept staring down the street, trying to prevent his mind from playing tricks to make the shadows into enemies. It was silent expect for the murmured whisperings of Knight Eren as she worked on whatever she was working on.

As he was standing there, a thought occurred to him. While he had been attacked, that did not seem to be the other adventurers' general case. Weren't there supposed to be thousands of Hemlock Guards in the city? Where were they all?

Surely they should have encountered more resistance than the isolated pocket John had run across.

John gripped the hilt of his sword, trying to steady himself. He couldn't let his mind get distracted. They were standing in the open in hostile territory, and at any moment, they could be attacked.

"Contact," one of the Knights' voices drew his attention, causing him to turn slightly.

In front of the Knights some distance away still, he saw a familiar red carapace of a Hemlock Guard emerge from the darkness, followed by another one, and then another.

Tens of the red carapace guards marched slowly out from the darkness, their boots tramping across the ground with an audible sound in unison. The tens grew to hundreds as more and more emerged into the light.

John wavered as he tried to comprehend exactly how many of the Hemlock Guards had appeared. They continued marching forward slowly, and John noticed that for some reason, their movements were slower than before.

John drew his blade, readying himself, though a part of him had already realized that they couldn't hope to stand against so many. He glanced to the sides as he saw that the rest of the Knights were mirroring his actions. Long halberds, swords, and a battle axe joined his sword pointed at the approaching Hemlock Guards.

Knight Jaeth spoke a command, "Hold steady. Don't let a single one of them break through."

John glanced back to check if Knight Eren had made any progress on disarming the trap, but she seemed just as focused, brown light shifting through the air.

He turned his attention back to the oncoming onslaught, bracing his hands on his sword's hilt. In a single moment, the Hemlock Guards collided with them, and John found himself in a flurry of steel.

The guards' movements were slow, at least in comparison to the forces of the Baron's, which gave John the ability to fend off the onslaught of blades, if only just barely. For every sword he blocked, a spear would thrust through to pierce him, and for every spear he blocked, he would have to dodge an ax.

Desperately he tried to keep the onslaught at bay, his sword moving in flashes of blue, his magic flaring wildly through his arms. For a moment, they managed to hold against the onslaught, not pushing back the tide but not collapsing from its strength.

He heard a cry from behind him and saw a flash of light as a magic barrier shattered and a metallic thud and their circle tightened. John desperately wielded his sword, sweat beginning to burn at his vision as he attempted to keep the Hemlock Guards back. His world had narrowed to his opponents as he wove his sword in sweeping strokes, parrying what bladed instruments he could.

His magic would flash with every weapon he missed, and he could feel his reserves dropping as he was unable to keep up with the sheer number of weapons.

"I got it, run!" a voice shouted, which he realized was Knight Eren's.

He broke from his opponents, thrusting his hand forward, unleashing a chunk of blue magic outward, blowing the Hemlock Guards in front of him back before he turned, running backwards with the rest of the Knights.

Knight Jaeth had taken the lead as they sprinted down the street.

John risked a glance backwards and saw that the Hemlock Guards were slowly beginning to give chase, their movements showing the same strange inhibitions from before.

Knight Jaeth began to lead them through the streets, seemingly turning at random. John noticed that they seemed to be growing closer to the metal ring in the city center. The tramp of armored metal steps behind them had only faded slightly, but as he risked another glance behind him, he saw that the Hemlock Guards were still giving chase even while the Knights outpaced them.

They turned into a wider street where John now saw that they were directly in front of the ring. They were running towards it, entering the site of construction implements that surrounded it.

Knight Jaeth looked about, surveying the site with a critical eye before she pointed to a building that stood relatively intact at the side of the construction site.

"We need to climb," she ordered. She ran over and demonstrated that she, too, knew how to use the climbing technique that John had been taught. The rest of the Knights and John joined her, climbing up the side of the building with frantic energy.

John was still not entirely comfortable with the technique, but he shoved those fears to the side as he pulled himself higher and higher, resisting the urge to glance back and see if their pursuers had caught up with them.

It was only as he reached the edge of the building where he pulled himself over onto the flat top that he risked looking downward.

The sight was empty but only for a couple of moments before their pursuers began to stagger in, milling about the site. Strangely John saw that none of them seemed to be looking about for them. They moved about the site, but they made no move to go inside the buildings, shift equipment, or just look up.

"What's wrong with them?" Knight Eren said in a calm voice, and he realized she was kneeled next to him, also looking down.

"I don't know." John shook his head. "They didn't act like this when we first encountered them."

The Hemlock Guards milled about the area for some time. Knight Jaeth was talking into her radio, quietly reporting back on their circumstances.

The structure caught John's attention as he realized that it looked finished far more than before. The metal was smoothly joined together, and the center strobed with the red light pulsing infrequently.

It couldn't be complete yet, John told himself. If it was, whoever had constructed it would have already used it to open the door for the Kings.

That was unless they needed something else to trigger the invasion.

It was as he was momentarily distracted by this thought that his attention was drawn to a red shimmer in the air. He could see red seeping through the air from the gateway, instead of giving off light, it emitted black shadows across the ground.

It was spreading further out, slowly creeping through the air. John's stomach twisted, and John gritted his teeth as the feeling that usually came from looking at the portals magic seemed to double in intensity.

"What is that?" Knight Eren whispered.

The crowd of Hemlock Guards had cleared a space right before the portal, and a hunched figure had stepped forward. They had a pale sallow face, wrinkled like a prune shaded in a large dark hood, hiding most of their features. They were dressed in dark robes and clutched a great staff, whose end shone brightly the same red color as the portal.

They moved slowly through the crowd of Hemlock Guards who parted until they had walked to the head of the portal.

The man set the staff down onto the ground, impaling the stone underneath him. The staff pierced straight through the stone with no resistance, standing upright before the portal. The Hemlock Guards nearest the portal keeled over, their armor crumbling off them in clouds of black smoke, revealing people who then collapsed to the ground. The effect spread through the ranks of the Hemlock Guards, more and more of them collapsing to reveal the people whom John could only assume had been the residents of the city.

The effect soon spread until not a single one of the Hemlock Guards remained, leaving the bodies of the people scattered about the site.

The portal light strobed brighter, casting its malevolent light outward over the entire city.

"Everyone, drop down. We're going to engage them," Knight Jaeth said softly.

The rest of the Knights moved closer to the edge of the roof.

Knight Jaeth took the lead, jumping down and cushioning her fall with a brief blast of yellow magic. The rest of the Knights and John followed her lead, leaping down and cushioning their falls with magic.

As John's blue light died from around him, he saw that the figure holding the staff did not so much as move to react to their presence. They began to move towards him, weapons drawn. As John's foot collided with the ground, he felt his body freeze, and he was no longer able to move. As if any motion he tried to make an equal and opposite force pushed back against him.

The other Knights similar to him were caught in a haze of dark red light, identical to the portal misting around their bodies.

"Forgive me, but I do not have the inclination to deal with you right now," a deep masculine voice emanated from the hooded figure. John could see, unapparent, at first glance that the red energy from the staff had seeped into the ground and was coiling around their feet.

Perhaps that was what was keeping them in place.

Yet John had nothing he could do with the knowledge; he couldn't move a single muscle in his body.

"What you see here is the culmination of centuries of planning and thought," the man spoke again; it didn't seem quite as if he was addressing them, more as if he was talking to the world itself, "Lano the Grand Mage thought to prevent the rule of the Six Kings. He thought that by creating a barrier, he could stop their dominion from extending over the remaining Seven Realms. The arrogance of mortals."

The man released his staff and raised his hands to the air.

"I speak to the Kings immortal and true. The rightful rulers of all Realms. I humbly offer you this realm in exchange for one request.

That I, Kar Dun, be granted a place amongst your number as the Seventh King!"

CHAPTER 22

THE MAN WHO WOULD BE KING

For a moment, the world was silent. Not a single sound disturbed the air.

Then a sound like nails on metal scratched through the air as what was clearly laughter from the same space the magic occupied.

"You would seek to command us?"

Voices intermingled with each other rung out through the air.

"We who are Kings?"

The man, Kar Dun, replied undaunted, "I speak to you as one who wishes only to be your equal."

"You say you are such, but bring the Slayer! We are not fools! We will not be tricked into meeting our end!"

For the first time, Kar Dun seemed taken aback by the course of events. "The Slayer? My Kings, I would do no such thing."

"Are you so foolish as not to know what stands behind you?"

The man turned back to them, looking at the Knights and John. "One of them is the Slayer? My Kings, a thousand apologies I did not know."

"An arrogant fool you are, but truthful. We will bargain. In exchange for this Realm, you will have your reward. That is, you must destroy the Slayer before you do so."

"I will do as your will commands, my Kings," Kar Dun gestured, and suddenly, their restraints were gone. He drew forth an ebony sword that seemed to suck in all light that fell upon it from his side.

They did not even have a moment to ready themselves suddenly; Kar Dun was in their midst, striking out with a speed that was little more than a blur. The barriers of the two of the Knights fell, and they were struck down.

John attempted to rally with the Knights, drawing his blade, but as he drew himself up to attack, he had to suddenly defend as the man's sword flickered forward, slamming against his own, knocking him back.

John rolled to his feet to see three Knights working together in a coordinated display of swordsmanship to slice the man down. Still, the man weaved and blocked with seeming ease before unleashing another flurry of slashes that cut one of the Knights barriers down to nothing and then cut through the Knight, sending them to the ground.

The remaining Knights, Jaeth and Eren, fell under his onslaught, and John rushed to help them, pouring his magic through his body, not even attempting to conserve it. As Eren was about to be hit by Kar Dun's sword slash, John caught his blade with his, parrying it to the side.

Even with the angled parry, he still felt the strain on his arms from the sheer strength contained within the man's arms. How much magic did this man have?

The onslaught continued, and John found himself along with Jaeth and Eren driven back under the man's strength and skill. A part of John's mind realized that this was actually like fighting Bernard.

He was utterly outclassed in strength, speed, and skill, not to mention magic.

John was caught off balance by a sword slash aiming for his gut, only for Jaeth to parry the blow to the side, stepping slightly forward. John moved around her, parrying the second blazing-fast strike.

The third slash warded them back, and they retreated. Eren followed their retreat, but they could not make any real distance between them as the man advanced after them with a speed that made him blurred.

John gritted his teeth as he engaged the man with Eren and Jaeth swords clashing and magic heating the air as it flashed about them. It was taking every ounce of the skill Bernard had imparted into him to attempt to hold the man back even with the help of Eren and Jaeth. Any opening that appeared Kar Dun would exploit ruthlessly, and it was only together that they had managed to prevent the man from ending their lives.

It was a losing battle, though, and John knew it.

Kar Dun ripped his free hand downward. A swirling pillar of red fire erupted from it and roared towards them. There was no escape.

The fire blasted John backward, and for a moment, all he could see was the red fire that mercilessly ripped into his magic shield, eating at it hungrily. His back collided with a wall that crumbled underneath the force.

He rolled backward, finally free of the fire.

His magic had been reduced to under half of his reserves. He realized that he must have been sent quite a distance as he was now some distance from the portal. He glanced around, trying to find the other fighters. Immediately he spotted Eren and Jaeth also collapsed about the street they had been launched into.

They didn't stir. John pushed himself to his feet, shaking off the feeling of weariness that was eating at him. He rushed to Eren's side and was relieved to find that she was still breathing, although unconscious. He saw that Jaeth was in the same condition.

Kar Dun would soon hunt him down. This brief respite was only temporary; John knew it.

Turning to the nearest building, he kicked open the door before picking up Jaeth and deposited her inside, followed by Eren, making sure to place them out of sight of the broken open door. He turned back around and ran back outside, pelting down the street as fast as he could.

All he could do was try and make sure that the Hemlock Guards wouldn't find them. He was the target. The book had said the Slayer wielded the Blade of Knights. He wielded the sword; ergo, he must be this Slayer.

He just wished he knew why exactly he had to die.

John shook the thought free from his head; he needed to stay focused. Kar Dun would be pursuing him; what could he do?

John spun around the corner of a street only to come face to face with a group of Hemlock Guards engaged with a group of Knights.

John grimaced. He doubted that these Knights would be any match for the man he was running from. He was about to turn and run away before a red light ripped forth from the Hemlock Guards, soaring over his head.

John, unwilling, turned to look at the sight of Kar Dun glowing with the red energy.

“I understand fleeing from death, boy. It is only natural for a mortal to fear their end. You cannot outrun me, though. I am, but one step away from a King, and you will not stop me!” Kar Dun roared.

John knew he was right.

Still, he couldn’t surrender. He wouldn’t.

John gripped his sword tightly, feeling a small comforting trickle of warmth come from the hilt.

If he let Kar Dun win, that would be the end of the Realm. It would be the end of his friends. It would be the end of Aysel.

Kar Dun charged at him, and John readied his blade, only managing to deflect the first strike of his onslaught. The second strike collided cleanly, grinding against his magic, sending blue sparks flying. The third was sent at equally blazing speed, racing at his neck, and John knew his barrier wouldn't hold as Kar Dun's sword flared red.

CLANG!

A blade interjected, blocking Kar Dun's sword. A familiar-looking blade.

"Don't you touch him," a familiar, deep voice said.

John didn't need to look behind him to know who had saved him.

Bernard, in full armor, stepped forward, managing to push Kar Dun back through sheer strength. Kar Dun backed away a couple of steps, looking at Bernard without a hint of fear in his eyes.

John was reminded of Bernard's stories of the warriors of old who fought in the great wars that had shaped the nations as they were today. Bernard's sword was positioned at an angle away from his body.

The silence seemed to have fallen over the area, and John dimly noticed that the other Knights were gathering behind Bernard as the Hemlock Guards had collapsed into piles of inert armor.

Kar Dun laughed. "Really? You fools think you can stop me?" He twirled his sword before launching himself forward in a blazing fast strike, turning at the last second from Bernard to attack another Knight to the side.

He shattered the Knight's magic barrier in a single strike and went for the kill only to have to retreat under the onslaught of three more Knights cutting at him. Despite his retreat, he easily parried their strikes away as he almost seemed to be waiting for something.

The tramp of heavy footfalls reached John's ears and emerging from another street, a horde of the Hemlock Guards ran at the Knights.

The forces collided in an instant, turning John's world into chaos as the fight began. Swords flashed, axes swung, and arrows soared as the air filled with metal seeking death. John found himself next to Bernard, fighting together to push back against the tide. Desperately he tried to look about as he fought, trying to spot where Kar Dun had gone.

He found himself in the fight, though he couldn't make heads or tails of where anyone was. His world had narrowed down to his immediate surroundings as he deflected the metal flying at him and responded in kind.

His blade struck through red barriers, causing armor suits to collapse, but the space they occupied was just filled with more of the Hemlock Guards.

He found himself in a gap in the fighting and spotted Bernard for the first time since the fight began. He was engaged head to head with Kar Dun, his green magic flaring brightly against Kar Dun's dark red in massive explosions of light.

Bernard brought his sword up, and the air began to swirl with a green light. He swung down, and a gale of green wind ripped across the space between him and Kar Dun, sending the Hemlock Guards that got in the way flying into the air.

Kar Dun responded by swinging his blade, stirring a storm of blood-red fire to sweep forward, burning through the wind increasing in size as it burned towards Bernard.

Bernard responded by stabbing his sword into the ground, causing a spout of water to shoot up, soaring into a geyser that doused the flame and turned into a wave that crashed down upon Kar Dun.

This was nature magic on a scale that was far beyond Zayne's usage of earth or anything else John had ever seen; magic that he had never even learned the basics of how to use.

In this battle, John knew he could do little more than observe the destruction.

More of the Hemlock Guards fell upon John. Channeling his magic through his left hand, he sent a blast of force forward, sending two of the guards flying into the air as he brought his sword to bear on the other two opponents. His magic-enhanced strength caused his sword to cave in the armor of the Hemlock Guards.

They kept coming until he beat their armor in enough for the armor's magic containment to fail and a cloud of red magic to release from the armor dissolving into the air. He saw that the rest of the Knights were managing to hold the Hemlock Guards at bay, but for every one they struck down, more would appear running from the side streets.

This wasn't going to work, John realized. It was a battle of attrition, and they didn't have the numbers. He could see the collapsed form of Knights down from magic exhaustion or worse from where he stood.

They needed to deal with Kar Dun.

John's reserves were still low as any magic he had regenerated he had poured back into his limbs to keep fighting.

A shadow swept down over him, and John found himself suddenly launched through the air, battered by an incredible force to the side. He rolled across the ground, eventually coming to a stop, his magic reserves even lower.

He pushed himself to his feet against the cold street and looked up to see a familiar skeletal dragon standing amid the Knights. It casually batted the Knights around it to the side, its singular baleful red eye tracing over all of them.

The skeletal dragon raised its head to the sky and roared.

The sound ground against John's eardrums painfully, and he winced, doing his best to cover his ears while still maintaining a grip on his sword.

Then as the dragon's roar ended, he heard more howls.

From the dark rock above the city, skeletal dragons swept down. Another two dragons joined. The dragons swept through the Knights, sending them flying through the air, their baleful red eyes glowing, as they howled.

John felt a growing pit in his stomach. They couldn't win. How could they?

His skin felt cold. He couldn't breathe. He—

His hand that still clutched his sword suddenly felt like it had been dipped in fire. A flickering blue light lit up his hand, burning so brightly John had to avert his gaze.

The fear had disappeared, he realized. It was replaced by a heat that burned through his whole body. He pushed himself back to his feet and realized with a strange calm that a dragon was charging towards him, raising its claw to strike him down. John replied with a slash of his blade, cutting with ease through the bone in a single slash of his sword, blue light trailing his blade's movement. The dragon roared, losing its ability to stand.

The eye, he remembered, Silvia had struck the eye.

John leaped up and stuck his sword into the red orb, and with a blue flash, the eye erupted, and the skeleton ceased moving, falling to the ground.

John turned his attention to the other dragons. Even with this second wind, he didn't think he could take out these dragons by himself. His magic reserves were low. Still, his mind didn't even consider another option as he readied his sword.

A dragon charged at him at speed, sprinting across the ground, and John braced himself even though he knew there was no way to stop its charge.

A bright familiar red light shot through the air. It erupted in a blinding explosion against the dragon, not just destroying its eye but causing the beast to collapse with half of its skull seemingly obliterated.

"Ha! That makes us even!" a familiar voice called out, and John saw Martin perched on top of one of the buildings, a second arrow already drawn.

Knights began to pour into the street, pushing back against the Hemlock Guards, reinforcing the formerly faltering, overwhelmed Knights.

Three of the Hemlock Guards charged at John, but before he could even ready his blade, one was cut down in a flash of silver as Aysel shot out from the Knights in a streak. She cut down the second with a backswing and deflected the blows of the third before throwing a blast of silver magic at them, sending the guard flying into a wall cratering it.

She turned to John, and John felt his heart leap into his throat by her sheer beauty. She stepped to him, and for a moment, he didn't even register the words she had said.

"Are you okay?"

John nodded dumbly, awed by the fierce expression on her face.

It took him a moment before he responded, "Yeah, I'm okay."

John wanted to say something else, something more, but more of the Hemlock Guards were pouring in, and he and Aysel found themselves in the midst of battle. They fought side by side, moving about to prevent any attacks on the other as they attempted to push back their opponents.

They were soon joined by Martin and Silvia, who joined their fight, and slowly they managed to push the Hemlock Guards back enough to give them some breathing room. During the fighting, John had lost track of Bernard and with some space; he looked about, catching sight of him still engaged with Kar Dun.

The street around them had been ripped apart with great chunks torn as green and red clashed in the air. Kar Dun fought with massive sweeping movements, summoning crimson fire that roared forth only to be met with giant geysers of water that were beginning to fill the streets. Still, despite all of Bernard's skill, John could see that he was being driven back. For every strike that Bernard landed, Kar Dun would hit even harder.

Bernard was wearing down, and even as Knights attempted to help him, they were sent back by blasts of fire as Hemlock Guards congealed around Kar Dun to defend him. Two of the remaining dragons were still raging about the street as the Knights attempted to bring them down.

"Enough!" Kar Dun roared, audible despite the roar of the battle.

He raised his hands, and dark red currents rumbled through the streets, and the ground began to shake. The rumble traversed through the area, knocking down Hemlock Guard and Knight alike.

Kar Dun split off from Bernard, his Hemlock Guards taking the opportunity to attack Bernard and inhibit him from following, and began to charge at John, bowling any Knights in his way to the side with incredible force.

Martin fired an arrow at him, but the man gestured, and a barrier rose in front of him, blocking the arrow and subsequent explosion from impacting him. Silvia sprinted across the ground from the side, attempting to bring her long daggers to bear against their opponent, only to be sent flying by a red wave of magic.

John and Aysel braced themselves, and Aysel stepped forward, meeting Kar Dun's first sword strike, which nearly jarred the sword from her hands. John attempted to join her, launching his attack and slicing his sword forward in a crescent arc of blue silver, which impacted the man's magic shield, glancing off in a shower of red sparks.

Kar Dun merely laughed. "You're centuries too early to even think of contending with me."

He parried John's follow-up slash to the side and sent a roaring blast of fire at Aysel, sending her flying away from the inferno he conjured with a negligent wave of his hand.

John once again attempted to attack, only for the man in an impossibly fast move to grasp his wrist before he could strike.

"My skill lies in magic, boy. You can't possibly hope to compete."

John tried to struggle, but he felt the magic within him begin to drain. Blue energy drained visibly from him down the man's arm, who grinned at him viciously.

He tried to struggle, to move. All in vain. The strength that had been flowing through him was nowhere to be found. He collapsed to his knees, and his sword tumbled through his now weak grip that could no longer hold up the blade.

His reserves hit zero, and his barrier dropped. He felt weak. The world seemed to have narrowed. Kar Dun's dark eyes glared at him viciously, and John could see his lips quirked up in a smile as he looked down at him.

"Why even try?" Kar Dun hissed, and in a burst of speed, his sword struck through him.

John choked, unable to comprehend for a moment what had just happened. He collapsed to the ground, unable to move, feeling cold sweeping through his limbs. Distantly he saw the man be forced back by a raging green light as Bernard roared in fury as he attempted to strike Kar Dun down.

Even the roar was distant as the sounds around him seemed to dull.

Ever so distantly, he felt his body shift as a beautiful face hovered above him, mouthing words he could no longer hear. Aysel looked upset, he realized.

He tried to smile, to say something but only warm liquid bubbled up from beneath his lips.

CHAPTER 23

THE FIRST DEATH IS ALWAYS THE HARDEST

John awoke, gasping for breath frantically clutching around his chest only to find no wound even though he very distinctly recalled that there should be one.

He was high in the air, he realized, sitting on a large flat rock that overlooked a body of water that seemed to expand infinitely into the distance. The light that warmed him came from the sun hovering over the horizon, lighting up the water before him.

He stood up and looked about, trying to get his bearings. The large flat rock he was on seemed to be a pillar of stone that rose from the water below. Looking around, he saw no other forms of solid ground, only the deep blue water.

Where was he?

"Am I dead?" he found himself saying aloud.

"Yes," a voice sounded out, and John spun, trying to find the location of the speaker.

He saw no one. He saw the only thing in the center of the stone platform he stood on was a sword impaled into the stone. A very familiar sword, he realized.

It was the sword he had pulled from Treemor's cave, the sword he had been wielding.

He slowly approached it, walking across the flat stone.

John reached out his hand for the blade but stopped before he pulled it. He looked around once again, trying to get his bearings. John had never seen a place like this before in his life. He had never even seen an ocean, which is what he assumed he must be standing above.

After a moment of consideration, he spoke again, "Where am I?"

"You are in the in-between, a place between life and death," the voice spoke again.

John waited, but the voice did not elaborate.

After a moment, John said, "So that's it, then." He couldn't quantify the emotion in his voice. In truth, he hadn't expected it to end like this. Now that it had, well…

He looked out over the water below, watching the waves. They were distant, and the sound that carried up to him seemed somewhat muted. He could hear no signs of life of any sort, no birds crying, nothing. He had never been to the ocean, but from what he had read that was what he should have expected.

It was sinking in that perhaps he wouldn't be able to do a lot of things he had hoped.

"No."

John turned, knowing no one was there.

"No?" he questioned.

"You are the Slayer; you cannot pass into death."

John was struck by the term "Slayer" again, so much so that he didn't quite process the last part of what they said at first.

"What is the Slayer?" he asked.

"It is your destiny and duty. You are the one who will serve as the Chosen One's Knight."

"The Chosen One," frustration bled into John's voice. "What do you mean the Chosen One?" he was tired of the incomplete information he had been trying to make do with.

"The Chosen One is the one who will decide the fate of the Thirteen Realms, whether the Kings will be destroyed or if they will finally rule all."

"Who is the Chosen One?" John asked the air.

"Aysel Lyn." The voice responded.

"Aysel," John parroted in shock. Was it her? But … even as he thought it through, he recalled what Aysel had said to him. Hadn't she said that she had spent her life being pursued? Was this why?

"How do you know all of this?" John asked the air.

"Because I was there when the prophecy was made." The voice responded.

"Who are you?" John asked.

"I am the Blade of Knights. I am your weapon," the voice said, and now a clue of who he was talking to struck John.

John paused before he asked. "Are you the sword I drew from that cavern?"

"Yes." The sword responded.

"What does it mean that you're the Blade of Knights?" John questioned.

"Merely that I am the sword destined to be wielded by you, the Slayer."

John nodded as he tried to process everything. He had thought that answers would make things make more sense, but now that he had them, he still didn't know what to do.

John's mind ran back to the first part of their conversation. "You said I can't pass into death?"

"You are the Slayer. You cannot pass on."

A glimmer of hope emerged in John's chest. He could go back. He could stop Kar Dun.

"How do I go back?" John asked.

"You merely have to ask," the voice responded, and John saw in the distance that the clouds were beginning to cross over the water, slowly beginning to enclose on the pillar.

"Is there a way I can beat Kar Dun?" John asked the air, desperately hoping for an answer.

"Yes."

The fog was accelerating. "What am I supposed to do?"

"Act."

The fog surrounded him, the thick white substance flowing over him to the point he could not see anything.

In the next moment, he realized he was lying on the cold, hard ground. Cracking open his eyes, he saw that he was lying on the street, though not precisely where he had fallen.

In the air, he could see a miasma of red energy flowing through the air only to grind to a halt as it met an equal and opposite blast of silver light that pushed back against it. Standing in front of the dark red magic, he saw the form of Kar Dun's hands raised to the air, directing a raging current of energy toward the silver light. Squinting past the brightness, he glimpsed the condition of Aysel. Within it, eyes narrowed in a glare at Kar Dun.

The Knights were scattered about, still doing their best to fight back the Hemlock Guard. They were desperately attempting to cut through the Guard, which blocked the path to Aysel and Kar Dun.

No matter how hard they pushed, they were held back, unable to overcome the sheer number of the Hemlock Guards. He realized that he was directly behind Kar Dun and almost unconsciously grasped his sword's hilt.

In a movement, he was up. His magic reserves were gone. It was nothing but him and his sword. He made his first step forward and then another till he was running, flying across the street.

In a second he had crossed the distance to Kar Dun.

He thrust his sword forth, spearing through the man, cutting through the sparks of a red barrier long since drained of magic from his battle with Aysel. His sword cut through cleanly, and the man dropped, ending the battle of light, which faded away.

He could see the gate's red energy turning from its passive glow into something chaotic before it erupted all at once, shooting through the air. The metal came apart with a tearing screech, and John thought he heard an inhuman cry ringing through the air.

The Hemlock Guards fell as one, as though their strings cut, and the armor fell apart, revealing them for the empty husks they were. John could see the other adventurers in the crowd looking about, confused at the sudden end of their fight. He had done it.

John's eyes fell upon a body lying across the ground a mere couple paces away from him, wearing the Knight's armor with an all too familiar face.

He stared at the broken form of Bernard lying dead upon the earth.

"No," he choked out in a whisper. With unwilling steps, he made his way forward, drawing up to Bernard's body. He collapsed to his knees, feeling strangely blank. The world had a strange feeling of unreality like he was watching something instead of experiencing it.

He looked at Bernard's face, serene in death. Bernard hadn't even known that John wasn't truly dead. There had been so much that John had wanted to ask Bernard.

It was too late now.

Anger stirred in his chest. He wanted to rage to destroy the person who had killed Bernard, but he already had. There was no sense of consolation in that thought.

John found himself sitting down heavily upon the ground, staring at nothing in particular. Noise and motion were going on around him, but he couldn't bring himself to care.

Idly he looked down at the blade in his grip and felt a sudden surge of anger. Why had he been brought back too late? If he hadn't, Bernard would still be alive.

He sat on the stone and stared off into the ceiling of the cavern above. He should be crying, he thought. He had just lost the person who was the closest thing to a father figure he had ever had, but his eyes remained dry.

He let his mind drift as he stared blankly into space. The voices around him had gotten more aggravated; he noticed distantly, but that was as much as he could tell. They were merely discordant notes in the silence of his mind as he lacked the will to put them together.

He was tired. His magic reserves were still negligible, and he considered falling asleep where he sat. Maybe when he woke up, this scene would have changed. Perhaps he was sleeping.

A familiar face blotted out his vision. Their pale skin was dirty, and their purple hair was a mess as they stared at him with piercing silver eyes. Their mouth was moving, and sounds emerged that he realized were probably words.

He stared blankly at them.

More sounds emerged, bothering his brain as they pulled at the comforting numbness that had settled over it.

"John," a voice broke through the jumble of noise around him, and John was confused for a moment till he realized the voice had come from his sword. A warmth enveloped the hand that held his blade, and with that warmth, John finally stirred.

The syllables and words that were spoken around him began to make sense again.

His vision came into focus, and he realized that Aysel had crouched down in front of him. Her hands were on his shoulders, and she was looking at him anxiously.

Martin and Silvia were on either side of him, and he could see the other adventurers clustered around. He breathed in a shaky breath as he tried to reorient himself, consciously avoiding looking down at Bernard.

"Are you—" Martin stopped himself. "Come on, let's get you out here." He offered a hand which John didn't take.

With his mind in a semblance of calm, John shook his head. "He … he needs to be buried."

Zayne nodded. "We'll take care of it."

John unwilling took Martin's hand, allowing himself to be pulled from the ground.

He stood shakily.

"How did he die?" John said, a part of him wanting an answer but another part of him not wanting to know.

"He was attacked by that man right after you went down." Martin gestured at Bernard, "Bernard managed to push him back for a while, but he was overwhelmed," Martin said.

John nodded, still not processing Martin's words. He looked down at Bernard, who, without the red stain that covered the front of his armor, could almost be sleeping.

He looked about the street and was struck by armor strewn about, from the Hemlock Guards' empty shells to the Knights who were being lifted and carried away by their compatriots.

He found himself wishing that he could go to sleep. He was exhausted to the point his thoughts and limbs felt like lead weights. A hand clasped his shoulder, and he blearily looked up to see that Grant was standing in front of him, a solemn expression on his wizened face.

"I know you are tired, John, but I need you to answer some questions for me," Grant said.

John looked tiredly back, and he must have nodded to Grant because Grant spoke again. "Are you injured?"

John furrowed his brow as, for a moment, his flighty thoughts didn't register Grant's words. He looked down at his torso and patted the hole in the center of his shirt, coming away with a sticky red substance. He felt deeper but did not come into contact with the hole that had previously been there.

He shook his head at Grant, whose face had twisted slightly at his actions looking like he wanted to protest.

"No, I'm fine," John responded.

Grant nodded. "Alright." He looked down to the hole in John's clothing, a strange expression on his face.

Grant opened his mouth to say something else, only to be cut off by Zayne.

"He's experiencing magic exhaustion. We should let him rest."

Grant turned to Zayne, a frown on his face before he sighed and nodded. "Yes, I suppose you're right."

John was led by his group away from the street, a low murmur buzzing around him, but he couldn't find it in himself to care.

He found himself in a building and lying on a bed, staring at the ceiling in short order. Though blank, his eyes refused to allow him to sleep, and his attention fell on his sheathed sword resting on a table by his bed. Reaching out, he grasped the handle and pulled the blade into the bed with him, and it was like that he was able to close his eyes and sink into a dream of nothing.

When he next awoke, he found himself staring at an unfamiliar ceiling.

He laid in bed for a while, staring at the ceiling, memorizing its off-white color that stretched on above him. He felt his mind attempt to drift, but he forcefully shut down that urge. The careful blankness he was experiencing was a far better place to stay.

Heat glowed in his palms, and he realized that he was still gripping his sword, and as he did so, events began to slip back into his conscious. The events had a haze to them as if they weren't quite real, as if they were imagined.

A knock sounded through the room, and he turned just as the door opened. Aysel stepped in, closing the door behind her. She turned to him and walked towards his bed. Their eyes met. Her face transitioned to a look of surprise. "John! You're awake?"

John considered her words for a minute before realizing that she had asked a question though it hadn't quite sounded like one.

"Yeah, I am," he said.

"Are you—" Aysel stopped herself, beginning again. "How are you feeling?"

John shrugged, marshaling his body to sit up in the bed. "Fine."

A frown crossed onto Aysel's face before she shook it away. "That's … that's good."

She sat down at a chair that was positioned by the bed.

"You've been out a while," she said. "The doctors say it was from magical exhaustion."

John nodded at the news, not feeling anything towards the fact one way or another.

"Bernard saved me back there," Aysel continued, and John looked up at her, surprised at the mention of the man who had occupied his thoughts whenever they had strayed.

Aysel continued, "After you…" she paused. "After you went down, he was like a man possessed. He attacked Kar Dun with magic I've never even seen. He pushed him back, but he seemed drained by the magic he was using. He wasn't able to block the last strike."

Aysel stopped speaking, and John nodded, processing her words. A question bubbled up from within him as his mind was drawn back to what he had seen.

"What magic were you using?"

Aysel looked surprised at his question before she responded, choosing her words carefully. "I'm not sure. I've only used it a couple of times before. All I know is that it's an attack that generates an incredible amount of heat, and when I've used it before, I've burned through anything in my path. I can't use it on command, though. It just happens."

John nodded. Was this because she was the Chosen One? It was possible. Part of him wanted to ask, but he wasn't quite sure how. Did Aysel know she was the Chosen One?

Putting together what she had told him from her past, it was possible.

Suppose she did know, how would she react to him telling her. Would she fear that he, too, would want to use her for her power? John did not know. Perhaps if Bernard were still around, he would have spoken to him and then used his advice to plot a path forward, but that was impossible now.

John only had himself to rely on.

“I’m leaving soon,” Aysel said, and her words struck John harshly.

She continued, “Marcila thinks it’s best if we move on as quickly as possible. It’s only a matter of time before the Knights of the Dawn discover who I am. Marcila believes we should leave before they do.”

John’s chest clenched uncomfortably. “I take it that means you would rather I didn’t come.”

Aysel smiled wanly. “Seeing you go down like that made me realize something. I can’t bring you into something like this. It’s probably for the best … I don’t want you to get hurt.”

“Isn’t that my choice?” John replied, a small fire flickering to life in his gut.

Aysel looked taken aback by his response. “I…” Aysel turned her gaze downward.

“I’ll miss you, John.”

She stood up from her seat and began to walk out of the room. John attempted to stand but found that his energy couldn’t support him as he collapsed to the ground.

Aysel turned, looking down at him, her bottom lip trembling. "Please, John, don't make this any harder than it has to be."

John pushed himself up, shakily with his arms. He focused his gaze on Aysel. "Even if you leave, I promised I'd help you. I won't go back on that promise."

Aysel looked struck for a moment, her eyes meeting his, and John could see unshed tears in her eyes. "Goodbye, John," she said softly and then walked from the room.

CHAPTER 24

THE END OF THE BEGINNING

Days passed before John was well enough to walk on his own. Whatever the sword had done to revive him had left him with little strength, and his magic reserves had recovered far slower than they should have.

Martin and Silvia had visited him and other members of their group except for Marcila and Aysel.

He discovered from them that most of the city population was still alive and, once freed from their prisons of armor suits, had remembered little of their ordeal. Trams had been sent back to the City of Lights, and the people had begun to rebuild together. Karat had found herself forced into leadership to help the people rebuild as the previous City Council had been lost in the battle.

The Adventurer's Guild had contracted with other adventurers to help keep any monsters away from the city. They had still visited, and now without the overhang of their mission, John found the conversation enjoyable in a way it hadn't been before.

Zayne had even offered him a spot in his Guild, the Raven Fallows, which John considered seriously. Martin and Silvia had already accepted membership on the spot and prepared to head off on an expedition. They were to deal with the monsters that had been encroaching onto the City of Lights.

Once John could move again, he talked with the bank that oversaw Bernard's assets and discovered that Bernard had willed everything he owned to him. It was just another reminder to John of the man he had lost. As he had gone through Bernard's possessions, of which there was remarkably few, he had come across a series of journals which, upon closer examination, he realized to be details of the man's previous adventures and his time with the Knights of the Dawn. He hadn't looked through them much as he found them too poignant to read. He had thus stored them away.

John found himself rather aimless as he moved through the days. Without the mission over his head, he thought he would have felt free. He had even gone to the mission boards at the Guild office and looked over the possible missions. But nothing had looked right to him.

He was staying at the Knight's Rest Inn, taking advantage of the cheap accommodations. He knew he could have stayed at the Western Workshop, but he had no desire to go back there.

So it was that John found himself walking the streets of the City of Lights. He couldn't help but feel a strange hollowness. It was weird not having Aysel, Martin, and Silvia with him.

He had thought that having spent so long on his own that returning to that state wouldn't bother him, but it did. He continued down the streets, observing the buildings still under repair and the ordinary commerce that occurred up and down the streets.

His attention fell upon a beaten storefront, emblazoned on the window were the words, "The Garage." Through the window, he spotted a row of cycles lined up and gleaming. In particular, one caught his attention, a deep blue one that had a sleek frame somewhat smaller than its compatriots.

Somewhat on a whim, he entered the store, hearing the bell jingle as he entered. A woman with dark red hair and grungy clothes stood at the shop's desk, fiddling with the pieces of what John could only assume was a cycle.

On his entrance, the woman looked up and gave him a welcoming smile. "Hello, how can I help you today?"

John was caught off guard even though he probably shouldn't have been. Of course, she expected him to be a customer. This was a shop. Well, if he was in here anyway…

"That cycle by the window," he pointed at the blue bike, "how much is it?"

The woman looked at the cycle he pointed at. "That one's 4000 denarii."

John reached into his pocket and pulled out his wallet; taking out the card linked to his bank account; he handed it over to the woman.

"I'd like to buy it if that's all right," he said.

The women nodded and proceeded to ring him up at the register. After taking his card back, the woman handed him a set of keys and helped him take the cycle off the display and roll it out of the store.

Bidding her farewell, John proceeded to walk down the street as he began to consider his actions. It wasn't like he couldn't afford the bike. Even discounting the payment he had received for completing his mission, he had inherited Bernard's considerable assets.

He continued down the street, walking the cycle through the crowd of pedestrians. John stopped by a store that sold foodstuffs and proceeded to purchase a large amount of food and a bag that would keep it fresh as long as he charged it with magic. He exited the store, and after filling up the bag and charging it, he placed it into one of the two saddlebags at the side of the cycle.

He walked for another while before he arrived at a store that sold travel items. He stepped inside and purchased a sleeping bag and a tent. He exited and then proceeded to continue with more purpose till he found a store that sold devices. He browsed through the aisles before finding a portable gaming device and, after consideration, a handheld terminal. He exited the store once again, storing his purchases.

John continued through the city before he found that he had arrived at one of the exits, and as he stepped through the gate, he took a deep breath of the air.

He swung his leg over the cycle and channeled magic through the handles, and he felt the cycle thrum.

John hesitated a moment, looking back at his home.

Then he looked back out over the valley, seeing the road that traversed through it, leading out into the world beyond. He engaged his cycle and sped off down the road, not looking back once as his home began to disappear into the distance.

He would find her.

www.ingramcontent.com/pod-product-compliance
Lightning Source LLC
LaVergne TN
LVHW041107080826
845145LV00007B/1719

* 9 7 8 1 7 3 6 3 9 9 8 0 4 *